M000046331

INTO THE FIRE

ALSO BY JODI McISAAC

The Thin Veil Series

Through the Door

Into the Fire

No longer property of the
Dayton Metro Library

INTO THE FIRE

Jodi McIsaac

47N⬤RTH

The characters and events portrayed in this book are fictitious. Any similarity to real persons, living or dead, is coincidental and not intended by the author.

Text copyright © 2013 Jodi McIsaac
All rights reserved.

Printed in the United States of America.

No part of this book may be reproduced, or stored in a retrieval system, or transmitted in any form or by any means, electronic, mechanical, photocopying, recording, or otherwise, without express written permission of the publisher.

Cover Illustrated by Gene Mollica
Published by 47North – Seattle, Washington

ISBN-13: 9781477808696
ISBN-10: 1477808698
Library of Congress Control Number: 2013936773

FOR LAUREN

PRONUNCIATION GUIDE

The guide below is meant to help you pronounce some of the trickier words that pop up in this story. But, seeing as there is little agreement as to the "proper" pronunciation of most of these words even among native Irish speakers and scholars, feel free to say them any way you like.

Aiofe—*EEF ah*
Airgetlam—*AR get lum*
Brighid—*BREE yit*
Conchobhar—*KON cho var*
Cúchulainn—*koo CULL in*
Dian Cecht—*DEE an KAY*
Ériu—*AY roo*
file—*FEE luh*
Fionnbharr—*FYUN var*
Fionnghuala—*fyun OO la*
leannán sí—*LAH nawn SHEE*
Lia Fáil—*LEE-ah FOIL*
Manannan mac Lir—*Man na non mac LEER*
neamh-mairbh—*NEE uv MAOW* (rhymes with "now")

Nuala—*NOO uh la*
Ruadhan—*ROO awn*
Scone—*SCOON*
sidh—*SHEE*
sidhe (plural of sidh)—*SHEE*
Tara—*TAH ra*
Tír na nÓg—*TEER na NOHG*
Toirdhealbhach MacDail re Deachai—*TUR a lakh mac DOLL ray DAW hai*
Tuatha Dé Danann—*TOOa ha DAY DONN an*

PROLOGUE

She waited until darkness fell. There were no stars tonight, no moonlight to illuminate her waves of red hair as she crouched on the edge of a wood, beneath the tangled branches of a hawthorn tree. The tree was dead, like all the trees in Tír na nÓg, and provided little cover. It didn't matter; no one had come looking for her. But it was only a matter of time. They would come, and they would want revenge.

Fortunately, chaos was on her side. Her mind was still reeling from how quickly her fortune had turned the moment the High King's head had been separated from his body. Lorcan was dead, and she no longer needed to waste her time or her power on bending him to her will. The throne was hers for the seizing, but she had to act quickly.

Tentatively, she stepped out from under the cover of the wood. There was no light to guide her, but she knew this path by heart. The dry grass crunched beneath her feet as she crossed the clearing, glancing behind to make sure she was not being followed. A small mound rose before her, and her hands quickly found the polished stone set in its side. She pressed firmly and watched as the side of the hill dissolved and was replaced by a door of wrought silver. She was home.

CHAPTER 1

Cedar McLeod was contemplating her mother's secrets as she prepared to leave them behind. She stood alone in the empty living room of her childhood home. The lace curtains swayed toward her, carrying the smell of the ocean, taunting her. *Stay,* they seemed to say as they reached out for her. *Discover the truth about the woman who lived here.* She walked over and shut the window, forcing the stubborn latch closed. *I have to go,* she told herself. She pushed the curtains aside and looked out through the glass. The evening sun seemed to hover over the water in the bay, as though it might rest there for a while before disappearing beneath the waves. Cedar had always loved the passage from day to night; it was a time when the air felt thick with mystery.

She walked through the old house one more time, saying her good-byes. She had never been particularly sentimental . . . but she had also never traveled so far away without knowing if and when she would return. And so she closed her eyes and tried to savor the memories this house held for her. She felt the soft, plush carpet under her bare feet and remembered losing Barbie shoes and marbles in its depth, and the scoldings she'd received when her mother—when Maeve—had stepped on them. She ran her hand along the polished banister as she slowly climbed the staircase, avoiding the creakiest spots by habit. It was a path she'd memorized as a teenager when she was going through what Maeve had called "her rebellious stage." Sliding down the banister had always been the easiest escape; coming back home had been another matter.

She reached her bedroom and sat down on the edge of the bed, smoothing the threadbare quilt beneath her fingers. She was tempted to lie down, to stare at the ceiling and think about all the reasons for doing what she was about to do. But no, she had to go home. Finn and Eden were waiting for her. She had made her decision. And so she picked up the last box and carried it downstairs, her arms sore from a weekend of packing and cleaning the old house. She locked up and then squeezed the box into the trunk of her car.

Only the workshop was left.

She walked around it for what must have been the dozenth time. It was such an ordinary building on the outside: white clapboard with only one door and a small square window. It had sat there in their front yard, just off the gravel driveway, for as long as she could remember. She'd never been allowed to enter it. "It's nothing that would interest you," Maeve would say. "Just a desk and a chair and a few books. I'm entitled to a little privacy."

When she was fifteen, Cedar had tried to break into the workshop with one of her friends. But Maeve discovered them, and Cedar had never seen her in such a rage. Cedar was grounded for a week, and when she was finally allowed out, she discovered that her friend had suddenly moved to the city. After that, whenever Cedar was tempted to try again, she'd find herself remembering an urgent test that needed to be studied for, or a drawing that she'd been meaning to work on.

But now she knew better.

She finished her circuit around the outside and stopped in front of the door, which refused to open. She knew now there must be some sort of spell on it and that whatever was inside had something to do with Maeve's secret life as a druid. But now Maeve was dead, and whatever secrets she still held were buried with her. Cedar rattled the doorknob, knowing it wouldn't work.

She had tried to get in several times since Maeve's death three weeks ago. She had brought a locksmith out, but his tools had broken on the first attempt, and then he'd been too busy to try again. She'd tried to break the window with a crowbar, but it hadn't even scratched the glass. A curtain covered the window, and she could not see inside, except for a small ragged space in the corner—but even then all she could see was dust and darkness. She had asked Finn to help her, but he had just warned her to not drive herself crazy. Some mysteries were best left unsolved, he had said, and meddling in the affairs of druids never turned out particularly well.

She glanced at her watch and knew she had to get going. But she hated the thought of not knowing this side of her mother. She felt certain that if she could only get inside Maeve's private sanctuary, all of her questions would be answered.

She placed her hand on the rough wood of the door. "Open," she whispered, feeling foolish. She glanced over at the tree under which Maeve was buried, then turned back to the door. "Mum?" she whispered. "It's okay now. You can let me in. Let me in." Nothing happened. Cedar kicked at the door in frustration, and the wood creaked. Encouraged, she kicked it again. Then she took several steps back and flung herself shoulder-first into the door.

She was not expecting the explosion. A loud crack like a rifle shot ruptured the silence of the evening, and a force like a hot wind sent Cedar flying backward through the air. She landed hard on the gravel driveway amid a torrent of red sparks. Her head hit something hard, and she felt the darkness close in on her.

When she opened her eyes again, something was obscuring her view. She could see a rim of light in her peripheral vision. It surrounded the object in front of her like a halo. She recognized it as the porch light. The sky was black; night had fallen. She started to sit up and winced as a sudden burst of pain shot through her head.

"Wait," the object said. "Let me help you."

She felt herself being gently lifted into a sitting position. The world swam around her, and she closed her eyes, waiting for the pain in her head to subside. After a moment she opened her eyes again and blinked a few times. Gradually, the object in front of her came into focus. It was a man. He was kneeling beside her, his light gray eyes fixed on her with concern. He was handsome, though old enough to be her father. His shaggy brown hair was generously flecked with gray, his long face was lined and pale, and he was wearing a worn brown leather jacket over beige pants and a buttoned shirt. Behind him, the workshop looked as intact and impenetrable as always, despite the blast that had knocked Cedar off her feet.

"How do you feel?" the man asked.

"Um . . . surprised," she answered. "Who are you?"

"You hit your head pretty hard," he said. "You might want to get it checked out."

"No, I'm fine, thank you," Cedar said. She slowly got to her feet, running a hand over the large bump on the back of her head. She waited for him to introduce himself, feeling increasingly uncomfortable, but he only gazed at her silently. Finally, she said, "I'm Cedar. And you are . . . ?"

His gaze slid from her face to the tree behind her, where Maeve and Kier were resting among the roots.

"Cedar," he said, more to himself than to her. "Well, that's certainly fitting." His voice was soft and slightly accented. Irish, she thought. Then his eyes returned to her. "I'm Liam," he said.

She waited again for him to elaborate, but this time he walked past her and knelt down at Maeve's grave, which was covered in wildflowers.

"Thank you for your help, but why are you here?" she asked, suspicion in her voice. As far as she knew, Maeve hadn't been friendly with any of the neighbors. In fact, she wasn't sure that her mother had had any friends at all.

"I came to pay my respects," he said simply.

"After dark?" she asked.

"It was better this way," he replied. "I didn't anticipate finding anyone else here."

He wove his fingers through the grass and the delicate stems of the evening primroses and mayflowers. "She loved wildflowers," he murmured. In the dim light, Cedar could see that his face was wet with tears. Quietly, he spoke some words in a language she didn't recognize. Small green tendrils pushed up from the ground through his fingers, spreading upward with a life of their own and growing longer and thicker. He lifted his hand from the ground and watched as leaves grew on the branches, expanding up and out until the bush was the size of a small child. Then blossoms erupted from every branch in shades of red, white, and pink. "She also loved roses," he said, not looking at Cedar. "It will bloom every year on the anniversary of her death."

Cedar gaped at him in astonishment, wondering if she had hit her head harder than she'd thought. "How did you do that?" she asked. "Who *are* you?" She was about to ask if he was one of the Tuatha Dé Danann but stopped herself.

He stood and brushed a few specks of dirt and grass off his knees. His eyes were wells of enormous sadness when he answered, "I'm no one of importance." He started to walk away but then stopped. "I would stop trying to get in there if I were you," he said, indicating the workshop with a nod of his head. "It won't open for you, or anyone for that matter. I know the spells she used, and they'll only get nastier the harder you fight them. It is impossible for a human to get inside. And if you somehow managed it by magic, you would likely find yourself unable to get out. Just leave it be."

"What do you mean? How do you know all of this?" Cedar demanded. Her mind was racing. If this man knew about Maeve, then maybe he also knew about Eden, and she didn't like strangers knowing her daughter's secret. She had to find out who he was and what he wanted.

He ignored her questions and turned his back on her, starting to walk toward the road. She ran after him and they almost collided when he abruptly stopped and turned around. She grabbed one of his arms to balance herself and didn't let go. "Who are you?" she said again, tightening her grip.

He stared into her face for a long moment, as though trying to memorize it. His voice caught when he tried to speak. "Someone who cares," he said. "Don't go back there, Cedar."

"Where?" she demanded.

"You think it's a place of safety, but it's not. There is nothing but pain for you in Tír na nÓg." Then he wrenched his arm out of her grasp and walked briskly down the gravel driveway and around the corner.

"Wait!" she yelled, and ran after him. But when she reached the end of the driveway there was no sign of him, nor of any vehicle. There was only a small cloud of dust rising up from the dirt road and into the breezeless night.

❧

When Cedar opened the door to her apartment, she was met by a flurry of activity. Eden, who had been sitting on the sofa reading *The Hobbit*, squealed, "Mummy!" and ran toward her. Finn and Jane were up to their elbows in boxes, setting out lamps, picture frames, and *Star Wars* figurines on Cedar's bare bookshelves and end tables. Most of Cedar's belongings had gone into a storage unit, except for her deluxe espresso maker and a few pieces of furniture. Jane was dancing to the sound of Milo Greene on the stereo, but she stopped mid-groove when she saw Cedar.

"Hey, look who's back!" Jane said, a wide grin on her face. Her hair was completely shaved on one side of her head, and the other side hung down over her eyes, which were lined with turquoise today. Bright red streaks stood out from the black hair around them. A series of small skulls adorned her ears and hung like gruesome trophies from a bangle on her wrist. Cedar started to say hello, but then Eden barreled into her and she winced, her body still tender from her collision with the gravel driveway.

"Hey, there, Honey Lime," Finn said, coming in for his own hug as Eden returned to her book on the sofa. "Honey Lime" was his new favorite nickname for her, out of several that he'd tried on for size. He said it was the color of her eyes when she was happy. Jane said it sounded more like a margarita and pretended to gag whenever he used it around her.

"Are you okay?" he asked, running his hands gently along her sides where Eden had squeezed her. Cedar nodded and laughed. She couldn't get a paper cut without Finn noticing. Ever since her miraculous return to life he had barely left her side, or Eden's. He had wanted to accompany her to Maeve's house this weekend, but Cedar had been worried about bringing Eden there. On the surface, Eden seemed to be coping fine with what had happened, but Cedar had heard her crying out for Gran in her sleep. Taking her back to the place where Maeve had been killed and buried might be too much right now. So she'd convinced Finn to have a daddy-daughter weekend in Halifax, and he had reluctantly agreed. Cedar was tempted to keep what had happened at Maeve's a secret, to avoid encouraging Finn's overprotective tendencies. But the temptation was fleeting. They had promised each other that there would be no more secrets.

"Something strange happened, actually," she said. She told Finn and Jane about her encounter with Maeve's workshop and about the strange man who had come to pay his respects.

"Super weird," Jane said.

"He didn't say anything else?" Finn asked. He looked troubled.

Cedar shook her head. "No, he just told me to stop trying to get into the workshop and that we shouldn't go back to Tír na nÓg. I thought you might know who he was. Is he one of the Tuatha Dé Danann?"

"I don't think so," Finn said. "I don't know anyone called Liam, though that might not be his real name. But if he knew our plans to return to Tír na nÓg, one of the others might know him. I'll ask around. I, for one, want to know who he is and how he knows so much about us."

"Why do you think he'd warn you against going to Tír na nÓg?" Jane asked. "Not that I disagree with him," she added, arching an eyebrow. "I think Tír na nÓg is *far* too dangerous for you. The three of you should just stay here with me."

Cedar grinned. "Wait a second, did you pay this guy to scare me off?"

"It's not funny," Finn said, frowning. "Without knowing who he is, it's hard to know how seriously we should take him. But my guess is that he's a druid. I didn't think Maeve was in touch with other druids, but maybe she kept that a secret too. If he *is* a druid, his warning shouldn't be taken lightly."

Cedar glanced over at Eden, who appeared to be reading but was more likely hanging on their every word. "Hey, Eden, do you want to watch a quick show before bed?"

Eden looked over the cover of her book and said, "I'd rather know what you guys are talking about."

"Nothing. Boring, grown-up stuff," Cedar answered, rifling through a stack of DVDs and putting in *Secret of the Wings*, Eden's new favorite. Eden's fascination with fairies had grown exponentially since she had discovered that she technically was one, although she considered her lack of wings to be a tragic oversight. Cedar had tried to explain the difference between the Tuatha Dé Danann and the pixie-like fairies of cartoons and toys, and Eden had seemed to understand. But every once in a while Cedar found her daughter staring wistfully at her Tinker Bell doll or racing around her room wearing the wings from last year's Halloween costume and jumping off her bed in the hopes that she'd suddenly be able to fly. *Tír na nÓg will be good for her,* Cedar thought. *And it will be good for me too.* Both of them had a lot to learn about the world they belonged to by birthright, if nothing else. And Tír na nÓg would be safer. . . . If they stayed here, it would be impossible to keep Eden's ability hidden from friends, teachers, babysitters, and other parents, who wouldn't be able to ignore the sudden appearance of a portal to wherever Eden happened to be daydreaming about at the moment.

Eden begrudgingly settled onto the sofa, and Cedar led Jane and Finn to the kitchen.

Jane poured them each a glass of wine and raised her own glass after serving her friends. "To my best friend, Cedar; her long-lost lover, Finn; and their magic baby, Eden, who are abandoning me to this mundane world and going off to assume their true identities as fairies in the not-so-mythical-after-all land of Tír na nÓg. Wow. It sounds so strange when you say it out loud. But here's to living in crazy times. And now for my only word of Irish: Sláinte!"

Finn clinked glasses with them but was still frowning. Cedar poked him in the ribs. "Come on, you're not really worried, are you? How could a random druid possibly know what awaits us in Tír na nÓg? It's like listening to a fortune teller." Now that she was drinking wine in her brightly lit kitchen in the company of friends, the man's warning seemed insignificant, comical almost.

"How many druids are there, anyway?" Jane said. "I thought Maeve was the only one."

"No," Finn answered. "There are many, or at least there used to be. Their numbers have certainly diminished since the exile."

"Exile?" Cedar asked. Every day, she was learning new information, stories, legends, and facts about her people. She knew it would take years to get up to speed.

"Like Maeve, druids are . . . complicated," he said, measuring his words carefully. "Their magic is very powerful, and they used to hold a very important position in our society. They were the teachers, philosophers, historians, and judges. And they used to live and work very closely with us. Not only with us, of course; there were many druids who served the kings and chieftains of this world as well."

"You said they 'used to' live and work closely with you—not anymore?" Cedar asked.

"Sadly, no. The story goes that many years ago, when the druids still lived in Tír na nÓg, a druid stole away the lover of one of the Tuatha Dé Danann nobles. This flew in the face of convention; you see, druids were not considered our equals. It would be like the Queen of England running off with one of her servants. The noble was heartbroken and furious, and the High King at that time owed him a favor. So at the noble's bequest, the king banished all druids from Tír na nÓg. It was a very harsh punishment for the fault of one man, especially considering the centuries of service they had given us."

"Have they ever gone back?" Cedar asked.

"No. We have paid for the king's rash decision. The druids had grown proud, and they felt that their exile was an insult too great to bear. They swore never to return unless they were given equal status with the Tuatha Dé Danann, including the right to assume the High Kingship. Of course, because my people are even prouder, we have refused, even though it would greatly benefit our land and society if they were to return."

Secretly, Cedar could understand why the druids felt the way they did. It hadn't escaped her notice that the Tuatha Dé Danann did not play well with others, be they humans, Merrow, leprechauns, or druids. Perhaps she could help change that, she thought. But out loud she asked, "So if Liam's a druid, why would he have warned me to not go back?"

"I don't know, but it worries me. As I said, druids have no great love for our kind. Maybe he knows how important you and Eden are to the rebuilding of Tír na nÓg, and he was trying to frighten you into staying here. But how would he *know* that unless one of us told him? On the other hand, it sounds like he really cared for Maeve. Maybe he was trying to protect you for her sake. Many druids *do* have the gift of foresight. But if that's the case, I don't understand why he didn't give you more information."

"I don't get it either," Cedar said. "He just walked around the corner and disappeared. But honestly, I think we still need to go. The longer we stay here, the greater the chance that Eden will slip up and open a sidh, and I can't keep her cooped up in this apartment forever. Let's just be extra careful while we're there. If something happens, we can always come back. Lorcan's dead. Nuala is still around, but she can't hide forever, and we're more likely to find her if we're there."

"Are you sure?" Jane asked. "Maybe you should just lie low for a while and let them sort things out over there in Tír na nÓg. You could come to the comic con in Vegas with me instead!" She was leaving in a few days, and had been talking about the trip for weeks.

Jane's face was so imploring that Cedar had to laugh. "Oh, my dear," she said, "I would love to go to Vegas with you, but the longer I put this off, the harder it will be. No, we're leaving in the morning, vague warnings be damned. I want to get us all settled in and started on our new life. So you go to Vegas and have a blast, and if everything goes well, maybe I'll come back for a visit in a couple of weeks."

"You better, or I might just slip up and forget your alibi," Jane said with a wink. Cedar glared at her. "Oh, don't worry, I'm just kidding. I remember the whole story: You got back together with Eden's dad and are moving to Australia so you can be together. You got a great job, are very happy, blah blah blah. And I'm subletting your apartment until you decide to sell it, whenever that might be. Thanks, again, by the way. This place is way nicer than my dingy hole in the wall."

"No worries," Cedar said. "Hey, maybe we can fix you up with one of the Tuatha Dé Danann."

Jane rolled her eyes. "Puhleeze. I can barely handle human guys, let alone a fairy-god-man. Besides, they're all . . . you know, gorgeous and shit."

Cedar laughed. "And so are you, my friend. In your own funky way."

CHAPTER 2

Cedar woke up alone in her bed to the sound of breakfast being prepared in the kitchen. She heard Eden's excited chattering and smiled. Finn must be telling her stories again.

Finn had immediately bonded with their daughter, and his presence had gone a long way toward helping Eden feel safe. She never spoke of her kidnapping unless prompted, and even then she tended to only answer direct questions. Cedar didn't want to push her for more information than she was ready to share, so she focused on showering her with love instead.

Together, Eden and Cedar loved to pepper Finn with questions about their "real" world. He seemed to enjoy answering as much as they enjoyed asking; the stories he told them about the Tuatha Dé Danann sounded like fairy tales, but he swore they were all true. Cedar's desire to know more about the world of her birth parents grew stronger each day, and although her first priority was to take Eden somewhere safe, it wasn't the only reason she was looking forward to going to Tír na nÓg. She wanted to help transform her homeland from the dry and barren place she had seen back into the paradise it had once been. She didn't know what to expect when they returned. Would the land have rejuvenated itself in the weeks since Lorcan's death? Or was there more work to be done? There was only one way to find out.

"Good morning!" she said brightly as she walked into the kitchen, trying to mask the fluttering in her stomach. Eden waved enthusiastically, her mouth filled with toast and peanut butter. For some reason, she was wearing a sparkly silver mitten on one hand. Jane, who had slept on the sofa, stuck out her bottom lip and took another sip of coffee.

Cedar filled her mug and then kissed Eden on the head. "Are you pretending to be Michael Jackson?" she asked, looking pointedly at the silver mitten.

"Who's that?" Eden asked. "I'm Nuadu of the Silver Hand!"

"Who?"

"Our ancestor!" Eden exclaimed, waving her silver hand around. "His hand got cut off in a battle, so the doctor Dian Cecht gave him a silver one to wear instead. Kind of like Anakin Skywalker, except Anakin's was black. But then Dian Cecht's son, who was an even better doctor, gave Nuadu a new hand—a real one—and he became king. All Anakin turned into was Darth Vader."

"Yes, I see where the comparison breaks down," Cedar said, stifling a smile. "How are you enjoying your father's history lessons?"

"Great!" Eden replied, her face lighting up. "Guess what else I learned? There are four magic treasures in Tír na nÓg. There's a pot that's always filled with food, a sword that can never be beaten, a spear that never misses, and a big stone that roars."

"A stone that roars? That seems like an odd treasure," Cedar remarked over the rim of her coffee cup, one eyebrow raised.

"They're not all in Tír na nÓg," Finn corrected his daughter. "Our people brought them here to Earth when we first arrived from the Four Cities, and then to Tír na nÓg when we lost the battle with the Milesians. The sword, the spear, and the cauldron are still there, but the stone was lost. It's called the Lia Fáil, the Stone of Destiny."

"Well, our destiny is to finish packing and head out on our own adventure," Cedar said, ruffling Eden's hair. "Finish your breakfast, and then go brush your teeth."

∾

A couple of hours later they were ready. Cedar had gone over their alibi with Jane one more time to make sure she had it straight. Eden had packed her favorite stuffed animals and books into a backpack and was wearing what she thought was her most fairylike dress.

Before his parents had returned to Tír na nÓg a couple of weeks ago, Finn had given back to his mother her half of the starstone so that they'd still be able to communicate. He activated it now and waited for her response.

Cedar was glad to hear Riona's voice. "Are you ready?" Riona asked through the stone.

"We are," Finn responded. "Where shall we meet you?"

There was a pause, and then Riona answered, "By the white tree, I think."

There must have been something strange about her expression, because Finn leaned closer to the stone and asked, "Is everything okay?"

Cedar edged in to see Riona's face. Catching sight of her, Riona gave her a nod and a small wave.

"Things are . . . interesting. I'd forgotten how the politics of this place can be. But I'll explain everything when you get here." She waved her hand again and was gone.

"Well, shall we?" Cedar asked.

Eden ran up and took her hand, squeezing it tightly. Cedar knelt down and hugged her daughter. "Remember, baby, I'm with you this time. It's going to be such an adventure, and we're all going to be together—you, me, and Daddy—so you don't have to be afraid of anything."

Cedar stood up, trying to keep her legs from shaking. Despite her encouraging words to Eden, she was more than a little nervous. The last time she'd been to Tír na nÓg, it had literally been the death of her. Eden's experience hadn't been much rosier—she'd been taken there against her will, like a sacrificial lamb. And Finn had fled the place when he was only twelve years old, driven out by war and a tyrannical leader. But now they were all going back. They had changed everything about Tír na nÓg the last time they were there, and now it was home—or it very soon would be. She took a deep breath, knowing that her life would never be the same once she walked through that door.

"I'm ready," Eden said. "The white tree."

Cedar gave Jane another quick hug. "Be safe," Jane whispered, her eyes filled with worry.

Eden reached out to grab the doorknob to her bedroom. They had discovered that while she had used a tree and an archway to open the sidhe in Tír na nÓg, she still needed to use a door on Earth. She closed her eyes and then pulled the door open. The air behind it shimmered, moving in waves like heat off asphalt. Through it, Cedar could make out the vague outline of a white tree with several figures gathered beneath it. Grasping Eden's hand tightly in one hand and her small suitcase in the other, Cedar walked through the door. She sensed Finn's presence directly behind her.

The first thing she noticed was the change in the air. It felt lighter, thinner somehow, though she could breathe just fine. She tried to remember if it had been this way the last time she'd been to Tír na nÓg, but so much had been going on that she'd hardly taken the time to notice the quality of the air. She was surprised to see that the landscape looked much as it had before—brown, dry, and barren. The grass crunched beneath her feet, and the uniform gray of the sky did little to defuse the dead atmosphere. But she barely had time to register these thoughts before she was swept into a bone-crushing hug by the most beautiful man she had ever seen. He was tall and lean, with blond hair that looked as if a woman's hands had just been run through it. His straight nose and chiseled cheekbones provided the perfect setting for a pair of piercing blue eyes that were twinkling with mirth. She could feel the muscles rippling in his chest as he hugged her, and she hoped she wasn't blushing. He didn't show any signs of letting go.

"All right, Felix, let her breathe," Finn said.

"Felix?" Cedar gasped, pulling away to get a better look at him. Gone was the old fisherman she had known, with his bushy white beard and small beady eyes. In his place stood this godlike creature, who suddenly flashed her a wide grin. "You kept your teeth!" she exclaimed. Instead of the perfect smile she'd expected to go with the rest of his gorgeous body, Felix's grin was still punctuated by two gold teeth and one black one.

"Just for now. I wanted you to recognize me," he said, laughing. "Damn, it's good to see you. And you, too, little fairy," he said, bending down to greet Eden.

"Eden, this is Felix," Cedar explained. "He used to look like an old man, with a big white beard. But that was just a costume—a very good one. Do you remember him?" Eden nodded and smiled shyly. Felix had doted on her while he was supervising Cedar's recovery in the days following their return from Tír na nÓg.

One day, Eden had discovered a wounded bird at the playground. She had brought it back to Felix, begging him to heal it. When he did, that had sealed the deal for Eden—she and Felix became fast friends. She had taught him how to play Go Fish, and he'd tried to teach her how to pronounce his real name, Toirdhealbhach MacDail re Deachai. It had come to no one's surprise when they'd decided she would keep calling him Felix. He had come back to Tír na nÓg only a week ago, once he was certain that Cedar and Eden were both in perfect health.

"Why do you look so different?" Eden asked him.

"Well, when I was in Ériu, in your other world, I thought it might be fun to pretend to be someone else for a while. I don't get to do that too much around here. But now that I'm back home, I figured I should probably look like myself."

"You sound different too," Eden said, looking puzzled.

"Aye, do I now, young lassie?" Felix said, putting on the heavy accent he'd adopted while living in Halifax. "Don't worry, I'm still the same lovable guy, just without the beard and the strange words. It was great fun, though—definitely my favorite disguise yet. Here are some other people you might not recognize at first." He stepped aside, and a slim, graceful woman rushed forward to hug them. It was Riona, but she looked thirty years younger than when Cedar had seen her last. With her dark hair and fair skin, she could have easily passed for Cedar's sister. Molly was there too, looking like her usual teenage self.

"Hello, Cedar. Hello, Eden," Riona said. "It's so good to see you. Do you recognize me, Eden? I know I don't look like a grandma anymore, but I still am. Remember how I turned into a kitty for you?" Eden smiled and nodded. "This is Molly—she looks just the same, but I think you met her only once or twice, so you might not remember her. Molly was born in Halifax, just like you, so you're not the only one who's new here."

Cedar was encouraged by Riona's words. She hadn't thought of it before, but the rebels had been away from Tír na nÓg for more than two decades. Some of the younger children had never seen their homeland before, and Finn and his brother, Dermot, had spent the majority of their lives away from it. Even those who had spent centuries in Tír na nÓg must have felt disoriented. So much had changed, so little was as they remembered. Cedar wasn't the only one who felt like a stranger in this place.

Just then, she heard a loud voice call out, *Cedar! Welcome home!* Cedar spun around, looking for the source of the voice. Finn burst out laughing. "What . . . ," she started to ask, and then spotted a tiny figure running toward them from off in the distance. She heard the voice again. *I'm coming! Hang on!*

"Nevan!" Cedar cried, realizing that the voice she'd heard had been Nevan speaking to her telepathically. In a few moments the pixie-like woman was upon them, hugging Cedar and Finn and laughing.

"I hope I didn't scare you!" she said, out loud this time.

Cedar grinned. She had liked Nevan from the beginning. "No, I was just surprised, that's all. I keep forgetting you can do that."

"It's *very* good to see you." Nevan beamed. "And . . . don't worry. We're going to sort everything out. Hey, Eden!" Nevan knelt down so that she was at Eden's level.

"Hi, Nevan," Eden said, smiling.

Nevan and her partner, Sam, had been two of the last to return to Tír na nÓg after Lorcan's downfall. Nevan had fallen in love with Cedar's homeland and had been reluctant to leave it, especially for the gray skies of Tír na nÓg. But Sam had convinced her that they needed to play a part in their world's renewal, and so they had returned.

Taking in Nevan's words, Cedar frowned. "What needs sorting out?" she asked. Nevan stood up abruptly, her playful smile sliding from her face.

After a moment of silence, Riona was the one who spoke. "Eden, why don't you show Molly what you brought from home? Are there any stuffed animals in your backpack?" she asked. Molly took the hint and knelt down beside Eden, who had already starting pulling toys and books out of her bag. Moving a few paces away, Riona signaled for the others to follow her. When they were far enough that they could speak privately, she said, "I'm sorry to have to ruin your first day here with bad news. Nuala has returned."

"Returned," Cedar repeated, her heart seizing. "From where?"

"From wherever she was hiding," Riona answered. "She has presented herself to the Council and made them an offer they are finding difficult to refuse. You've come just in time to stop them."

"Stop them from what?" Cedar asked.

"They're going to make her queen."

Cedar's legs and lungs were burning by the time they arrived at the Hall. The great building was as imposing as ever, its twisting white spires piercing the sky, their colored banners hanging limp against the dull backdrop. She shuddered at the memory of this place. Finn put his hand on her arm as they approached the main entrance. "Just wait a moment," he said, "and catch your breath." He didn't look tired at all, and Cedar was reminded of how frail—how human—she was compared to everyone else in this world.

She was baffled by Riona's revelation. Why would the Council want to make Nuala queen? Nuala had tried to help Lorcan. She was the enemy. She must be using her power of persuasion on them, but surely the Council of the Tuatha Dé Danann would not be so easily deceived.

Riona had urged Cedar and Finn to go to the Council without delay. Finn's father, Rohan, would be waiting for them there. In the meantime, Nevan had offered to show Eden around before bringing her to her new home, where Riona would get her settled in. Cedar had been reluctant to leave her daughter behind, but Eden had seemed perfectly happy to stay with her new friends.

Cedar drew in another deep breath and wiped a few beads of sweat from her forehead. "Remember," Finn said. "You are the daughter of Brogan and Kier. You are one of us, and you killed Lorcan. "

"Technically, *you* killed Lorcan," Cedar pointed out.

Finn cupped her flushed face in his hands. "I'd be dead if it weren't for you . . . all of us would be. You're the bravest person I know. I don't think she'll try anything, not with the Council around, but even if she does, she can't use her power on me, remember? I'll stay right by your side, and I'll help you resist her." He paused. "I know it's going to be hard to be near her," he said. "Believe me, Cedar, I want to rip her apart with my bare hands, and I will if I get the chance. But if she's under the Council's protection, we can't touch her. Not now. But you don't need to be afraid of her."

"I'm not afraid," Cedar said. "I'm angry." Eyes flashing, she straightened up and walked briskly through the entrance to the Hall. They passed several other Danann as they made their way to the center courtyard. No one tried to stop them, though several stared, and some called out greetings. Cedar felt bolstered by this. They had friends here.

They finally reached the soaring marble arches and stately birch trees that surrounded the spacious courtyard. The members of the Council were sitting on carved wooden chairs in a small circle in the center of the courtyard. There were eight of them, five men and three women, all of them elegantly dressed, though their faces were drawn and pale. A few Danann were in the courtyard as well, sitting on small white chairs arranged outside the circle or milling around amid the arches. Cedar's eyes skimmed over them without taking much notice—she was looking for only one person.

And then she saw her. Nuala was sitting on one of the thin white chairs just outside the Council circle, wearing a long ivory dress trimmed with gold, her flaming red hair loose around her shoulders. Delicate strands of ivy were woven throughout her tresses, something Cedar was sure would look ridiculous on just about anyone else. On Nuala, it looked regal. She wasn't bound or restrained in any way, and she looked quite relaxed as she sat there smiling at the members of the Council who were facing her.

Cedar felt as if hot lava had been poured into her stomach. She almost doubled over with the intensity of her hatred for this woman who had endangered her daughter's life and killed her adoptive mother. She struggled to regain control, well aware that Nuala could use even this hatred against her. The Council members stirred at their arrival, and a tall, handsome man who had been pacing the courtyard rushed over to them.

"Fionnbharr, Cedar, you have arrived," he said.

Cedar looked more closely at the man, who was wearing deep green robes that did nothing to hide his powerful build. "Rohan?" she asked in disbelief. Like his wife, he appeared thirty years younger than when Cedar had last seen him.

"Aye, aye, it's me," he said gruffly.

"What's going on?" she started to ask. "Why is—"

"Not now," he interrupted. Then he turned to the Council. "May I present my son Fionnbharr, who slew Lorcan with his own sword. And this is Cedar, daughter of Brogan and Kier, who gave her own life to secure our freedom from that tyrant."

Cedar looked around at the faces in the circle. She wasn't sure what she had been expecting, but it wasn't this. Some of the members of the Council leaned forward to get a better look at her, others raised their eyebrows, as if they, too, had been expecting something more. A couple leaned toward each other to exchange whispers. Only one stood. A short, stocky man with curly brown hair strode over to her, knelt, and kissed her hand.

"I owe you my life," he said as he stood. "I was one of the souls freed by your sacrifice. It is a gift I can never repay."

"Cedar, this is Gorman. He was killed by Lorcan a few years ago for his shield of protection. I think you are familiar with it?" Rohan said.

Cedar took an instinctive step back. "Do not fear," Gorman said quickly. "It activates only on my command. I was a fool to let my guard down around that monster. I don't deserve a second chance but am grateful for it all the same." He bowed at Cedar again and then resumed his seat in the circle.

Another member of the Council, a tall, reedy woman with thin blonde hair that fell past her waist, nodded at Cedar but did not stand. "So this is the human to whom we owe our thanks," she said. Though her words were gracious, she did not smile, and her lip curled up slightly when she spoke.

"Cedar is not human. She is one of us, a Tuatha Dé Danann and the daughter of the High King," Finn said. Rohan shot him a warning glance.

The woman inclined her head slightly in Finn's direction, as if to acknowledge that he had, indeed, spoken. "Yes, one of us, I suppose, though quite masked in humanity. She clearly has no Lýra. Tell me, is she immortal?"

Cedar could sense Finn shifting nervously beside her. It was clear that he hadn't been expecting an inquisition. She stepped forward. "To be honest, I don't know," she said. "I suppose only time will tell, quite literally. And it's true that I don't have the Lýra, but that was done to hide me from Lorcan. I have killed him and have returned home to be with my people."

The blonde woman gazed at Cedar steadily. "You did kill him," she agreed. "And I believe few of us will miss him. His aims were noble and just, but his ways were . . . brutish, shall we say?"

"'His aims were noble and just'?" Cedar repeated incredulously, ignoring the pressure of Finn's hand on her arm. "His aim was to destroy humanity. There's nothing noble about that!"

"Spoken like a true . . . human," Nuala said, rising to her feet. The folds of her gown fell to the floor, and she looked like a bride on her wedding day as she walked confidently into the center of the circle. "Hello again, Cedar. I was so happy to hear that you were alive."

"What's she doing here?" Cedar said through gritted teeth, unable to restrain herself any longer. "Don't you know who this woman is? What she's done?"

"The Council has heard Nuala's position," said another member of the Council, a huge, strongly built man with a dark goatee.

"What position could she possibly have?"

"Oh, Cedar," Nuala said, shaking her head. "I feel so sorry for you. You've been through so much, I understand how upsetting this must all be. Can someone bring Cedar a chair? She's looking rather frail." Cedar ignored the proffered chair and glared at Nuala, who continued. "You've been horribly misinformed, I'm afraid. Let me explain, just like I did to the Council. It's true that I brought Eden here, but it was because I—like many others— believed she was the dyad, the answer to the prophecy. With all due respect to Ruadhan"—she nodded in Rohan's direction—"I found his leadership weak. I did not think he would have what it took to bring the child here and challenge Lorcan. So I did it myself. Like everyone, I believed the lie Ruadhan spread. . . . I thought that Lorcan had been unable to absorb the gift of the sidhe when Brogan died. I never imagined that he might want to kill Eden."

Cedar looked disbelievingly around at the members of the Council, most of whom were listening intently, even nodding. She glanced at Finn, whose brow was deeply furrowed. "Is she . . . ?" Cedar asked.

"I don't think so," he answered in an undertone. "She doesn't seem to be using her ability—not now, at least. But she's also naturally persuasive."

Rohan cleared his throat. "The Council knows where I stand. We're all aware that Fionnghuala has a silver tongue and can persuade those around her to see the world as she would have them see it. But I am immune to such power and have borne witness to her actions, which reveal her true character."

The Council member with the goatee spoke up again, standing this time. He was a head taller than any of the others in the courtyard, and Cedar could see his muscles straining beneath his robes. He looked like someone you would not want to anger. "Yes, but we have used the goblet of Manannan mac Lir, which you returned to us. She tells the truth—she acted in what she thought were the best interests of our land and people. And she did not intend for the child to die."

"She brought the child here to help Lorcan, not to fight him," Rohan argued.

"She was Lorcan's prisoner," said the blonde woman.

"Then why did she run as soon as he was killed?" Finn interjected.

Nuala stepped forward. "Perhaps it's time we look to the future, instead of dwelling on the past," she said in a silky voice. "Has the Council considered my proposal?"

"What proposal?" Gorman, the man who had kissed Cedar's hand, looked at his fellow Council members in confusion.

"Ah, yes, you were absent when she first approached us," said the tall, reedy blonde. "Fionnghuala, would you care to repeat what you told the rest of us? I'm sure our newcomers will be interested as well."

Nuala smiled ingratiatingly. "Gladly, Sorcha. The goblet of Manannan mac Lir does not lie. My intentions were—and are—noble. I had hoped that the child Eden could fulfill the prophecy by returning me here to Tír na nÓg, where my people were in great need. While I was on Ériu I realized that *my* ability could be used to defeat Lorcan, whose bloodlust was a danger to us all. I hoped to use my gift to persuade him away from an all-out war against the humans—a war that he did not seem to understand would have been far more difficult than the ones we fought with them millennia ago. The humans have grown numerous, and are well armed. I had a different plan, and still do—a plan that will give us what we deserve without sacrificing the lives of our people in a long, drawn-out war for which we were poorly prepared.

"My plan would have worked but for Gorman's shield of protection. I went through great trials to return home and was dismayed to discover that Lorcan was immune to my power. I became his prisoner, but I did not give up hope. He kept me close because of my knowledge of the rebels. I knew he'd eventually lower his guard around me, and then I'd be able to convince him to change his ways, and save our people. But before I could do so, Eden's human mother arrived and did what only she could have done—used her druid-given gift and sacrificed herself, destroying Lorcan. She has been reunited with her child, which is exactly what she wanted." Nuala paused for a moment and nodded graciously at Cedar, who stared stonily back at her. Then Nuala swept around the circle, her voice rising dramatically.

"Now we need to start rebuilding our great society. I ask that you consider my plan: Crown me your queen, and I will use my ability to convince the humans to make war—on each other. Not a drop of Danann blood need be spilled. Indeed, the humans are nearing the brink of another catastrophic world war even now. A few well-placed words in the right ears will tip the balance. I will encourage them to use weapons that will not damage the land, so once they are done destroying their own kind, we can claim what is rightfully ours. Why fight the humans when they are so willing to fight each other?"

Nuala cast her piercing green eyes around the circle. "There is one more thing," she said. "I was not idle during my time on Ériu. I made contact with several key druids and gained their respect and trust. The druids have agreed to return to Tír na nÓg to live alongside us as they once did, contributing their considerable skills to the rebuilding of our land. While we are settling Ériu, they will try restoring Tír na nÓg to its former splendor. If they succeed, we will have dominion over both worlds."

For a moment, there was complete silence. Then Gorman asked, "And what, exactly, do they want in return?"

Nuala's voice was steady and full of confidence. "Nothing more than the knowledge that someone they know and trust is on the throne. They *will* come back—when I am queen."

Cedar had heard enough. "Say something," she hissed at Finn. "They respect you more than me. They'll listen to you!"

But it was Rohan who cleared his throat and approached the circle. Nuala regarded him coolly, but he didn't even look at her as he addressed the Council. "Hear me, and accept my words as truth. This woman has been part of my company for the past two decades, and I know her well. She despises humans as much as Lorcan did. Their means may be different, but their goals are the same and equally despicable: the destruction of a race that has no quarrel with ours. The humans won Ériu as their own thousands of years ago. *This* is our home now, and it requires our care and attention. We should leave the humans in peace and focus all of our abilities on healing our own land."

Another of the Council stood, a man with a swarthy complexion and a long black beard. "You have become soft, Ruadhan. The humans may have won their last battle with us, but there's no reason why we should not win the next one. Why should we remain defeated forever? Perhaps our time in Tír na nÓg is over. I, for one, would not waste the druids' skills here. With our strength and with the druids by our side, we can create a new Tír na nÓg on Ériu, as splendid as in the days of our fathers."

"You would wipe out an entire race for a better garden?" Gorman exclaimed, rising to Rohan's defense. "Give our land some time; it has not yet been a month since the poisoner was defeated. We must be patient. We must not abandon this land that has given us so much."

"And what if the land never heals?" asked a curvy woman with dark auburn hair and milky-white skin. "We cannot stay in this barren place forever. What about our children? We must bring the druids back. Their skill with the land is unquestionable. Give them a chance, and if they fail, we should do as Fionnghuala has suggested and reclaim Ériu."

Cedar stared aghast at the members of the Council, most of whom were now standing and arguing loudly. She shook off Finn's arm, which had been wrapped around her shoulders, and strode into the center of the circle to stand beside Rohan.

"No," she said firmly. To her surprise, the arguing voices trailed off and went silent. She took a deep breath and continued. "This woman kidnapped a child—*my* child, Rohan's granddaughter and the granddaughter of the last true High King. She didn't do it for the benefit of your people. She did it to save her own skin. Maybe she's telling the truth when she says that she didn't think Lorcan would kill Eden, but that doesn't negate the fact that she captured an innocent child and put her in danger to achieve her own ends. Lorcan would have killed Eden if I hadn't intervened. *Think about it,*" she urged. "Do you really want someone with Nuala's ability ruling over you? She could have whatever she wants, whenever she wants it." She stopped, breathing heavily, and waited for a response.

After a moment, the blonde reedy woman whom Nuala had called Sorcha stepped forward. "We have known Fionnghuala for many years, and she has not once used her gift for her own benefit. Do not presume to tell us what to do. We will consider her proposal. Now leave us. There is much to discuss."

Cedar turned to Rohan, looking for his support. But he just shook his head. "We'd best leave," he said. "The Council must deliberate."

Cedar felt fire burning in the pit of her stomach again. "You're making a huge mistake," she snarled, and then turned abruptly and walked out of the circle, her body rigid and her head held high. She knew Finn and Rohan were keeping pace behind her, but she kept on walking until she was outside the Hall. The cold, dry air hit her in the face, and she finally stopped, breathing hard.

"We have to go back," she said, swiveling around to face Finn and his father. "We need to talk to them alone, when Nuala's not there."

Rohan exhaled loudly and reached out a hand to stop her. "I wish it were that simple, Cedar. I've always hated the politics of this place. Brogan was able to keep all of these egos in line, but . . . ," he trailed off, his expression cloudy.

"I've tried talking to them. So have Felix and Anya. But Nuala got here first, and she planted seeds of doubt in their minds. We were gone for many years and were in hiding for years before that. We've been branded as traitors, and there are many questions about what we were doing while we were on Ériu. Lorcan was not as reviled as you might think. He did not rise to power by violence only. There were many who supported him, who believed that we should take back the land we once called home. But he was too blood-thirsty, too power hungry, and by the time the others realized that, he was too powerful to stop.

"Nuala's timing is impeccable. The Council is glad that Lorcan's gone, but his death created a vacuum. She can give them what they've always wanted without the bloodshed and civil unrest. She may be using her power on them, but I don't think so. I don't think she *needs* to . . . she's offering something most of them want. And Sorcha is right—I never saw Nuala use her ability until we were in Ériu. They trust her, and with her ability, she can hand them what they want on a silver platter. If they have to make her queen in order for that to happen, well . . . as you see, she doesn't have much opposition." He looked at her sadly. "I'm sorry, Cedar. I know this is not the welcome you expected. But I don't think talking to the Council is going to help us."

Cedar frowned. "Do you think we can fight them? Or just go after Nuala directly? Because we *need* to stop her."

Rohan and Finn exchanged glances. "We do," Rohan said slowly. "But starting another civil war is not the answer, and targeting Nuala would be too dangerous given our precarious position here. There is another solution."

"What?" Cedar exclaimed. Her blood was still pounding through her veins, and she was ready to do whatever it took.

"We need to present the Council with an alternative to Nuala as queen. Someone with a very strong claim to the throne, who would have the support of the people. That person is you, Cedar. We need *you* to become queen of Tír na nÓg."

CHAPTER 3

W ell, that was certainly interesting," Nuala said as she strolled
by the dry banks of the river. Her companion, the imposing
Council member with the dark goatee, laughed softly.

"That's one way to put it," he said. She could feel the weight of
his gaze on her, but she pretended to be absorbed in the flora
around them, even though there was nothing of beauty to draw her
eye. Let him look . . . and desire.

"Do you have a better description, Deaglán?" she asked with a
lilt in her voice.

"You, for one, were as captivating as always," he answered. "I
know I'm not the only one who's glad to have you back. And I'm
grateful that you weren't here for the worst of it."

Nuala arched an eyebrow at him. "The worst?"

"I was proud to support Lorcan at first," he said, furrowing his
brow. "He had lofty ambitions. He wanted to see our people rise to
greatness again. Brogan was happy for us to stay as we were—
outcasts. He didn't see the shame in our defeat. I know you were on
Brogan's side, so I will not speak ill of him—"

"I was on no one's side. I merely wanted to avoid bloodshed,"
Nuala interrupted. "I believed there had to be a better way than
sending our people to war. I still believe it."

He nodded. "I agree. And you were right to escape Lorcan. He
grew mad with power, and ruthless. He started turning on his own
supporters if they had a gift that could benefit him. No one was
safe. You certainly wouldn't have been."

Nuala feigned a shudder at the thought. "Yes, I believe he would have killed me sooner or later. I had hoped to best him when I returned, but with Gorman's shield . . . well, the human woman did us all a favor." *She certainly did,* Nuala thought to herself. She had never dreamed that things could turn out so well. With Lorcan gone, there was very little standing in her way. The return of Rohan and the rest of her pursuers from Ériu was inconvenient, but she had been pleasantly surprised by how easy it was to discredit them. Lorcan's propaganda had done its job for her. "And now that the madman is gone, we must move forward. Do you think the other Council members agree with me?"

"Well, I can't speak for the others, of course," Deaglán demurred. "But I believe your plan to be an excellent one. There is the small problem of your family history, of course, which may give some of them second thought. Gorman in particular is being rather prickly about that issue. But to my mind it makes perfect sense that your plan should be put into action, and making you queen is a necessary step. I don't think it will take the Council long to reach a decision. Despite the prophecy and Lorcan's death, the land has not healed. We cannot stay here much longer, not the way things are."

"I'm glad that we are of a like mind," Nuala purred. "You have great influence on the Council."

"You have great influence on everyone," Deaglán said, casting her a knowing glance.

Nuala blushed. "I would never use my ability on the Council—surely you know that. I've sworn to never use it to gain an unfair advantage, whether in matters of politics . . . or love." She lifted her eyes to meet his, and let them linger there until her meaning was impossible to misunderstand. "What exactly do they say about my family?" she asked once he had finally looked away.

He stared at the ground as he answered. "Only that you do not come from one of the great houses, and that your ancestors were more servants than masters. Well, and there is talk that there has been the occasional . . . instability, shall we say, in your family line."

"I see," Nuala said, but she could hardly deny it. Everyone knew the stories.

"And then there is the matter of your parents, of course. A very tragic situation, to be sure."

"It was," Nuala agreed.

Deaglán hesitated and then asked, "May I be so bold as to inquire as to exactly what occurred there? There appear to be some . . . variations on the tale, you might say."

Nuala looked across the riverbed to the bank beyond. She didn't enjoy discussing or even remembering her family. But a little bit of sympathy would certainly not hurt her cause. She decided to use her pathetic story to her advantage.

"My ability came from my mother's side," she said. "She could see deep into the hearts of others and uncover their true desires, even those they wouldn't admit to themselves. She could use her power to persuade a person to do something or think something, as long as it aligned with something true inside that person's mind or heart. But she was gentle and kind, and never used her ability to her own advantage, even though she could have achieved anything she wanted. My father, as I'm sure you have heard, was neither gentle nor kind. He was vain and brutish and constantly paranoid that my mother was casting a spell on him, making him do things that he couldn't remember. Why he married her in the first place I don't know—he knew she had this power. She never hid her ability from him and had always promised that she'd never use it on him. I don't believe she ever did. But he could not be convinced otherwise."

She glanced over at Deaglán to see how her story was being received. His eyes were gazing back at her with compassion, so she took a deep breath and kept talking. "I was eight when we discovered that I shared my mother's ability. I was arguing with a friend over the last elderberry tart, of all ridiculous things. She was determined to have it, but I told her to give it to me. Suddenly, her eyes glazed over, and she handed me the tart and then walked away. I told my mother what had happened, and she was horrified. She knew what it meant. She had hoped it would skip my generation, or die out with her. From the very beginning she warned me not to use it or let anyone know about it, particularly my father. She said that no one would ever trust me once they knew the truth about my talent. I didn't believe her; I had more faith in people than that, and I was determined to prove that I could be trusted. That I could be loved."

She spared another glimpse at Deaglán and saw that he was blushing slightly. She mentally rolled her eyes. This was too easy. He was like a dog desperate for a walk; all she had to do was dangle the leash in front of him. She exulted in the fact that she didn't even need to use her ability; in some cases, apparently, feminine wiles were enough.

Nuala was grateful for her mother's warning; in all her years in Tír na nÓg she had been cautious and had used her ability sparingly and only in secret. Her restraint had paid off. She had proven herself trustworthy, and the Council did not suspect that she would ever be so bold as to try and influence their decision. And—so far—she hadn't. As long as they were cooperating, she saw no need to risk being caught using her power on them. If they became difficult, however . . .

Her thoughts were interrupted by Deaglán. "You deserve both trust and love, fair Nuala," he said. "And so did your mother."

"She did," Nuala agreed. "But my father did not think so." She could not keep the bitterness from her voice. "I used to come home to find my mother battered and bruised. She would never fight back, not even to protect herself. I used to beg her to let me use my ability to deal with my father, to get him to leave her alone. But even then she forbade me to use my gift. She told me that the only way I could live a normal life was to act like I didn't have it—just like she did. I know that she was afraid I'd become the target of my father's wrath if he found out what I could do. I obeyed. And then one day . . . I came home to find her dead on the floor. My father had killed her. He was ranting and raving about how she had bewitched him into marrying her and was keeping him under her control. I ran away, terrified. When I had gathered my courage to return, he had hung himself."

Nuala allowed her voice to break on the last sentence, and felt Deaglán's warm hand caress her arm. It was almost true, except for the bit about her father. She had not run away, terrified. She had looked him deep in the eye and had, for the first and last time, shown him her power. It hadn't been difficult to persuade her father that his life was meaningless, and that he'd be much happier swinging from the branch of the rowan tree that grew on the far edge of their land.

"You were not to blame for your father's actions," Deaglán said softly. "You have overcome the challenges of your background admirably."

Nuala smiled and covered his hand with her own as they continued to walk together. "You are very kind," she said. "We can only hope that the others feel the same way."

◦◦◦

Cedar was not in the mood for jokes. "Rohan, you're not serious."

"I *am* serious," he said. "You're the daughter of the last High King."

"The last one who wasn't a psychopath, at any rate," interjected Finn.

"Yes, but that doesn't matter. You told me the throne isn't hereditary," she said.

"It's true that it isn't *always* hereditary," Finn said. "But unless there's a good reason for the throne not to be handed down from parent to child, it often is."

"But there *is* a good reason," Cedar said. "They all think I'm human, remember? And I have no desire to be queen of Tír na nÓg or anywhere. Let's go, I want to get back to Eden, and we need to talk to the others and make a plan. A *real* plan."

They walked in silence, Rohan leading the way, while Cedar trailed behind, her mind a mass of slippery and contradictory thoughts. She was starting to wonder if coming to Tír na nÓg had been a mistake after all. Maybe she and Eden should return to Halifax. She knew that Finn would come with them if she asked—at least, she thought he would—but she also knew how committed he was to rebuilding his people and his land. She didn't want to ask him to make that choice, and she could never live without him. . . . She also couldn't bear the thought of giving Nuala the satisfaction of seeing her run away.

Maybe she could warn the world leaders in Ériu? But that was clearly no solution. She'd be dismissed as a crazy person and locked up in a psych ward. But what if she showed them what Eden could do? It would be definitive proof that another world existed. But no, she couldn't, *wouldn't* put Eden at risk like that.

Her mind returned to Rohan's suggestion: that she become the queen instead of Nuala. She knew that would never work, but what if someone else mounted a serious challenge to Nuala's claim? Rohan, maybe; he had been close to Brogan. Or someone who had been Lorcan's enemy here in Tír na nÓg. It could be anyone, as long as he or she was willing to put a stop to Nuala's blood-crazed plan.

After a while they came upon a small steep hill that was covered in scraggly grass. Cedar was surprised to discover that an ornately carved door was set in its side, like the one at the Fox and Fey pub back in Halifax.

Without warning, the door burst open and Finn's brother, Dermot, appeared. Cedar jumped and then quickly recovered herself. "You live in a hobbit hole," she said without thinking. Dermot laughed.

"Nice to see you again too, Cedar!" he said, giving her a hug. "Welcome home! We've cleaned the place up as best as we could, even though the front rooms were a disaster. I even found our old chess set, and it's your move." Dermot punched Finn in the arm. "Now if you'll excuse me, I'm off to find my ladyfriend Dáiríne. We're building a little hobbit hole of our own," he said with a wink, heading off in the opposite direction.

"I'll leave you two to get settled in," Rohan said. "But Cedar . . . think about it. We don't have much time." He caught up with Dermot in a few long strides. Cedar turned back to Finn, ready to launch into all the reasons why Rohan's plan was a bad one. But Finn was standing with the door open, gesturing for her to go in. She stepped through the doorway into darkness, but it grew light as soon as Finn closed the door behind them, even though there was no obvious source for the illumination. They were in a small, empty room about the size of an elevator. Before Cedar could ask about it, the ground beneath them began to drop, and she gasped in surprise. Finn put his arm around her to steady her. "Don't worry," he said. "This just takes us down to the house." His face was bright with excitement, and Cedar remembered that this was his first trip home in twenty years.

They continued to descend until they came to a gentle stop. When Cedar looked up, she couldn't see the door they had used to enter. They were in a small, dimly lit archway in front of a carved door. It opened easily at Finn's touch, and they stepped through it.

Cedar looked around in amazement. It was a large sitting room, and it reminded her of the living room at Rohan and Riona's house in Halifax. The furniture was all constructed of gleaming wood that twisted and turned seamlessly. Woven tapestries of vibrant colors hung from the walls on golden rods alongside several instruments, some of which were familiar, some unrecognizable. She looked up at the arched ceiling, which was the color of ivory. It gave the room an expansive, airy feeling, even though Cedar knew they must be several feet underground.

"The door in the hill and the one that leads to this room are enchanted to only let family and friends inside," Finn said. "Lorcan's minions tortured my uncle to get in this far, to the common areas. When my parents came back, this part of the house was in ruins. But even my uncle could not open the door to the rest of the chambers. Come, we'll see if it's as I remember."

They passed through several other rooms, which showed signs of having recently been put back together, and then they came to another richly decorated door, which glowed golden.

"It's not—?" Cedar began.

"A sidh? No. But only members of the immediate family, or those who have been freely invited by them can get past this door."

He pressed both palms to the door and then stood back. It swung open with a series of small chimes, and Finn and Cedar stepped inside. To Cedar's astonishment, they were standing in the middle of a sunny, circular courtyard. Smooth, flat stones shone beneath their feet, reflecting light from above. Cedar looked up and squinted against a bright yellow sun in a clear blue sky. Willow trees lined the courtyard, their branches swaying in a non-existent breeze, and a waterfall cascaded out of thin air into a small pool in the center of the room. Cedar felt a rush of incredible warmth through her veins and her muscles relax.

"It's incredible," she said. "It's so . . . alive. This is how Tír na nÓg used to be, isn't it? Why is it so different in here from what's outside?"

"It's an illusion of sorts," Finn said. "Or a reflection, you might say. Like a recording, or a hologram. Only here, it's tangible. You can touch the trees, drink the water. Still, it's just a memory of what was. I'm glad it's here, though. It gives us something to remember, and something to strive for. Come, let's find Eden. Riona was going to show her her new room."

He ducked under the branches of one of the willows, and Cedar followed. She realized now that the courtyard was in the center of a large, round room with four doors evenly spaced around its edges. "Each of these doors leads to a private chamber. My parents share a room, and there's one for each of my siblings. But since Dermot has moved in with Dáiríne, my family has redesigned his chambers for you and me. And Eden will have my old room, which is through here." He led her through one of the golden doors, which looked heavy but swung open effortlessly at the barest touch of his fingertips.

Cedar gasped and looked down. They were standing on a thick branch, high up in a huge tree that had to be at least fifty feet off the ground. "Don't worry. I would have broken my neck a hundred times if it were possible to fall from this tree," Finn said with a grin.

"Eden!" he called. "Are you in here?"

"Daddy!" Eden called back, and Cedar had to crane her neck to see where their daughter's voice was coming from. Eden's head was peeking out from behind a branch several yards above them. Further up were more branches and then a dark sky dotted with bright stars. A full moon gave the scene a soft, ethereal glow.

"Be careful, Eden!" Cedar cried instinctively.

"I am! Come on up. . . . It's amazing!" Eden called back.

They walked along the branch until they reached the trunk, which was so thick that the three of them wouldn't be able to wrap their arms around it. A narrow staircase was carved into the trunk, spiraling upward. As they climbed it, Finn pointed out his favorite branches, one with a wicker cage where his pet gnome had lived and another that was strung with child-sized musical instruments.

Dresses and robes in various shades of pinks and purples and yellows now hung from a few of the other branches.

"Riona's been busy," Finn said. "She still thinks this room is too boyish for Eden, but I think she'll like it okay, don't you?"

Cedar smiled at the uncertainty in his voice. "Are you kidding? This is like a dream come true for her. She loves climbing trees. There's not a child alive who wouldn't think this is the best room ever."

At last they reached the top, where Eden and Riona were waiting for them, sitting on a sky blue cushion that was cradled in the tree's uppermost branches. Cedar laughed when she saw that Riona was reading Eden's copy of *The Hobbit* to her.

Eden had changed her clothes; she was wearing a moss-colored dress decorated with fine gold thread. It set off the olive tones in her skin and the gold flecks in her eyes. Her wavy brown hair was loose around her shoulders instead of in its usual ponytail. She looked older than usual, and though she had only arrived in Tír na nÓg a few hours ago, she already looked as though she belonged in this place.

"This is my bed, Daddy!" Eden said with a giggle.

"I know," Finn said, grinning. "You look beautiful, baby." Cedar could feel the pride and joy emanating from him. She knew how much it meant to him to have them both here in his ancestral home.

Riona was beaming too. "I showed her where her clothes are, and the books and toys, and where she can wash. You quite like it, don't you, Eden?"

"Yes! I love it!" Eden said.

Riona stood up. "I didn't show her the bell yet," she said to Finn. "How about you bring Eden and Cedar to *your* new room, and then we'll talk once you're done looking around." She gave Cedar's arm a quick squeeze before heading down the spiral staircase.

"What bell?" Eden asked, her eyes wide.

"Well, this is where you'll sleep," Finn said. He reached over and picked up a small silver bell that was resting on a large green leaf beside Eden's bed. "But if you need us for any reason, all you have to do is ring this little bell, and it will automatically transport you into our room. You could make a sidh, of course, but the bell is enchanted so that its sound will echo throughout our room as well, and it will give us a little, uh, warning that you're coming. Want to try it?" He passed it to her, placing one hand on her shoulder and holding Cedar's hand with the other. "Just give it a ring."

Eden rang the bell softly, and Cedar felt herself grow warm all over, like she was being wrapped in a soft, heated blanket. The tree and the room around them grew dim and faded out of focus. Seconds later their surroundings came back into focus, but they were no longer in Eden's room. They were in a field of poppies, huge flowers that came up to Cedar's waist, waving in the gentle breeze as if in greeting. A cacophony of color spread out before them—reds and purples and oranges and yellows, with their bright, fuzzy green stems. On a sudden impulse Cedar bent down and took off her shoes. The grass was as soft as the plushest carpet, and the sky above was bright blue and dotted with puffy clouds. She could hear birds singing and a waterfall in the distance. The field of poppies ended at the edge of a wood, out of which flowed a stream of clear water that danced and glittered in the sun.

Cedar felt tears springing to her eyes. "I love poppies," she whispered, barely able to speak.

"I know," Finn said. "I remembered all the poppies you painted on the bedroom wall at your old apartment, so I thought you might like this."

"I do," she said, lost for more words. They walked through the field, past a long table surrounded by woven chairs with bright blue cushions.

"The dining room," Finn noted with a grin.

Eden was running pell-mell through the field of poppies, spinning in circles and falling on the soft grass. She squealed with laughter every time she fell, then jumped up and spun again.

They entered the wood, a welcoming collection of oaks, beeches, alders, and birches. The light dimmed as they followed a gently curving path through the trees.

"This reminds me of Narnia," Eden said, catching up to them.

Finn smiled. "Many humans believe that there must be worlds beyond their own and have tried to imagine what these otherworlds might look like. A few humans have even been to Tír na nÓg over the years."

"Maybe the man who wrote Narnia visited here, and he copied it!" Eden said.

"I don't think so. It has been a long, long time since a human stepped foot in Tír na nÓg. But sometimes the veil between the worlds grows thin, and humans are able to catch a glimpse of Tír na nÓg in a dream, or in a particularly magical place. Speaking of magical places . . ." Finn gave Cedar a tender look as they reached a clearing. There was a wide, smooth pond with lily pads floating on the surface and a large willow tree dipping its branches into the water's edge. She could see the glittering shapes of fish swimming languidly through the water. Eden immediately ran to the pond and knelt down, admiring the fish and giving them all names.

Next to the pond was the most beautiful bed that Cedar had ever seen. It was made of some gleaming white material she didn't recognize. It was as polished as marble, but she knew at a glance that it would be soft to the touch, not hard and cold. The frame curved and twisted into intricate, never-ending knots. The linens were white too, and almost incandescent. They looked so delicate that she was sure they would tear at the lightest touch. She walked over to the bed and ran her hand along the covers. It was like touching a cloud. She felt her cheeks grow warm at the thought of the nights she and Finn would spend in this bed.

"What do you think, Honey Lime?" Finn asked.

"It's perfect. *You're* perfect."

"No one's perfect," he replied. "But maybe, just maybe . . . I'm perfect for you."

Cedar reached up and kissed him. "You are," she whispered.

At times she wondered how she could have managed so many long years without him. But she knew how. She had shut her heart away behind walls of bravado and stubborn independence. She'd gone through the motions, building her career, spending time with friends, and raising Eden as a single mother. But life had been all about the business of daily survival, a dull, mechanical forward march through time. Eden had been the only spot of color in her life, and she'd experienced no deep, lasting joy. In her quest to shield herself from pain, loneliness, and rejection, she'd also walled herself off from delight, gratitude, and meaning.

Eden's disappearance and Finn's return had woken her from her self-induced emotional coma, and she was determined never to go back. She wanted to experience everything life had to offer, and she wanted to embrace love, even while knowing loss could be lurking around the next corner. She wasn't going to run anymore, not from anyone or anything. And that included Nuala.

"Let's go find your mother," Cedar said suddenly. "I want to know what she thinks about Nuala's plan and how we can stop her."

❧

When they returned to the willow-lined enclosure, they found Riona sitting on a bench near the fountain. Her eyes were closed, as if she were meditating. Cedar marveled again at how young she looked. She ran a hand through her own hair absentmindedly, as though she might feel any gray strands. Then she chided herself for worrying about such things. There was nothing she could do to stop herself from aging, and there were larger issues at stake than her own mortality. When she heard them approaching, Riona opened her eyes and stood, and Eden ran over to her to tell her about the poppy fields and the pond of fish.

"What did you think? Do you like your new home?" Riona asked.

"It's breathtaking," Cedar admitted. "More beautiful than I could have imagined."

Riona beamed. "I'm so glad," she said. "Now come with me, we've arranged a little welcome party for you."

"A welcome party? But shouldn't we—" Cedar stopped, not wanting to mention Nuala around Eden.

"We'll deal with that, yes," Riona said with a knowing nod. "But there are many people who would like to see you first."

Cedar gave Finn a look, but he just shrugged and wrapped his arm around her shoulder. "I think this will help us," he said. "The more people we share our story with, the better."

He had a point. The Council hadn't seemed to care too much about their side of things, but if they could get enough people to support them, the Council members might be more inclined to listen.

They climbed back through the door that led to the common room. In the short time since they'd been there, it had been completely transformed from a cozy sitting room into an expansive atrium flooded with light. Bright banners hung from the ceiling, and a trio of instruments hovered in the corner. No one was playing them, but delightful music flowed from that part of the room, and the instruments quivered and swayed in time with it. Tables filled with food and drinks lined one long wall, and Cedar's stomach growled at the tantalizing smells. "Whoa . . . ," Eden breathed, looking around with an open mouth.

In between the music and the tables was a crowd of people. A loud cheer went up when Cedar, Finn, and Eden entered the room. Cedar looked back at Riona, who shrugged innocently.

"It's a welcome party," she said. "At first we thought it might be limited to those of us you already know. But then word spread, and, well . . ." She gestured at the crowd, all of whom were looking at Cedar with great interest. "You saved a lot of lives, Cedar. I know your reception at the Council was less than warm, but to most people, you're a hero."

Cedar stared around in amazement. She hadn't expected a hero's welcome, but the animosity she'd experienced at the Council had given her second thoughts about even being part of this world. It felt good to know that so many of the Danann wanted her to be here in Tír na nÓg. It was exactly what she needed.

"Did you know about this?" she asked Finn. He tried to look innocent but then broke into a wide grin. "I wanted today to be special for you," he said. "It didn't go exactly as I had planned, but . . . we still have a lot to celebrate." He tugged her into the crowd, where Riona was waiting to make introductions.

"Wait," Cedar said. Someone had caught her eye across the room. She pulled away from Finn and made her way over to where Anya stood against the wall. "Hello, Anya," she said.

Anya smiled at her, but her face was heavy with grief. Cedar couldn't blame her. It had been only a few weeks since she'd lost her son Oscar in the battle against the Merrow. "Hello, Cedar," Anya said. "I'm sorry about your loss. I know that Maeve meant a lot to you and Eden."

"Thank you," Cedar said. "How . . . how are you doing?"

"As well as can be expected, I suppose. It's difficult to see all of these souls who were brought back to life after Lorcan's death, knowing that my son will never be one of them. But he died for a noble cause. I see that now," she said. "I'm glad you're here. I've heard about Nuala and how the Council is thinking of making her our queen. I, for one, will die before that happens. You *must* challenge her, Cedar."

"We will, somehow," Cedar assured her, not knowing what else to say. "We'll figure out a way to stop her."

Anya looked at her quizzically. "'Figure out a way'? You mean you're not planning to claim the throne?"

"Is *that* what people are expecting?" Cedar asked. "Rohan mentioned it, but I didn't really think he was serious. I thought Rohan might be a better contender, actually."

Anya laughed—a short, bitter sound. "I think we did too good of a job on you, Cedar. We didn't even want you involved with the search for your own daughter. 'Just a human,' we said. Now we want you to be our queen, and you don't think yourself worthy."

"I'm just being realistic," Cedar said. "I want to stop Nuala more than anything, but I don't think this is the way to do it."

At that moment Anya's other son, Sam, arrived with Nevan. "Hey, Cedar," Nevan said. "Did Eden tell you about all the exploring we did?"

"Not yet," Cedar said with a smile. "But she's hardly had time to catch her breath. I'm sure I'll hear all about it later. Where is she, anyway?"

"She's with Felix," Nevan answered, pointing over at the long tables of food. "He's letting her try one of everything."

"Thanks," Cedar said, and headed in Eden's direction. But before she could get too far, she was stopped by a group of people she didn't know.

"Welcome to Tír na nÓg!" one of them said, grabbing her hand and shaking it enthusiastically. "I knew your father. He was a great king. And your mother was a wonderful woman too." The others in the circle nodded and murmured their agreement. "We're sure that you'll make a wonderful queen. The Council can hardly refuse you! Brogan's blood runs in your veins."

Once again, Cedar found herself at a loss for words. "I'm not sure—" she started, and was mercifully rescued by Riona, who wrapped her arm through Cedar's and led her away after making their excuses.

"I'd like you to meet my friend Seisyll," Riona said, leading Cedar over to a robust woman whose hair was pulled back in a series of tight twists that emphasized her sharp facial features. "You met her husband, Gorman, at the Council."

"Oh, yes! It's a pleasure to meet you," Cedar said.

Seisyll grabbed Cedar's hand and clutched it tightly in her own. "You have no idea what you have done," she said fervently. "You not only saved my husband, but you've given us all a second chance."

"Oh . . . um, thank you," Cedar said. She was beginning to feel like she was an actor in a play and that she was the only one who hadn't been given the script.

"Can I get you a drink?" Seisyll asked, and before Cedar could respond, she waved her hand in the air. A crystal goblet filled with wine soared toward them, pausing just in front of Cedar, who reached out and plucked it from the air.

"Thank you," she said, taking a sip. "How did you—"

"We all have our special gifts," Seisyll said, floating a plate of food toward them as well. "But what was I saying? Ah, yes. I was just telling Riona that she and her friends put us to shame. We should have joined the resistance too, but we weren't foresighted enough. By the time we realized our mistake, it was too late. And then Gorman was taken in for questioning—they knew about our friendship with Rohan and Riona, of course—and he never came back out. Until you arrived, that is," Seisyll said, squeezing Cedar's arm.

"Those idiots on the Council need to have their heads knocked together—look at the welcome they've given you! What do we want with a world like Ériu, anyway? We were only there for a few hundred years—we weren't the first to conquer it, nor the last. We hardly have a 'claim' to it, as they say. And, really, while I'm sure

Ériu is lovely, it surely cannot possibly compare to Tír na nÓg, even now. What are your thoughts, dear?"

"Uh . . . well, they are both very beautiful, I suppose, in their own way," Cedar answered. Finn had walked over to join them and had wrapped his arm around her waist.

"Well, I say it's the very best thing that could have happened, you coming here," interjected Seisyll. "Both when that monster was still in power and now. You're the only one who can help us, Cedar. Surely you must realize that."

"Actually, I think there are others who might be better suited for leadership," Cedar said, starting to feel like a broken record.

"Cedar isn't entirely convinced that she's the right person for the job," Finn told Seisyll.

"Not the right person?" the woman exclaimed, her voice traveling up an octave. "Whatever do you mean? Don't you understand what's at stake here? You have the strongest claim to the throne of any of us. Brogan and Kier were *adored*. And your daughter has the gift of opening the sidhe, which means that if it weren't for that pesky human thing, you would surely have it too! That's a *very* good sign. You were meant to be the queen, just like your father was the king."

"Really, Mum?" Eden asked, and Cedar jumped, not realizing that Eden had joined them. "You're going to be the queen?"

"No, I'm not," Cedar protested, shooting the rest of them a warning glance. "I understand the need to deal with you-know-who, believe me, but I really don't think this is even an option. The Council wouldn't give me the time of day, and we're wasting our time if we think there's a chance they'd appoint me as queen. Yes, my father was king, but I never knew him, and I know nothing about your world or your people. That makes me the least qualified person here!"

To her surprise, Seisyll threw back her head and laughed. "When did being qualified have anything to do with it? Besides, from what I've heard, you're *very* qualified—you're brave, intelligent, and stubborn. That's all you need to rule this lot. But you're also the only one among us who truly understands what it's like to be human." She glanced down at Eden before continuing, patting the girl on the head. "He wasn't the only one who despised humans, you know. There are others like him—too many if you ask me—who think that humans are only ants to be crushed.

"People wonder why the land's not healing itself now that he's gone. But the prophecy just spoke of 'poison'—and I think there's still plenty of that hanging around. Your job here isn't done. Having someone like you on the throne could do a lot to correct the damage that was caused by you-know-who, not just to our land but to our people. Having *her* on the throne will only make it worse."

Cedar remembered the prophecy well. *The dyad that should not be will rise from the ashes and purge the land of the coming poison.* They had thought Eden was the dyad, but it was Maeve who had realized the truth, and almost too late. It was Cedar—both human and Danann—who had been able to defeat Lorcan.

"I still think there are others who are more capable," Cedar said. She didn't understand why Seisyll was pushing her so hard. "What about you? You're obviously sympathetic toward humans. Or Gorman? Or Rohan? Riona, you'd make an amazing queen! You're so wise and kind and strong."

"Thank you, Cedar," Riona said, smiling softly. "But none of us have the claim you do. Rohan was Brogan's steward, and you are his daughter. That's a big difference. I agree with Seisyll. You're the best hope we have. And with all of us rallying behind you, I think you may indeed have a chance."

◦‿◦

Later that night Finn and Cedar lay exhausted in each other's arms. The gossamer sheets, so soft she could barely feel them, were tangled around Cedar's legs. She closed her eyes and trailed her fingers along Finn's chest. This was all that she wanted—peace and quiet with the man she loved. Was such a thing even possible in this world? Earlier they had tucked Eden into her new bed and sat by her side until she fell asleep. Cedar had wanted to keep Eden with them, but Finn had convinced her that their daughter would be perfectly safe in her own room. He'd had other plans, and now Cedar was happy that she'd listened to him.

She opened her eyes and looked up at the sky above them. It was a deep indigo, shot through with bright silver stars. "I don't want it," she said.

Finn rolled onto his side and propped himself up on one elbow. He tucked a stray strand of dark hair behind her ear. "I know," he said. "And no one will force you. It's a decision only you can make. But for what it's worth, I know that you'd make a great queen. You might not see it, but you have what it takes."

"How can you say that? I wouldn't even know where to begin."

"Cedar, I know you better than anyone. There's much more to you than what you realize. The others see you as Brogan and Kier's daughter, and they make a good point—you do have the strongest claim to the throne. But I see more than that. I see a passion and strength that's all your own. You work hard, you learn quickly, and you're willing to do whatever it takes to protect the people you love. You have a strength they do not yet see."

Cedar lay silent, considering his words. It seemed so impossible to think that she could be the queen of this magical world. She was telling the truth when she said she didn't want it. She already had more than she'd ever dreamed possible. But if her parentage really did give her some influence, she could at least use it to support someone other than Nuala as the new king or queen. They just needed the right candidate.

Earlier that evening, Rohan had reluctantly agreed that if Cedar refused to step forward, he was the next best choice. She would give him her support at tomorrow's Council meeting, which had been called to consider any other claims for the throne. Cedar was relieved that the Council hadn't accepted Nuala's proposal right away. It meant that there was still a chance to stop her.

She snuggled into Finn's side and closed her eyes, her body longing for sleep but her mind still racing with everything that had happened over the last couple of days. Had it been only last night that she'd met that stranger at Maeve's old house? She wondered again who this man called Liam was and if he was one of the druids Nuala had claimed to have met while on Earth. Why had he told her to stay away from Tír na nÓg?

Just as she was about to drop off to sleep, another question popped into her mind, one that had been plaguing her for weeks. Somehow she'd never found the right moment to ask.

"Finn?" she whispered, not sure if he was still awake.

"Mmm?" he mumbled, cracking one eye open to look at her.

"What was Kier's ability?"

He opened both eyes. "You don't know? I thought Riona must have told you."

Cedar shook her head.

He looked at her intently. "It doesn't surprise me at all, you know. I can see it inside of you, even through the mask of your humanity."

"What was it?" she asked.

"Fire."

"Fire," she repeated. Somehow, the news didn't surprise her either. "What could she do with it?"

"Anything she wanted," he answered. "She could create it, wield it, extinguish it . . . anything. If only she'd been around on the day we met," he teased. "Do you remember?"

Cedar smiled at the memory. "Of course I do. You saved my life. Well, it felt like that anyway."

"You were so . . . intriguing," he said. "And gorgeous. I wanted an excuse to talk to you again."

It was Cedar's first major art show. She'd exhibited at smaller shows before, but this was the first one where she was the featured artist, where people were coming primarily to see her *work. She had been speaking to an elderly gentleman when a soft, rich voice from behind her said, "Your work is beautiful." She turned to say a polite thank-you, expecting to see another middle-aged patron of the arts. Most of the people her age in Halifax hit the bars on Friday nights, avoiding places like the prim art gallery on Sackville Street. This man, however, was not the typical gray-haired, pinstriped-suited admirer she had been expecting. He was tall and athletic, with wavy brown hair that tumbled effortlessly down to his stubbled jawline. A hint of a smile played on his face, and his deep brown eyes sparked with gold. Cedar opened her mouth to say thank you, but all that came out was "Ah."*

The elderly man with whom she had been speaking chortled, made an excuse, and walked away. Quickly realizing that she looked ridiculous, Cedar forced a smile and thanked the newcomer for his compliment.

"It's amazing," he continued. "So evocative. You have a rare gift."

That was when she really smiled, and she felt a jolt of pleasure course through her body.

"You are very kind, um . . ." She held out her hand, and he took it.

"Finn," he said. "Finn Donnelly."

"Nice to meet you, Finn," she said. "I'm Cedar McLeod."

"I know," he said with a wink. "Your name's on all the paintings."

She grinned. "Well, not all of the ones here are mine. But I'm so excited—okay, maybe a bit terrified—to be part of this show. It's a huge milestone for me."

He smiled down at her and started asking her questions about her various pieces. He seemed almost as knowledgeable about her paintings as she was. She was about to ask him why he was here at an art show instead of out drinking with his buddies when the ear-splitting shriek of the fire alarm ripped through the air.

Everyone in the gallery froze in place, wondering if it was a false alarm. Some were covering their ears. Then came the acrid smell of smoke, and Cedar's stomach sank. "No," she whispered. "Not here, not tonight . . ."

One of the gallery officials was shouting instructions and herding people toward the exit. Cedar ran to lift the painting closest to her off the wall, but Finn grabbed her arm. "There's no time!" he shouted over the alarm, which was still shrieking. "You have to get out of here!"

"Not until I save my paintings!" she yelled back, trying to jerk her arm free.

"It's not safe!" he said, half-dragging her toward the exit. "Go!"

Cedar went, buffeted by the crowd that was tumbling out of the exits and onto the sidewalk. It was November, and the air was chilly. She stood on the other side of the street and watched as the fire crews arrived and poured into the building, letting loose their great hoses of water on the flames that were visible through the windows of the gallery. She wondered vaguely where the handsome man who had liked her paintings had gone, but thoughts of him were driven from her mind by the unmistakable smell of burning paint.

Without realizing it, she had started crying. The hot tears mixed with the cold air as they dripped off her chin and the tip of her nose. She knew her mascara was running, but she didn't care. She thought of her now-destroyed canvases one by one, each with its own history, its own personality, its own special world. The crowd was starting to grow, and she was shivering from the cold, yet she couldn't make herself walk away from those small deaths.

And then she heard her name. At first she looked around at the faces of the people who were standing the closest to her, but she didn't recognize any of them. Then she heard her name again, from behind. She whirled around and caught a glimpse of movement in the alley between the two neighboring buildings. Hesitantly, she wove her way out of the crowd of bystanders and walked toward the alley.

Standing there in the darkness, great clouds of air bursting out with every breath, was Finn. He was grinning so widely his teeth sparkled with the light of the nearby streetlamp. At first she just stared—she didn't know what he was doing there—and then she looked down. Stacked neatly beside him were her paintings. Every last one.

And that was the moment she fell in love with him.

CHAPTER 4

The next morning Finn and Cedar arrived back at the Hall. The courtyard was crowded with people; several rows of the thin white chairs had been added outside of the Council circle, with standing room only beyond that. Cedar caught sight of Riona and Rohan, who waved to them and pointed to the empty seats beside them.

Earlier that morning Cedar had discovered the Tír na nÓg equivalent of a walk-in closet in her room—a huge carved wardrobe that seemed to grow bigger when she stepped inside of it. Dresses and robes of every color hung on either side, and toward the back were drawers filled with jewelry, ribbons, and fresh flowers for her hair. She still preferred her worn blue jeans, but she had dressed for this more formal occasion in a beautiful charcoal dress with bell sleeves and light blue embroidery crisscrossing the bodice.

They'd left Eden in the care of Riona's friend Seisyll, who had promised to show her how to play some of the instruments that were hanging from the music branch in her room.

Cedar looked around the courtyard and saw a few friendly faces. Felix was sitting a couple of rows away from them, looking as gorgeous as he'd appeared yesterday, and Dermot was next to Dáiríne, whom she'd met at the party the previous night. Murdoch and Anya were present too, and they nodded in her direction when she smiled and waved at them.

Cedar! Behind you!

Cedar swiveled around and caught sight of Nevan's grinning face. Sam was sitting next to her, his arm draped around her shoulders.

Many of the Danann in the crowd looked at her with undisguised curiosity. If last night's welcome party had been any indication, they all thought she'd be making a competing claim for the throne today. She looked around for Nuala and found her in the seat directly behind the blonde councilwoman, Sorcha, who had so readily dismissed Cedar the day before. Her stomach tightened, but she knew she was surrounded by friends.

The goateed councilman stood and cleared his throat. Riona leaned over and whispered, "His name is Deaglán. Did you meet him yesterday?" Cedar nodded, scowling at the memory.

"The Council has already heard one claim for the throne of Tír na nÓg," Deaglán continued. "This meeting has been called to determine if there are any others who believe they possess the qualities necessary to lead us. If you wish to be considered, please step forward and present us with your claim."

A silence fell over the room. Cedar held her breath, waiting to see who would step forward. After a few moments, a man stood and walked into the center of the circle. Cedar's spirits rose. He looked like a great warrior, strong and powerful, but with a kind face framed by a thick beard. Surely the Council would choose him over Nuala.

"Conchobhar," the councilman said. "What is your claim?"

Cedar listened as Conchobhar began to recite the great deeds he had done, wars he had fought in, and enemies he had destroyed. Her spirits started to sink as he spoke of Tír na nÓg's weakened condition and the human "threat."

"The swords and spears of the Tuatha Dé Danann have grown dull!" he thundered. "We need a warrior king on the throne once more if we wish to regain our former glory—one who is noble and does not abuse our own people, but also one who is victorious!"

After Conchobhar sat down, Cedar cast a worried glance at Finn. She wasn't sure who would be worse, Nuala or Conchobhar. And if Nuala could accomplish the same goal without taking the Tuatha Dé Danann to war, surely the Council would choose her.

There was another long silence as the Council waited for any additional claims. Cedar noticed that people were looking at her expectantly. She studied her hands in her lap, trying to ignore them. She felt Riona nudge her. "Are you certain?" Riona asked. Cedar nodded. Riona whispered something to Rohan, who immediately stood.

"I wish to make my claim," he said. He spoke of his close friendship with Brogan and how he fought against Lorcan, refusing to accept a tyrant as king. He spoke of his years on Ériu and of the time he'd spent searching for the half-human, half-Danann of the prophecy. He spoke of finding Brogan and Kier's lost daughter and helping to save the sidh-child Eden. She was surprised that he didn't openly criticize Nuala's plan, and she wondered if the Council had forbidden him to speak of it. Instead, he spoke of living in peace with humans and reminded the assembly of the many great humans they had befriended over the years.

There was a long silence after Rohan finished speaking, and then Deaglán rose again. "Thank you. If there are no other claims, the Council will—"

He was cut off by the sound of a child screaming. Recognizing the voice at once, Cedar jumped to her feet. Eden was standing beside one of the white marble arches at the edge of the assembly, which was slightly glowing. Her face was distorted with fear, and her terror-stricken eyes were trained directly on Nuala, who sat stock-still.

"Mummy, help me!" Eden screamed. "It's her! Don't let her get me!" Eden started to run toward her parents, but Finn was faster. He scooped up the hysterical child and swept her out of the Hall.

Cedar began to follow, but then she stopped. Every nerve in her body was burning, as if she'd been lit from within. Suddenly, all of her protests sounded weak to her own ears. Nuala had put her child through unimaginable horrors and killed Maeve, and now she wanted to terrorize every mother, father, and child on Earth.

It didn't matter that the Council didn't like Cedar, and it didn't matter that she wasn't qualified. It didn't even matter that she didn't want to be queen. The only thing that mattered was stopping Nuala—and everyone like her—for good.

Fearlessly, she strode into the center of the ring. "Is this who you'd choose to be your queen?" she asked the Council, gesturing toward Nuala. "A woman so vicious that she terrifies an innocent child?"

Sorcha stood up. "This Council is assembled to hear claims for the throne," she said, her eyes burning into Cedar's. "Are you making a claim of your own?" There was a challenge in her voice, and Cedar's resolve stiffened all the more.

"I am," she said, letting the words hang in the air over the silent crowd.

"She offers you much," Cedar continued, jerking her head in Nuala's direction. "But she has no true claim to be your queen. Just empty promises delivered on a silver tongue. She says she has the druids on her side, but she murdered one of them, Maeve McLeod, who was a great friend to the Tuatha Dé Danann. It was Maeve who cared for Kier as she lay dying, and Maeve who selflessly raised Kier and Brogan's child as her own, keeping her safe from Lorcan. How did Nuala repay her for this great act of service? She shot her. With a gun. A *human* weapon.

"You know who I am. I am the child of the High King Brogan and his wife, Kier. They were strong and proud, and the Tuatha Dé Danann flourished under their reign. They both lost their lives fighting Lorcan, trying to save all of you and this beautiful world you've created together. To repay them by putting one of their enemies on the throne would be unthinkable.

"I killed Lorcan, and I won't stand for seeing his spy sit on this throne. Choose me, Brogan's only child, and I will continue his legacy. Together, we will restore Tír na nÓg to its former glory, without preying on weaker races. It's true that I have a strange gift—not fire like my mother, or opening the sidhe like my father and daughter. But it was this gift, this gift of humanity, that freed us from Lorcan's bondage. So make your choice. Do you want more of what you've had for the last several years? More war? More decay? Or do you want to start anew and restore the great society that's known throughout all the worlds for its nobility, compassion, and strength? I leave that choice to you."

With that, she turned and walked out of the Hall, feeling the eyes of every single person in the courtyard on her back.

❦

She found them sitting by what had once been a lively stream. Now it was little more than a muddy ditch, but a trickle of water was still forcing its way through, as though refusing to completely give up the ghost. Finn and Eden were sitting on the bank throwing rocks, which landed with a soft *splat* at the bottom.

"Hey," she said softly, and they both turned around.

"Mummy," Eden said, holding out her arms and starting to cry again.

"I calmed her down," Finn said. "But she wanted you. Where were you?"

Cedar gathered Eden onto her lap and held her close. "I did it," she said. "I made my claim for the throne." Finn watched her intently but said nothing. "When Eden started screaming, something inside me just . . . snapped," she continued. "I realized that we need to stop Nuala no matter what it takes. I can't just sit back and hope that someone else will do it." She kissed the top of Eden's head. "I'm so sorry you were scared, baby."

"I want to go home," Eden said, sniffing.

"I know," Cedar said. "Sometimes I want that too. But we have an important job here, and we can't run away, even if we really want to."

"What job?" Eden asked.

"Well . . . you saw that Nuala's here. And she's kind of like a big bully. She wants to hurt other people, and we need to tell her and everyone else that it's not okay for her to do that. If we don't stand up to her, she'll be able to do whatever she wants. I know you're scared, but Mummy and Daddy are right here, and we won't let anything happen to you. This world needs us—all three of us. Some of the people here don't like humans or even fairies who've spent a lot of time with humans. So we have to show them that humans are really great people and we should be friends with them. Can you be brave with Mummy and Daddy?"

Eden nodded. "I think so," she said.

Finn leaned over and kissed them both. "I'm proud of you," he said to Cedar. Then he looked down at Eden with a twinkle in his eye. "How would you like to go for a pony ride?" he asked.

"Yeah!" Eden said, scrambling to her feet. "But where will we find a pony?"

"Oh, I don't think we'll have to look very far," he said, and then, with a swirl of sparks, he transformed into a child-sized pony that was pink from head to hoof. Cedar laughed as Eden ran over to the pony and hugged it. She helped lift her up onto her father's back and watched as the two of them trotted away down the riverbank.

"Well, that was touching," came a voice from behind her. Cedar swiveled around to see Nuala standing just a few feet away, leaning against a slim tree, her arms crossed and a bored expression on her face. "The thing I like about you, Cedar, is that you can never hear me coming."

"What are you doing here?" Cedar asked, her eyes narrowed.

"I realized that I haven't welcomed you to your new home yet," Nuala said. "You seem to have settled in nicely. Lovely pep talk you gave the little one. I suppose I should thank you for calling me a bully instead of a kidnapper and murderer."

"That's because she already knows that's what you are," Cedar said through gritted teeth.

Nuala ignored this. "I also came to tell you that you're in way over your head. I've been planning this for a very long time. You don't think I wasted all those years on Ériu, do you? Not like everyone else. Except for Finn, I suppose, who was off doing who-knows-what to try and mend his poor broken heart." She pouted, and Cedar wanted to strangle her.

"No, *you* don't know what you're up against," Cedar said. "You think you can just bat your eyelashes and get whatever you want, but there are a lot of us who know the real story, and we're going to stop you. *You* should be the one who's afraid."

Nuala rolled her eyes. "Oh, yes, I'm terrified," she said. She straightened up and started advancing on Cedar, a wicked gleam in her eyes. "You can't stop me, Cedar. It's foolish of you to even try. You're only going to get hurt—you and the people you love—again. This is your last warning. Go and—"

"Get away from her!"

Cedar's mind suddenly cleared of the fog that had begun to descend on her. Eden was running straight at Nuala, her little hands balled into fists. "You leave my mum alone!" she screamed, flailing at Nuala. "Go away! Go!"

Finn was behind her, one foot still a pink hoof, his face pale.

The expression on Nuala's face was unreadable. Her eyes were wide wells of green and her mouth was slightly parted. For a second, Cedar could have sworn that she saw a flicker of sadness pass over the other woman's features. Then Nuala took a step back and said calmly, "Hello, Eden." She looked up at Cedar again. "Remember," she said. "That was your last warning." She turned and ran.

Cedar shook her head to clear the last of the cobwebs and looked at her daughter in amazement. Eden's fists were still clenched, and she was breathing heavily. "Was that brave, Mummy?" she asked.

Cedar dropped to her knees and wrapped her arms around Eden. "Yes, baby," she whispered. "That was very brave."

 ∾

It was early evening when the Council sent for her. Riona found Cedar in Eden's room, where she and Finn were listening as their daughter attempted to play a long, delicate wind instrument she had discovered on her music branch.

"Cedar," Riona said softly. "There's a messenger here from the Council."

Cedar stood up quickly, her heart pounding. "Have they decided?"

"I don't know," Riona said. "He just said that they need to see you. Only you," she added with a glance at Finn, who had also gotten to his feet.

Cedar turned back to Finn and took his hands in hers. "I'll be fine," she said. "You stay here with Eden." Then she kissed Eden and said, "Mummy's got to go to a meeting now, but I'll be back to tuck you in."

She said good-bye to Riona at the door and greeted the messenger politely. "Can you tell me what's going on?" she asked as she followed him to the Hall.

"No," he said, "I'm just supposed to bring you to them." He was young, and she was reminded with a pang of Oscar, who had shown her the hidden entrance to the Fox and Fey on the night Eden was taken by Nuala. They walked the rest of the way in silence, but she could feel the boy's eyes on her. She tried to calm her breathing and slowed her pace by a fraction. She wanted to appear before them as a potential queen, not as a sweaty, nervous mess.

When they reached the center court of the Hall, the messenger bowed and indicated that she should go in alone. She walked forward slowly and deliberately. This time, only the eight Council members were in the room. There was no audience, not even servants. Gorman was smiling at her, but she noticed he was twisting his hands in his lap. Deaglán was also smiling, though not in a way Cedar found reassuring. Sorcha looked bored and didn't acknowledge Cedar's presence in any way. The swarthy man with the big beard gave Cedar a stony glare, his arms crossed in front of him. Then there were two others in the Council who had remained completely silent during the meeting that morning. Cedar looked at them curiously, wondering where they stood. One was a short, pixie-like woman with hair the color of ivy that was done up in braids and wrapped around her head. She reminded Cedar of Nevan. The other was a man who could have been her brother, thin and lithe, with long fine hair so blond it was almost white. They returned Cedar's curious glances with looks of their own, and then the man with the white hair stood up.

"Greetings, Cedar," he said. "We thank you for answering our summons." Cedar said nothing but nodded and waited. "I fear you have not been properly introduced to the members of the Council since your arrival in Tír na nÓg. I am Amras," he said, then rattled off the names of the other seven members of the Council. "Ruadhan has withdrawn his claim and has given you his unconditional support. And the Council has decided that Conchobhar is not the right person to lead us at this particular time. So that leaves us with Fionnghuala . . . and you."

Cedar tried to keep her expression neutral, while inside, her stomach was clenched and her heart raced. She willed herself to stand perfectly still and wait for their decision.

"You are aware that some have reservations about the fact that you were raised as a human and have had the, er, 'gift' of humanity bestowed upon you," Amras continued. "But there is also the matter of your parentage, which is unquestioned. There are many who believe someone with Brogan's and Kier's blood in her veins is not to be taken lightly. Your claim has a great deal of support among the people, who regard you as a hero. In destroying Lorcan you have proven yourself both brave and selfless, which are noble qualities in a leader of the Tuatha Dé Danann."

Cedar could feel the knot in her stomach lessening. Maybe they were going to choose her after all.

"However," he said, and then paused. She held her breath. "By your own admission, you know little of our people and our customs. And we know little of you. It is a difficult choice indeed. Two divergent paths have been laid out before us, and it saddens me to say that we have never been so divided as a Council, nor has the correct path ever seemed so unclear. Fionnghuala offers much. The return of the druids and the promise of Ériu are no small things. What do *you* offer your people, Cedar?"

"Peace," Cedar answered immediately. "Dignity. Freedom from tyranny—because tyranny is what you're going to get if you choose her. As I recall, that didn't work out so well for you last time."

"Words," said Deaglán with a disdainful snort. "You offer nothing but words."

"She offers *hope*," Gorman retorted.

Amras raised his hands to quiet them both. "Your claim is strong," he said to Cedar. "But you are untested, and it is uncertain how your rule would benefit our people. We have come to a decision, but it is an unorthodox one." Cedar held her breath, waiting for him to continue. "We have a task for you, Cedar," he said. "Complete it, and you will prove yourself worthy of our throne, just as your father did many times over. Fail, and we will choose Fionnghuala as our queen."

Cedar was stunned, but she recovered quickly. This was completely unexpected. A task to prove herself worthy? She struggled against the voice in her head that automatically shouted, *You're only a human!*

No, she told herself, remembering Finn's words from the previous night. *I have a strength they do not yet see.*

"And what is this task?" she asked, surprised by how calm she sounded.

Amras sat down and nodded at the pixie-like woman next to him. "I am Maran," she reminded Cedar gently as she stood. "Are you familiar with the Lia Fáil?"

The Lia Fáil. Cedar knew she had heard those words before. She frowned, struggling to remember. Out of the corner of her eye she saw Sorcha smirking. Suddenly, the memory rushed back. Yesterday—had it only been yesterday?—Eden had mentioned it at breakfast, back in their apartment on Earth. "It's a stone," she replied. "One of the four treasures brought from the Four Cities. It's called the Stone of Destiny, and it . . . roars," she finished lamely, hoping she wasn't making a complete idiot of herself.

The pixie woman nodded. "It does," she said. "And do you know why it roars?"

"No," Cedar admitted.

"It roars when a true king or queen stands on it. It was once used as our coronation stone, and then, during the time of friendship between our peoples, we loaned it to the kings of Ireland for use in their coronations. Over the centuries it fell out of use and would roar no more. We do not know the reason—whether there were no worthy leaders left or the magic of the stone wore out. It has since been lost to history and myth. Your task is this: Find the Lia Fáil and bring it back to us. We have the other three treasures—the cauldron, the spear, and the sword. To have the lost Stone of Destiny would be a great gift."

Cedar's mind was racing. "How will I know it's the right stone?" she asked.

"As every child could tell you, the Lia Fáil grows warm at the touch of one of the Tuatha Dé Danann," Sorcha said. "But it should be obvious, shouldn't it? If you are truly destined for the throne, the Lia Fáil will let us know."

"Unless the magic has ended," Cedar pointed out.

Deaglán waved his hand impatiently. "I, for one, have confidence in the Lia Fáil's ability to prove who is worthy to be the ruler of our land and people." He gave Cedar a withering look. "No one is expecting you to succeed. But some believe we owe it to your parents to give you a chance to prove yourself. You have one week."

"*One week?*" Cedar asked, aghast. "To find a stone that has been lost for centuries?"

No one answered. They all watched her silently, awaiting her answer. She lifted her chin. "All right," she said. "I found my daughter against impossible odds. Now I will find the Lia Fáil."

ᕟᕟ

Finn was waiting for her outside the Hall. He swept her up into a tight hug as soon as he saw her. "You were amazing," he said. She arched an eyebrow at him.

"Were you eavesdropping?" she asked, and he nodded sheepishly.

"Butterfly," he said. "Yellow wings. Behind Deaglán's left shoulder. I was tempted to leave a few droppings on his robe but was worried that he might crush me."

Cedar laughed. "I'm glad you were there; you can help me make sense of all this."

Finn's eyes were glowing. "You should be proud of yourself. They threw you a real curveball, and you handled it beautifully. I think Sorcha and Deaglán were hoping you'd just give up right then and there."

"What do they have against me anyway?" Cedar asked as they walked back toward their home.

"They seem to have something against pretty much everyone," he answered. "I'm sure they'd both love to rule, but members of the Council aren't allowed to put themselves forward. My father says that Sorcha was a big Lorcan apologist in the early days. Of course, now she's claiming that he threatened her into submission, but I doubt that's what really happened. Deaglán's always played his cards close to his chest, and I'm not sure what his game is here. Maybe it's simple prejudice. It's hard for them to accept that you're one of them and that you killed Lorcan when no one else could."

"Do you think I can do it?"

"I told you, I think you'd be an excellent queen. And if you have what it takes to be queen, you definitely have what it takes to find the Lia Fáil."

Feeling heartened by his words, Cedar picked up the pace. She had expected to find the common room empty when she arrived back home. But her friends and family had gathered to hear what the Council had had to say. Rohan and Felix stood in a corner of the room, talking in low voices. Molly was reading a book to Eden on a long chaise longue draped in velvet while Riona looked on, and Nevan and Seisyll were chatting animatedly while sipping steaming mugs of tea. Seisyll was the first to see them enter, and she rushed over to Cedar.

"Cedar," she said, grabbing at her hands. "I am so very sorry about what happened this morning. One minute she was there, and the next she was gone. She closed the sidh the second she was through, or I would have followed her. I accept full responsibility—I should have been more vigilant when entrusted with the care of a sidh-child."

Cedar smiled wanly. "It's okay," she said. "Nothing bad happened. It's not the first time she's pulled something like that."

Seisyll smiled at her gratefully and then asked the question on everyone's lips. "So? What did the Council want?"

Cedar breathed out and looked around at all the expectant faces that were turned toward her like flowers to the sun. "They want me to find the Lia Fáil."

There was a moment of stunned silence, then Nevan said, "You've got to be kidding." She looked at Finn. "She's kidding, right?"

Finn shook his head. "I'm afraid not. They said she needs to prove herself worthy of the throne by finding the Lia Fáil and bringing it back. If she fails, they will give Nuala the crown."

"And I only have a week to do it. So . . . anyone know where it is?" Cedar asked, not expecting an answer. She was starting to feel slightly panicked, but she pushed the feelings down. Panic would not help her find the stone.

"There are several theories, of course . . . ," Nevan said, trailing off. "But I don't think anyone's even looked for it in, well, centuries. We've all just assumed it was lost forever."

"Well, what are some of the theories? Where was it last seen?" Cedar asked.

They all looked at one another, and then Riona said tentatively, "I heard that the human warrior Conn found it after it had been missing for quite a long time. He stepped on it by accident, and it roared."

"But didn't he break it in two when it failed to roar for Lugiad?" Nevan said.

"No, that was Cúchulainn, Lug's boy, way before Conn's time. And I don't think it broke—I think it just stopped working," Felix said. "They say it never roared again, except that once for Conn, which happened hundreds of years later. I assume that's why it got lost. It could no longer identify the true king, so it was just treated like any other ceremonial stone."

"When did all of this happen?" Cedar asked. "How long ago?"

There was another uncomfortable silence. "Um . . . I think it was before your race—the humans, I mean—started recording history," Nevan said, an apologetic look on her face. "I'm sorry, Cedar. It's just been so long since any of us have even thought about the Lia Fáil. The druids were always obsessive about history, not us. I'm afraid we're not going to be very helpful."

Then Finn spoke up. "The humans have some more recent stories about it. I did some research on it while we were on Ériu. I was curious to find out what the humans knew about our race. Some of it is . . . interesting, to say the least. Humans have a way of creating their own version of history based on their beliefs about the world.

"Some scholars believe the stone was used as a pillow by a man named Jacob, who was a great leader of a race called the Israelites. They say it gave him a vision, and he went on to found a new religion. Some believe it was taken and hidden in the monastery at Iona. Another theory states that it's the standing stone that still crowns the Hill of Tara."

"Where's that?" Cedar asked.

Finn shook his head. "County Meath in Ireland. It's the coronation site for the ancient Irish kings. But I've been to Tara in recent years and have touched the stone. If it was the real Lia Fáil, it would have grown warm at my touch.

"Then there is the Stone of Scone, which rings of truth, but seems . . . too easy."

Cedar waited for him to elaborated, and noticed that Eden was hanging on Finn's every word. A historian in the making, she thought.

"The story goes that the Lia Fáil was last used for the coronation of Murtagh mac Erc, the High King of Ireland, about fifteen hundred years ago," Finn continued. "Then he loaned it to his brother, Fergus the Great, who was being crowned King of Alba, or Scotland as it's now known. But shortly after his coronation, Fergus and all of his inner circle were killed in a storm off the coast of Antrim. So the stone was never returned. Instead, it stayed in Scone, which was the seat of the High Kings of Scotland at that time. It was used there in coronations until King Edward I of England conquered Scotland in 1296 and took the stone back with him to Westminster Abbey, where it has been used in coronations ever since."

"Is it still there? At Westminster Abbey?" Cedar asked. Maybe this wouldn't be so difficult after all.

"No," Finn replied. "It was stolen by a group of students a few years ago, and they returned it to Scotland. They got caught, and the stone was taken back to the English. But then the queen gave it back to the Scottish in a symbolic gesture, and it's now in Edinburgh Castle."

"Then that seems like a good place to start, doesn't it?" Cedar asked, not sure why Finn didn't seem more excited.

"It's just that the likelihood of it being the real Lia Fáil is slim to none," he said apologetically. "It's changed hands so many times; it's extremely likely that at least one copy was made, if not several. Who knows where the real stone is? It may be at the bottom of the sea with Fergus and his men. Or perhaps Murtagh sent Fergus a copy. Or maybe the monks at Scone gave Edward a fake. Even if they didn't, the chances that the real Stone of Scone was just sitting around in Westminster Abbey all this time are extremely rare. It's quite possible it's locked in a vault somewhere in a government facility or museum. There's no way to tell where the real stone is, I'm afraid."

Cedar was getting frustrated. "Well, we're not going to find it by standing around here talking," she said. "The first thing we have to do is go back to Earth." She felt a moment's hesitation as she looked at Finn, who was staring intently at Eden. She'd assumed he would come with her, but now she wasn't so sure. Would he want to stay in Tír na nÓg with Eden?

"We'll have to bring Eden with us," he said, and Cedar felt a wave of relief. "We'll need her to create sidhe for us so that we can travel quickly." Cedar hadn't thought about that, but he was right. If they only had a week they'd need to move as quickly as possible.

"We should all go with you!" Molly exclaimed. "The more of us who search for it, the faster we'll find it!"

Finn shook his head. "No, I think it should just be the three of us," he said. "It'll be too conspicuous for a big group of people to appear out of thin air. And I don't want to leave Nuala here on the loose. You need to stay and keep an eye on her in case she tries to take over while we're gone."

"Not so fast," Felix said, running a hand distractedly through his blond hair. "You have no idea what you'll find, or what you'll be up against. Finn, you've got a little girl to look after, and, well . . . no offense, Cedar, but you're still kind of, you know, human when it comes to strength and all of that. And if any of you are injured, my healing power will be useful. Everyone else should stay here, but I should come with you."

Finn started to protest, but Cedar said, "Thanks, Felix." She was glad he'd be coming with them. The more help they had the better, she thought, and if they did run into trouble, Felix could always bring Eden back to safety.

"Make sure you take the starstone," Riona said. "That way you can keep us updated on your progress, and we can let you know what happens here on our end."

"We should leave a sidh open for you," Finn said. "I don't like leaving you here with no way out, just in case things go . . . wrong. We don't know what game Nuala is playing."

"But what if she follows us through?" Cedar asked.

"I don't think we have to worry about that," Rohan said in his deep voice. "Eden's the only one who can open the sidhe, and she, Finn, and I are the only ones who can close them. I don't think she'd risk being trapped on Ériu. But there's no need to leave a sidh open. We're not going anywhere. Besides, we can contact you through the starstone if we need you to open one."

Cedar nodded. "Okay, if you're sure."

They all looked grim, no doubt remembering the years they'd spent searching for Brogan's hidden sidh as they evaded Lorcan. She hoped they wouldn't need such an escape this time.

Cedar said good-bye to Nevan and Seisyll, both of whom wished her luck and hugged her for just a little too long. Then she followed Finn, Eden, Riona, Rohan, and Felix into the house's willow-lined courtyard.

"We'll grab a few things from our room and open the sidh from there," Cedar told Riona and Rohan, gesturing to the door that led to the room she and Finn shared. Riona nodded and hugged her close. "Good luck, dear."

Cedar opened the door and held it ajar as Finn, Eden, and Felix entered. Then she waved at Riona and Rohan one last time and closed it behind her.

"Are we really going back?" Eden asked as they walked through the field of poppies.

"Yes, honey, but just for a little while. Your father and I need your help. There's something we need to find—"

"The Lia Fáil," Eden interrupted.

"That's right," Cedar said. "And we don't know where it is, so we'll need to look in a lot of different places. That's where you come in."

Eden nodded seriously. "I can help by opening the sidhe for us to go through."

"Think of it as a big scavenger hunt," Cedar said, keeping her tone light. If Eden saw this as a game, maybe she wouldn't mind being dragged all around the British Isles quite so much.

"Where do you want to go first?" Eden asked.

"Well, I think we should start by going home," Cedar said. "Our old home. An Internet connection would come in handy, and I can pick up my tablet to take with us in case we need to look up maps or pictures of where we need to go. Are you ready?" she asked as they approached the pond.

"Just a minute, I want to say good-bye to the fishies," Eden said, running over to look into the water. Felix followed her, and she started showing him her favorites.

Finn pulled Cedar in for an embrace as they watched them. "Ready to save the world?" he asked.

"Always," she said. She could feel the adrenaline pulsing through her veins. "But first, I want to change back into my jeans." She walked into her walk-in wardrobe and found her jeans and shirt toward the back, where they had somehow hung themselves up. When she emerged, the others were standing in a small group.

"I'm done saying good-bye," Eden said. "Where should we go? The kitchen?"

"It's as good a place as any," Cedar said. "I hope Jane's not walking around naked or something."

Eden giggled at this and then walked over to the wardrobe door and pulled it open.

Jane wasn't naked, but what they saw was even more surprising. Jane was sitting at the kitchen table with the man whom Cedar had met outside of Maeve's house. He stood up when he saw them.

"We meet again, Cedar," he said.

CHAPTER 5

"Cedar!" Jane cried, jumping up. "I didn't think you'd be back so soon! What's going on? Is everything okay?"

Cedar didn't answer. Instead, she gently pulled Eden behind her, her eyes glued on Liam. He held up his hands apologetically. "I'm sorry, it must be a bit of a surprise to see me here. But your timing is excellent. I was just asking Jane if she knew how I could find you."

He held his hand out to Finn, who was the closest to him. "You must be Finn," he said. "I'm Liam Neill."

Finn shook the man's hand but didn't smile. "So you're the mysterious Liam. Why were you looking for Cedar?" he asked, clearly disinterested in small talk. "And who are you? Cedar says you weren't exactly forthcoming the first time she met you."

Liam didn't seem offended. "I have to apologize for that as well. It seems as though I didn't make a very good first impression."

"You guys can come in and sit down, y'know," Jane interrupted. "You don't have to stand in the doorway. I just put on some coffee. Who's this?" she asked, jerking her chin in Felix's direction.

He bowed slightly and said, "Toirdhealbhach MacDail re Deachai at your service. You must be Jane."

Jane gave Cedar a wry look. "Is he for real?" she said.

"Oh, for goodness sake, just call him Felix. The rest of us do," Cedar said, and Felix straightened up and laughed.

"If you must," he answered with a wink at Jane. "But one of these days I'm going to meet a human who can say my proper name."

76

Jane scowled, and Cedar wondered if she had taken offense. Eden squirmed out of Cedar's grasp and ran off to play with the toys and books she had left behind in her room. The rest of them found seats in the living room, where Jane brought out mugs of steaming coffee. Cedar sipped hers gratefully. It had been another long day.

Liam accepted a mug from Jane and wrapped his long, slender fingers around it. "Again, I'm sorry for the unexpected visit—well, both unexpected visits," he said. "I didn't expect to see anyone at Maeve's house when I went to visit her grave. I'm glad I was there, since you seemed hell-bent on getting into that shed no matter what it did to you. But I'm afraid I wasn't very talkative that day." He stared down into his coffee. "I hadn't been back to that house in many years. It was . . . difficult."

"How did you know Maeve?" Cedar asked. Finn and Felix were both giving Liam wary looks, but Cedar was glad that he was here, glad that he'd come looking for her. She hated unanswered questions, and she'd thought about him a lot over the past couple of days.

"She was my student," he answered.

"Your student? But I thought Brogan was the one who taught her," Cedar said, surprised.

"No, he just arranged for me to do it," Liam answered. "I only met him a couple of times."

"So you're a druid," Cedar said. She felt like she was stating the obvious, but she needed to be certain.

"Yes," he said. "I was her mentor for several years. After her apprenticeship was over, we lost touch. She didn't want to have anything do with the druidic life after . . . well, after *he* left. By the time I learned what had happened to her, it was too late."

"How *did* you find out about Maeve's death? And how did you know Cedar was planning on going to Tír na nÓg?" Finn demanded.

"You of all people must know that the magical network is still vast here on Earth, even if it's mostly hidden. A battle between the Tuatha Dé Danann and the Merrow does not go unnoticed, especially one that results in the death of the Merrow queen. And it made even greater waves when the High King of Tír na nÓg was defeated at the hands of a human." He bowed his head at Cedar. "Your bravery is exceptional." Returning his attention to Finn, he said, "I did not know of your plans to return to Tír na nÓg; there is no spy among your ranks, at least to my knowledge. It was an educated guess. And I should have pressed my case harder. I came here today to warn you that Nuala wanders Tír na nÓg freely . . . but perhaps you already know that since you have been and returned."

Before Cedar could answer, Finn asked, "How do you know about Nuala?"

"I've known about her for many years," Liam answered patiently. "She attempted to contact as many druids as possible while she was here. I never spoke to her myself, but several of my kind did. Many of them were quite impressed. Rumor has it she's convinced some of them to return to Tír na nÓg once she is crowned queen. They say she is offering them equality with the Tuatha Dé Danann. I admit that I can see how that would appeal to some."

There was an awkward silence in which Finn and Felix exchanged loaded glances. Then Cedar asked, "Does it appeal to *you*?"

"No, on a number of levels," Liam answered. "For one, I'm quite happy here. Also, I don't put stock in the promises of the Tuatha Dé Danann—no offense. We had our time in Tír na nÓg, but here on Earth we serve no one but ourselves. Returning to Tír na nÓg would be a return to servitude, whatever Nuala claims. And if she thinks she can get all of the druids to return, she doesn't know us very well. There's no real organization or leadership. Most of us come and go as we please and are quite happily integrated into this world. We're humans, after all—we just possess certain abilities that other humans do not."

Felix stood up and started pacing the apartment. "It seems quite convenient that you were here exactly when we arrived, and that you showed up at Maeve's house the night before Cedar was supposed to leave for Tír na nÓg. How do we know you aren't helping Nuala?" he asked.

Liam nodded slowly, and when he spoke his voice was thick with emotion. "I understand why you might think so. But believe me, it couldn't be further from the truth. Maeve was my best student and a dear friend. If the information I've heard is true, Nuala killed her in cold blood. Now Nuala is playing some sort of game with my kind. I don't know what it is, but I don't trust her. Why does she want the druids back in Tír na nÓg so badly?" His brow wrinkled as he considered this.

"I can't give you proof if that's what you're looking for. But I can assure you I'm not helping her. She couldn't offer me anything that would make up for what she did to Maeve, not even the High Kingship of Tír na nÓg. I didn't come to spy on you—I came to warn you. Stay away from her."

"We can't," Cedar said bluntly.

"Cedar, she killed your mother," Liam said. "You have no idea what she—"

"I know exactly what she's capable of, and what she's planning," Cedar interrupted. "She's using the return of the druids as a way to convince the Council to make her queen. She conveniently forgot to mention the bit about offering them equality with the Tuatha Dé Danann. And when she's queen, she's going to use her ability to start a Third World War—or the apocalypse. Once all the humans have killed each other, Ériu will be ripe for the taking."

"Holy shit," Jane breathed. "Are you serious? Can she do that?"

"She can and will, unless we stop her. That's why we're here. We didn't come back because we were running from her," Cedar said.

"Then why *did* you come back?" Jane asked.

Cedar hesitated. It still felt too strange to say it out loud.

Felix was the one who answered. "Because *Cedar* is going to become queen, not Nuala."

Jane blinked at him. "No. Seriously?"

He frowned. "You don't think she is worthy?"

"She's my best friend, of course I do," Jane said, rolling her eyes. "Forgive me if the whole fairy-kingdom thing is still sinking in."

"But if that's the case, Cedar, why are you *here* instead of back in Tír na nÓg?" Liam asked.

Cedar swallowed. It was so much easier to accept these things when surrounded by the magic of Tír na nÓg. Here, it sounded ridiculous. But that didn't make it any less true. "Even though my father was High King, the Council has given me a task to perform before they'll make me queen. It's a test, to prove myself. I have to find the Lia Fáil."

Finn was still scowling, and Cedar could tell that he didn't like talking about this in front of Liam. But something deep inside of her trusted him. And she wanted him to stay. From the sounds of it, he had known Maeve a whole lot better than she had, and she had about a million questions for him.

"The Lia What?" Jane asked.

"Foy-al. L-i-a-f-a-i-l," Cedar spelled. Jane was already reaching for her laptop. "It's also called the Stone of Destiny. It's one of the four treasures of the Tuatha Dé Danann, but it's been lost somewhere on Ériu—I mean, Earth—for centuries. I have to find it. In a week." She gave Liam a wry smile. "You don't happen to know where it is, do you?"

Liam let out a long, slow breath. "Of all the things they could have asked of you . . . ," he said. "No, I don't know where it is. No one does. We—the druids, that is—have searched for it for centuries. It's an important historical and cultural artifact, even if it no longer has magical properties. But there are many large stones in sacred places around the world, and it could be any one of them."

"Great," Cedar said drily. "So we just need to go around and touch every stone in the world to see if it gets warm. Except it might not even work for me, being sort-of human and all."

"Well, that's where your Danann friends come in handy," Liam said. "Never hurts to have a god or two around."

Jane snorted. She was already online, her eyes flicking rapidly over the screen in front of her. "Okay, what do we know?" she asked. Quickly, Cedar filled Jane and Liam in on some of their theories, with Finn occasionally interjecting with additional information or to correct something Cedar had gotten wrong. Jane didn't look up from her computer's screen, her fingers clicking away on the keyboard as Cedar talked.

"What are you doing?" Felix asked Jane, peering over her shoulder.

She raised an eyebrow at him. "It's called a computer. Don't you have computers in Fairyland?"

He smiled, his blue eyes twinkling. "No, but I did learn to use one during the two decades I was living here. It's quite interesting, actually, watching human technologies evolve. It's another way you differ from us. Our technology, so to speak, has more or less gone unchanged since . . . well, since forever. Yours has changed radically since the last time I was here—before this most recent stint, I mean."

"When were you last here?" Cedar asked, intrigued.

"Oh, it's been a while," he said with a laugh. "Let's just say that the humans hadn't yet figured out electricity, let alone the Internet." He leaned back and laced his hands behind his head. "I like humans," he declared loftily. "Always have. Used to visit here quite a lot. I tried not to get too tangled up in the humans' affairs, but it was difficult. There was always someone who needed healing, especially with all the wars going on, and before you lot discovered things like penicillin and vaccines—which are brilliant, by the way. Of course, the human women are interesting too. There was this milkmaid once, in Derry . . . damn, she was beautiful. And she genuinely believed in the fairy folk."

"What happened to her?" Cedar asked. She glanced at Jane, who seemed to be studiously ignoring Felix. Her eyes were still fixed on the screen, but they weren't moving.

"She died," he said simply. "I went back to Tír na nÓg for a spell. I guess more time passed than I realized—it's so easy to forget that humans have such short natural life spans. When I returned, I found out that she had married, borne children, grown old, and died. But one of her daughters told me that her mother had always shared stories about the fairy she had once loved, so I guess she never forgot me."

Cedar was sure that any woman who had met Felix in his godlike state would have a very difficult time forgetting him.

Jane's expression took on a definite sour note. "You okay?" Cedar asked her.

"Huh? Yeah, I'm fine," she answered, sweeping a strand of black and red hair behind her ear. "Just reading."

Cedar yawned and stood. "I haven't heard Eden in a bit. I'm going to go check on her." She poked her head into Eden's room and found her daughter fast asleep, sprawled out on her bed among several books and stuffed animals. She thought about waking her to brush her teeth and then laughed to herself. The fate of the whole world was at stake, and she was still worried about Eden getting cavities. She grabbed a spare blanket from the closet tucked it in around her sleeping daughter's shoulders. "Good night, my heart," she whispered, kissing her gently on the forehead.

When she came back into the living room, Finn and Jane were huddled around the computer screen. Felix had tilted his head back against the sofa, his eyes closed and the hint of smile on his face— probably thinking of that milkmaid, Cedar mused.

"Young Eden seems very independent," Liam said, standing and stretching.

"She is—too much so, if you ask me," Cedar said. "I'm sorry you didn't get to properly meet her. I think she's just glad to be back home for a bit with her old toys again."

"So I cannot persuade you, then. You are going to search for the Lia Fáil and then return to Tír na nÓg."

"Yes," Cedar said firmly. "There's no other choice."

"I admire your perseverance," Liam said. "And forgive my intrusion . . . I know it's a decision only you can make. I just have your best interests in mind. Think of me as a concerned friend."

Cedar gave a half-hearted laugh. "I can always use more of those. And I do appreciate your concern." She tried unsuccessfully to suppress another yawn. It was late—very late.

"I think it's time for me to take my leave," Liam said. "I have to be on a plane back to Dublin very early in the morning. If you're determined to do this, I'd like to help. It's been a long time since my people have looked for the Lia Fáil, but I may be able to find some information that can help. And I'll try to find out more about Nuala's arrangement with these druids she claims to have on her side." He handed her a white business card. "This is how you can reach me."

Cedar looked at the card in her hand and then burst out laughing. "You're a librarian?" she said.

Liam cocked an eyebrow at her. "I am. And why is that funny?"

"I'm sorry, it's just that I always thought being a librarian would be a rather boring job, and you seem far from boring."

"I'll take that as a compliment. But being a librarian at Trinity College is far from boring. It's one of the most respected libraries in the world, and we have many priceless ancient manuscripts and artifacts in our possession. I also belong to the Irish Antiquities Society. But not to the Order of Druids, in case you were wondering."

"Why not?"

"Because they're all fakes," he said. "No true druid would ever flaunt his or her identity like that. Being a druid is a sacred trust, not a costume party at Stonehenge."

"Thank you for your help," Cedar said, walking with him to the door of the apartment.

"I almost forgot," he said, reaching into his pocket. "I was going to leave it here with your friend Jane in case you came back. But now I can give it to you myself." He held out a silver bracelet, from which dangled half a dozen tiny charms. "It was hers," he said, and Cedar didn't have to ask who he meant. "She let me keep it as a remembrance, but I think it belongs with you."

Cedar fingered the delicate charms and slipped the bracelet onto her wrist. "It's beautiful," she said. "Are you sure you don't want to keep it?"

He smiled. "I have many memories that will never tarnish," he said. "I know she kept secrets from you, especially about her years with me. Perhaps someday we can sit down and I'll tell you all about it."

"I'd like that," Cedar said. She closed the door behind him and went back into the living room, where she was surprised to find Jane and Finn arguing.

"It's still your place," Jane was saying. "You two should sleep in the big bed, and I'll kip on the sofa. Stop being so damn stubborn."

"No, I'm not going to have a lady sleeping on the sofa while I'm in a bed," Finn protested.

"Jane, can I talk to you for a minute?" Cedar said. Without waiting for an answer, she pulled her friend into the bedroom. "Are you PMSing or something? What's going on? You've been touchy all night."

Jane rolled her eyes dramatically and flopped down on the bed. "Oh, Ceeds, I'm sorry. It's just . . . that guy. He sets my teeth on edge."

"Who, Felix?" Cedar asked. "You just met him."

"Yeah, but I know his type," Jane said. "I mean, just look at him. He's so . . . gorgeous and preppy and cocky and bullshit."

Cedar raised both eyebrows at her friend. "Seriously? Are you sure you're not just flustered because he's really, really hot?"

"Of course not," Jane said, making a face. "I just know guys like that. They have their perfect lives and their perfect girlfriends and they don't understand why someone might want to pierce themselves or get a tattoo or color their hair. He's wearing khakis, for chrissakes. Believe me, I've known too many of his type. Remember Richard at Ellison?"

Cedar only vaguely remembered who Richard was. He had been a project manager at their workplace, Ellison Creative, for about a year, but she hadn't seen much of him because he was in a different department. Like Felix, Richard had been gorgeous in a Calvin Klein–model kind of way. "I think so. What about him?" she asked.

"Well, he was an asshole, for starters. He used to call me 'punk girl'—or worse—and ask me if I'd borrowed my clothes from Avril Lavigne. So I hacked into his computer and sent naked pictures of his girlfriend to his *other* girlfriend. Oh, and also to the HR department. He got fired for 'improper use of company computers.'" Jane snickered.

"Okay, so he was an asshole," Cedar agreed. "But Felix isn't like that. Just because he's good-looking—okay, really, *really* good-looking . . . and immortal—doesn't make him a jerk. He's actually quite fabulous. You didn't meet him before, when he purposefully made himself look like a crazy old fisherman. I bet you wouldn't have felt this way then." She was surprised to see this insecure side of Jane. To her, Jane was the ultimate example of a strong, confident, and independent woman. She sat down on the corner of the bed beside her friend and squeezed her hand. "And *you* are fabulous. Are you sure you don't want the bed tonight? It's either that or share the living room with your new best friend."

Jane looked at her, aghast. "He's staying here?"

"Where else is he going to stay?" Cedar asked, bemused.

"Oh, fine, but the sofa's mine. He'll have to sleep on the floor," Jane said, getting up off the bed.

"Whatever you say," Cedar said.

They headed out into the living room, where Finn and Felix were having a hushed conversation. They stopped when the women entered the room. "Everything okay?" Finn asked.

"Yep," Jane answered, heaving a pile of blankets from the linen closet onto the floor of the living room, as far away from the sofa as possible. "So, where are we going to start looking? And don't even think about leaving me behind. I've got a week of vacation coming, and I'd much rather go on a magical scavenger hunt than drink watered-down martinis with Trekkies at some Vegas casino. Besides, you might need someone with technological expertise."

Cedar knew there was no use arguing, and, truth be told, she'd be happy to have Jane come with them. "Edinburgh Castle?" she said. "We might as well start at the most obvious place."

"Yeah, but good luck getting your hands on that stone. I was reading up about it while you guys were yakking. It's in the same room the crown jewels. It's not like you'll be able to just walk up to it and step on it, or whatever you need to do," Jane said. "If I had more time . . . and I'd probably need to hire some help . . . I could possibly disable the security system. But it's hard to say without knowing more about it."

"One thing we don't have a lot of is time," Cedar pointed out. "Although we could probably find the money," she said, thinking about the precious jewels that were scattered all around her wardrobe back in Tír na nÓg. She could go back and get some, or maybe Riona could toss a few through a sidh. The thought made her smile.

"Here's my idea," Finn said, circling behind Cedar so that he could rub her shoulders. "Let's all go to bed and worry about it in the morning. We're not going anywhere tonight, and you, my dear, are starting to sway on your feet."

◌

"It feels strange to be back here," Cedar said, climbing into bed beside Finn after setting up beds for Jane and Felix in the living room and checking on Eden. "I know we were gone for only a day and a half, but so much has happened. . . ." She trailed off, staring up at the ceiling.

"Sometimes I wonder if my family and I should have just let you be," Finn said, propping himself up on his elbow so he could look at her. He was shirtless, and Cedar could feel the heat emanating from him. "Maeve wanted you to have a safe, normal life. That's hardly what you've got now."

Cedar smiled at him and trailed the tips of her fingers across his chest. "Normal lives are highly overrated. I love that we're a family again *and* that I finally know who I am." She pulled him down and kissed him softly, and then deeply, reveling in his body's response to her.

"Well," he said, his lips leaving hers and traveling down her neck, "I can promise you that you won't have to deal with any of this alone." He nibbled on her collarbone, his hand sliding along her side and pulling her close. "I will . . . always . . . be with you."

"Mmm, even when I look like your grandmother?" Cedar asked, arching her back and suppressing a moan.

She felt him smile, his lips against her skin. "I told you, we don't know what will happen. You're perfect, and you might stay this way forever. And if you do age . . . I'll just take some of Felix's aging potion and age right along with you." He was now kissing her stomach, and she wrapped her fingers in his wavy hair.

"You will not," she said. "I forbid it. I want people to think I'm some kind of sexy cougar grandma."

87

He looked up at her, one eyebrow raised. "You do, do you?" he said. "I'll show you sexy cougar—" He started to kiss her again but jerked away at the sound of screaming from Eden's bedroom. Before Cedar could even get up, he was out the door and running down the hallway. When Cedar caught up to him he was kneeling by Eden's bed. Their daughter was sitting bolt upright, her eyes wide open, still screaming at the top of her lungs, pausing only long enough to gulp for air.

"Eden! Eden!" Finn said. "I'm here. Eden, can you hear me?"

Cedar tried to lift Eden into her arms, but Eden started thrashing so violently that she couldn't hold her. "No, Mummy! No, Mummy!" she shrieked over and over again.

"What's going on?" Jane asked from the doorway. She stood there next to Felix, both of them wide-eyed with alarm.

"I don't know!" Cedar said. "Maybe she's having a night terror or seizure or something. Felix, is there anything you can do?"

Felix started to walk toward Eden, who was still flailing wildly and screaming. Suddenly, she launched herself off the bed and dashed out of the room, dodging Jane. She swung open the nearest closed door, which happened to lead to the bathroom.

"No!" Cedar cried as she caught sight of the tell-tale shimmering air. "Stop her!" Jane lunged for her, and Felix and Finn both moved so fast that Cedar could barely see them, but they were all too late. The door slammed shut and was once again the plain painted door of the bathroom. Eden was gone.

"Nooooo!" Finn cried out, pulling the door off its hinges and slamming it down on the floor. Cedar stared into the empty room, aghast.

"Did you see?" Cedar asked desperately. "Did anyone see where she went?"

They all shook their heads. "No," Jane said. "It just looked . . . dark."

CHAPTER 6

Eden opened her eyes and reached for Baby Bunny out of habit. But Baby Bunny wasn't there. She groped around for Elephant or another stuffed animal friend, but all she felt was grass. She sat up blinking in the darkness.

"What's happening?" she asked out loud. "Mummy?" There was no answer.

She stood up and then froze as she realized she was no longer in her room. At first she couldn't see anything, but then her eyes adjusted or it grew brighter around her—she couldn't tell which. She looked down at herself. She was wearing the same clothes she'd had on yesterday, a pair of jeans and a violet T-shirt. The last thing she remembered was lying down on her bed, wanting to read just one more chapter. . . . But this wasn't her home on Earth, she could tell that much. It felt different, strange.

Little lights started popping up in the grass all around her. She wondered if they were fireflies, or maybe fairies, the kind she'd read about in books before learning that she was one of them. The lights seemed to move and dance all around her, and she thought she could hear faint strains of music coming from them. Then she noticed another sound off to her left, a bubbling, laughing sound that was emanating from something that sparkled and glowed. Slowly, she walked toward it, the dancing lights moving with her.

When she got closer, she realized that it was a stream. The rocks glowed softly beneath the water, gently illuminating it. She saw something move and jumped. Small translucent creatures were playing in the water. They looked like little people but were only as big as her hand, with huge eyes and thin bodies. Their hands and feet were webbed, and they moved with a fluidity that didn't seem quite natural, as though they didn't have any bones. They looked up at her and laughed. "You've arrived!" they said in high-pitched voices, and then they dove into the water and disappeared.

"I have?" Eden said. "Where?" She didn't feel afraid, not exactly, though she knew she should be at home in her bed. She started to climb the hill beside her, hoping it would give her a better look at where she was. The grass was soft and cool beneath her bare feet. As she approached the top of the hill, she thought she could make out a form. It was a huge bed, and there were two people sleeping in it. Eden stopped, quite sure she shouldn't be here. But her curiosity got the better of her, and she tiptoed slowly forward, quiet as a mouse.

When Eden reached the bed, the first person she saw was a man with a dark goatee, sleeping with his mouth slightly open and one arm flung off the side of the mattress. She stared for a moment at the massive arm, its muscles bulging even in sleep. She didn't recognize him, so she tiptoed around to the other side of the bed, and then froze in terror.

Red hair was splayed out over the white sheets, spilling over pearl-white shoulders that rose and fell softly. For a moment Eden was frozen in her tracks, and she had to bite her lip to keep from crying out. Slowly, she took a step back.

Then Nuala opened her eyes. For a brief moment the two shared startled gazes, and then Nuala sat up suddenly.

"Eden!" she gasped. "It worked!"

Eden didn't wait to ask what had worked, she just turned and ran. She looked frantically for the doorway that had transported her here, but all she could see was grass and the stream. "Help me!" she screamed at the dancing lights, but they just skipped and twirled about her feet as she ran. She tumbled down the hill and chanced a look behind her. Nuala was right on her heels.

"Eden, wait! I'm not going to hurt you!" Nuala called. Eden dodged her grasp by a fraction of an inch and then closed her eyes and thought of home as she jumped feetfirst into the glittering stream.

∽

Nuala stared at the stream that ran through her bedchamber. The glowing rocks at the bottom sparkled and winked at her, but there was no sign of the little girl. She could still picture Eden's face as she crouched beside her bed. There had been fear, yes . . . but also hatred.

"Damn it," Nuala seethed. Her eyes were still fixated on the spot where Eden had vanished, but her mind was whirling. A strange sensation had settled into the pit of her stomach, and she struggled to place it. Surely she wasn't upset that the girl hated her. What did it matter? The girl was a pawn, a necessary part of her plan. No harm would come to her so long as her parents didn't do anything stupid. Still, she had thought that Eden might have enjoyed part of their adventure together. How many six-year-olds got to swim with the Merrow? Eden would probably never have seen Tír na nÓg if it hadn't been for her. *Stupid, ungrateful child,* she thought. Well, it didn't matter what the girl thought of her. What mattered was that her plan was working.

"Fionnghuala?" Deaglán came up behind her and wrapped his arms around her waist. "Is everything all right?"

She turned and looked him in the eyes. "Yes," she purred. "Everything is fine. Go back to sleep, darling." She watched as he walked up the hill and climbed back into the bed, falling asleep almost instantly. Then she reached inside her nightgown and pulled out a sparkling stone the color of merlot that dangled from a thin gold chain. Her lips moved rapidly as she softly sang the song that would unlock the stone's power and activate its other half. She followed the stream until she came to a delicate bench decorated with ivy that sat in the middle of a small copse of trees. She finished the song and waited. After a moment, the colors in the stone started to swirl, and then a face appeared.

✺

They were still pacing the hallway when Eden materialized out of thin air and fell onto the carpet at Cedar's feet. She was soaking wet. "Close it!" Eden screamed, and Finn rushed over to the patch of glittering air. They heard a loud roar, and then Finn waved his hand and there was silence.

Felix immediately took Eden into his arms and carried her over to the couch. She was shivering and pale. "Warm clothes," he said, and Jane ran to Eden's room. He cupped Eden's face in his hands and looked into her eyes. "Eden, it's Uncle Felix," he said. "Can you hear me?" Eden nodded. "You're safe now, and your mum and dad are right here."

Cedar crouched down next to the couch and clasped Eden's hand in hers. "Are you okay?" she asked. "What happened? Where did you go? Why are you so wet?"

"Let her rest for a moment," Felix said. He whispered some words and held his hands over Eden's forehead, then her chest, stomach, and legs. "She's fine physically," he said. "Just chilled. But let's help her feel safe and warm. I'll make some tea."

Jane handed Cedar some dry pajamas for Eden, then sat down in the armchair in the corner, hugging her knees close to her chest. Cedar helped Eden into the pajamas and then wrapped her up in a quilt and sat down next to her, holding her close. Finn was pacing the room, his eyes locked on his daughter.

When Felix returned, he handed mugs to both Cedar and Eden. "I have a feeling you could use some of this too," he said, and both mother and daughter accepted their tea. Finally, Cedar asked, "Can you talk about it now?"

"I don't know how I got there," Eden said. "I remember reading on my bed, and then I woke up outside. There were dancing lights and a stream with little fairies in it. I climbed to the top of a hill and saw two people in a big bed. One of them was Nuala. She woke up and chased me."

Cedar looked at Finn in alarm and saw that he had stopped pacing. His face was pale and drawn.

"How did you escape?" Cedar asked Eden.

"I just thought of home and jumped into the stream," Eden replied. "It was the only thing I could think of."

Cedar hugged her daughter close, her eyes filling with tears. "You did great, baby. I'm so glad you're safe."

"But how did I get there?" Eden asked.

"You don't remember waking up and screaming?" Finn asked. Felix had forced a cup into his hand as well, and Cedar was pretty sure that it didn't contain tea.

Eden's forehead creased as she frowned. "I wasn't screaming."

"You were, honey," Cedar said gently. "Your eyes were open and you were screaming and you wouldn't let me hold you. Then you ran out of the room and made a sidh. You closed it behind you before we could get to you."

Eden looked at her with big eyes. "I didn't do any of that! Honest, I didn't!"

"It's okay, Eden, you're not in trouble. You just don't remember doing it," Felix said. He glanced at Finn. "It could be an innocuous as a night terror . . . but considering where she ended up, I have my doubts."

"You think Nuala did this?" Cedar asked. "How? How could she get inside Eden's head like that?" The thought of Nuala being able to torment her daughter from another world was something Cedar hadn't even thought to fear. How could she keep her daughter safe if Nuala could get inside Eden's mind?

"I don't know," Felix said, a tortured look on his face as he stared at the huddled figures on the sofa. "I don't know."

CHAPTER 7

Cedar was afraid to sleep that night, convinced that Eden might somehow disappear from her arms. Finally, Finn asked Felix to make Cedar a sleeping draught so that she'd be at least somewhat well rested for their trip to Edinburgh. Cedar protested, but Finn promised to stay awake all night to keep an eye on Eden. Begrudgingly, Cedar agreed, knowing Finn required much less sleep than she did. It wasn't the first time she wished she didn't have the gift of humanity. *More of a curse than a gift,* she thought, but then checked herself. Her gift had saved Eden's life and rid the Tuatha Dé Danann of Lorcan. *Not that they were overwhelmed with gratitude,* she thought grumpily as she drifted off into an herb-induced sleep.

She was the last one up in the morning. Eden and Jane were chatting over bowls of Cocoa Puffs, last night's terror seemingly forgotten. Fascinated by the prospect of going to a real castle, Eden was bombarding Jane with questions about the princes and princesses who had lived there. To her credit, Jane was answering Eden's questions as patiently as she could, pulling up pictures and timelines and video tours on her laptop for Eden to watch.

"Good morning, sleepyhead," Finn said, handing her a cup of coffee.

"Morning," Cedar said. "You shouldn't have let me sleep so long."

He shrugged. "You needed it. And we don't *all* need to have an encyclopedic knowledge of Edinburgh Castle," he said, grinning at Jane and Eden.

"Mum, guess what?" Eden said. "They have a cemetery just for pets!"

"Very useful knowledge, I'm sure," Cedar said, smiling. "So? Are we ready to check this place out?"

"No photography or videos are allowed in the Crown Room, where the stone is," Jane said. "But I'm sure I can get around that if need be. And who knows? It might be easier than we think. It could just be a matter of distracting the guards and making a run for it."

"Think you can manage that without getting arrested?" Felix asked.

Jane shot him a dirty look. "I'm sure you could magic me out if I did," she said.

"Don't know that I'd want to," he replied under his breath.

Cedar raised her eyebrows at Finn, who shook his head and rolled his eyes. Cedar took this to mean that Felix and Jane had been bickering all morning. She stepped between them and clapped her hands.

"Okay!" she said brightly. "So we're going to act like normal tourists, but we'll head straight for the Crown Room. Jane will see what kind of technology we're up against, Felix will keep an eye out for any kinds of magical protection around the stone, and Finn and I will be glued to Eden's side." It made her nervous to take Eden out in public after last night, but if they didn't find the stone, none of them would be safe. No one would.

A few minutes later they were ready to go. Eden opened the sidh into a back alley on the Royal Mile, just outside the castle. It was early afternoon here, and the main street was crowded with the last flush of the tourist season. Cedar bought them all tickets at the admissions stand, despite Jane's protests. "Why are we buying tickets again?" she asked. "Why can't Eden just zap us into the Crown Room?"

"Because someone might ask to see our tickets inside," Cedar said. "I don't know how it works; none of us have ever been here before."

"Technically, that's not true," Felix said, strolling behind them. "I was here once . . . but it was before the castle was built."

"Show-off," Jane muttered.

They followed the map they'd been given at the entrance and walked through the Gatehouse, between the looming statues of Sir William Wallace and King Robert the Bruce. Cedar ran her hands along the stone walls, thinking about all of the other hands that must have touched them over the past several hundred years. She had always felt rather rootless growing up in the "new world," where almost everyone was from somewhere else. She'd had an Irish friend once in high school. She had asked her how long her family had been Irish, and, with a puzzled look on her face, her friend had answered, "Forever, I suppose." At the time, Cedar had envied such a heritage. How strange it was to realize that she belonged to a race even older than the Irish, an unbroken line that went back to the dawn of time.

They passed under a massive stone gate, trying not to run or look conspicuous in their haste. Eden kept pulling on Cedar's arm, trying to get her to go see the dog cemetery. "Later," Cedar told her. "We have to find the stone first." She had to admit that she, too, wished they could stop and look around. She'd never been to a castle before, and she vowed to bring Eden back here someday, when they could wander the nooks and crannies of history at their leisure.

After winding between ancient buildings and through clusters of tourists, they stepped into a large square courtyard in the heart of the castle. Stone buildings and towers surrounded them on every side. Cedar turned the map upside down so she that she could orient herself. "The war museum is that way," she said, pointing. "The royal apartments are that way, and it says the Crown Room is this way."

They followed a tour group through one of the doors and into a large hall. A man dressed in period costume was explaining what the hall had been used for in the sixteenth and seventeenth centuries. Cedar looked around for the stone.

"It's not in here. We have to head up these stairs," Jane said, leading the way. She scowled at the large signs that read, NO VIDEO OR PHOTOGRAPHY PERMITTED. When they reached the top, they passed through another doorway, one that was thick and heavy, and entered a small, dimly lit room. Cedar felt like she'd stumbled into an old university library. The walls were lined with dark wood, and the plush carpet muffled their footsteps. There were only a couple of other people inside, but the room was small and it felt close and crowded.

In the center of the room, on a raised platform cordoned off by a brass rail, were the Honours of Scotland, encased in glass. Eden's mouth hung open as she gazed at the crown, which was studded with pearls and gemstones. Beside it lay a long polished sword with an ornate, silver hilt. The scepter was no less impressive. It was gleaming silver and at least four feet long, topped with a dark polished stone and a single pearl. Lying beside it was a large rectangular block of stone resting on a deep purple cloth. The stone was about two feet long, a foot and a half wide, and a foot deep. It looked no different from the stones that she'd run her fingers across in the castle wall. She wasn't sure what she'd been expecting, but this stone appeared so perfectly ordinary that she didn't think it could possibly be the Lia Fáil of legend. Still, there was only one way to find out. She reached out a hand.

"Don't touch the glass, miss," came a voice from behind her. One of the castle guides was standing in the corner, frowning at her. Cedar nodded and pulled her hand back. After a moment Felix sidled up to the guide and started chatting casually with him.

"C'mon," said Jane, who had been staring into the corners of the room, probably trying to figure out where the security cameras were. "I want to look at the other side of the room." Cedar followed her to the opposite side of the display. It hurt to be this close without being able to do anything about it. All she—or Finn or Felix or Eden—needed to do was touch it to see if it grew warm. If it did, they'd be able to go back to Tír na nÓg and start setting things right immediately. If not, well . . .

Felix came striding up to them just then, rubbing his hands together, a huge smile on his face.

"You look like you have good news," Cedar said, her hopes rising.

Felix shrugged and winked at Finn. "I don't think we'll have too many problems," he said. "But it would be best if we went to get ourselves a pint so that we can chat about it somewhere more private. Let's go."

ᕦ

An hour later they were ensconced in the White Bull, one of Edinburgh's many tiny pubs. Eden was wolfing down a plate of sweet potato fries, accompanied by a Shirley Temple, while the rest of them drank their pints and listened to Felix. "It's amazing what people will tell you when they think you're a novelist," he was saying. "The security's heavy, for sure, but I don't think it's impossible."

"But there are cameras *everywhere*," Jane said. "Plus bullet-proof glass—"

"Bullet-resistant, actually," Felix corrected her. "There's no such thing as completely bulletproof glass."

"Whatever," she said. "There's bullet-*resistant* glass, steel blinds, the doors are reinforced with steel . . . and those are just the security features we know about. There are probably all kinds of bells and whistles we can't see. These are the most valuable artifacts in all of Scotland. Your little conversation with the guide hasn't changed any of that."

"Always the pessimist, aren't you?" Felix said. "They're expecting *humans* to try to steal the crown jewels. And we"—he indicated everyone at the table except for Jane—"are not human. We're faster, we're stronger, and we have a tricky little damsel right here who could get us into the queen's bedroom if we asked her nicely enough. Not that I want to know what's going on in there," he added, and everyone except Jane laughed.

"So what's your plan?" Cedar asked.

"First, we finish this lovely pint," he said, raising his glass in a salute. "Then we go back to your place and cool our heels until the castle closes and it's nice and dark. Later, Eden can open a sidh directly into the Crown Room. Finn will transform into something big and strong and decidedly nonhuman, bust open the case, grab the stone, and pop back into the sidh. Even if the cameras see him— which they no doubt will—and they lock the whole bloody island down, he'll already be back in Halifax, which is, frankly, the last place they'd think to look for him even if they somehow managed to recognize him, which they won't, because he'll immediately transform back into the handsome fellow you see sitting before you."

Cedar looked at Finn, who was smiling wryly at Felix. "Hardly sophisticated," he said, "but it should work."

"I like it," Cedar said. "Let's do it. But I don't like the idea of just cooling our heels while we wait." She checked the time on her phone. "We've got three hours before the castle closes, and probably another five or six before it's really dark. I think we should look somewhere else in the meantime, in case you're right and this isn't the real Lia Fáil. How about Scone?"

"It's a long shot," Finn said, "The abbey that was in charge of the stone was destroyed centuries ago. Still, it wouldn't hurt to do a little exploring."

Jane pulled her tablet out of her bag and did a quick search. "Scone Palace has a replica of the Stone of Destiny, and it looks like they recently found some of the ruins of the abbey. Wouldn't it be crazy if the real stone was built into the abbey? It could be part of the ruins."

"That would make sense if they wanted to hide it from the English," Cedar said, excitement in her voice. "Let's go check it out."

A few minutes later they were standing in a small grove of trees on the grounds of Scone Palace. The sun shone through the delicate green leaves so that the trees appeared to be dripping with jewels. They stepped out onto the pathway and looked around to get their bearings.

"The replica of the stone is up here," Jane said, pointing to a stone chapel on top of a small hill. Cedar cast her eyes about as they walked up the hill. There were other tourists milling around the grounds, but no one had seemed to have noticed their unconventional arrival. Scone Palace loomed in front of them, opposite the chapel. The palace's outer walls were draped in ivy, and a few leaves were beginning to redden in the late summer chill. "Here it is," Jane said.

The replica was a good one; Cedar couldn't tell the difference between the stone they had seen in Edinburgh Castle and the one that was supported by two pillars in front of the entrance to the chapel. It was the height of a bench, and Eden climbed up and sat down on it. Cedar placed her palm against the stone, which stayed cool to the touch. Finn and Felix followed suit, but both shook their heads. "Well, we *know* this one is a replica," Cedar said, feeling foolish for being disappointed. "The question is whether the original is still around here or if they actually gave it to the English." She shivered suddenly and told Eden to zip up her jacket.

"But I'm not cold," Eden protested. Cedar felt goose bumps travel up and down her arms, and was going to ask Finn if he found it unusually cold. She stopped when she noticed that he and Felix were staring straight ahead, looks of astonishment on their faces.

"What is it?" she asked.

"Oh, wow!" Eden exclaimed. "Cool! Look, Mum!" she said, pointing.

Cedar trained her eyes where Eden was pointing, but all she could see was an empty field. A group of Japanese tourists walked past them, chatting animatedly with one another. "I don't see anything," Cedar said.

"The church!" Eden said.

"What church? The church is behind us," Cedar said, pointing at the small chapel that the Japanese tourists had just entered.

"I don't see anything either," said Jane.

"You probably can't see it because you're human," Eden said in a matter-of-fact voice. "And because you're kind of human, Mum."

Finn turned to them. "You really can't see it?"

Cedar squinted at the field again. "No," she said. "All I see is a field. But it's bitterly cold. Aren't the rest of you cold?" They all shook their heads.

"Odd," Finn said. "Your human ability won't let you see them, but maybe you can still feel them."

"Them? Who?"

"The ghosts," Eden said in an awed voice. "Look! One is coming toward us!" She ducked behind Finn's legs and peered out around them.

"What's happening?" Cedar asked.

She felt Jane edge in closer to her. "Ghosts?" her friend whispered.

"Don't be afraid," Felix said, standing a bit taller. "You're safe with us."

"I'm not afraid," Jane snapped. "I just can't see a damn thing."

"A figure is heading this way," Felix explained. "And beyond him, I think it must be the old abbey. Jane, can you pull up the map of the grounds on your computer?"

Jane mumbled something about data charges, but pulled out her tablet and peered at the screen. "Yeah, according to the map, the abbey was located over there. What . . . what does it look like?"

"Like how you'd expect a ghost church would look, I suppose," Finn said. "It's not huge, maybe three hundred feet in length, Romanesque in design, I'd say. I think it was built in the 1100s. You can see through it, but it still looks solid enough to touch." He held up his hand, and they all fell silent. Finn, Felix, and Eden were staring at the same spot in the air in front of them. Then Finn bowed slightly. "And to you, friend. We did not expect to see this place."

There was another pause. Cedar could hear Jane whisper, "This is so bizarre . . ." beside her.

"Finn, who are you talking to?" she asked, unable to stay silent.

"Shh! It's the ghost, Mum!" Eden said.

"Forgive me," Finn said to the air. "But we have two humans among our party who cannot see or hear you. May I repeat your words to them?"

The ghost must have agreed, because Finn turned to Cedar and Jane and said, "This is James Abercrombie, who was the last abbot at Scone. He died in 1514. He recognizes us for who we are." The corners of Finn's mouth lifted up. "He says that death has a way of opening one's mind to the supernatural in ways that life cannot. He is the caretaker of this ghostly place and its people. The spirits here had a strong connection to the abbey and they died without peace. Once they make their peace with themselves, they move on."

"Move on where?" Jane asked.

"To whatever comes next," Finn answered simply. Then he turned back to the ghost.

"We are looking for the true Lia Fáil, which our forefathers brought to this world from Falias and entrusted into the care of humans. We know that there was once a great stone here on which many of your kings were crowned. They say it was taken by the English, but there are many who doubt that story. Do you know if such a stone still exists in these lands?"

Again, Cedar heard nothing but extended silence as the ghost abbot responded.

"He says there are more than a few ghosts from that dreadful time here in his abbey. Some betrayed their own people and country for English gold. Others failed to protect the innocent around them and sought to save their own lives instead. He says that if we go into the abbey, we'll hear many stories about the Stone of Destiny."

Finn, Felix, and Eden started walking across the field. Jane and Cedar looked at each other and then shrugged and started following the others. "How are we supposed to go into a church we can't bloody see?" Jane whispered. After a few paces, they group stopped abruptly.

Everyone was silent for a long moment, but Cedar could tell that the ghost must be talking, because Finn was nodding at regular intervals. Finally, he turned to look at her. "We're at the entrance to the abbey," he said. "The abbot says that he's willing to open your eyes so that you can see the spirit world inside these walls."

Jane looked nervously at Cedar, and then nodded.

"Yes, we would like that," Cedar said. She felt something cold pass through her, like she had been plunged into an ice bath and then quickly dried off. Suddenly, she was no longer standing in the middle of an empty field. A huge translucent stone structure loomed in front of her. She reached out to touch the wooden doors that were only a foot from her face. She expected her hand to pass right through it, but it stopped, and she could feel the grain of the wood beneath her fingers. When she withdrew her hand, the doors opened inward.

"Welcome," said the ghostly abbot, whom she could now see, a clean-shaven, unremarkable man wearing a plain robe that fell to his ankles. The only thing that stood out about him was the fact that he too appeared both solid and translucent. The top of his head was shaved bald. He smiled and bobbed at Cedar, and she smiled back. Feeling Eden grab for her hand, she knelt down to her daughter's level.

"How are you doing, baby?" she asked. "Does this scare you?"

"A little," Eden admitted. "But it's also really cool!"

"Well, I think all the ghosts here are friendly," Cedar said as they followed the abbot inside. The floor beneath them was stone, and Cedar wondered if the Lia Fáil could possibly be hiding here among the ghosts. There were many of them around, some standing in groups and talking, others kneeling on benches in prayer, some pacing and muttering.

They followed the abbot until he came to a stop at the doorway to a small chapel. "The man inside may be of help. His name is Thomas de Balmerino. He was abbot here when the English came. They imprisoned him for a time, but he returned to his position when he was released. I do not know what happened to him, only that the peace offered by our Lord has not been sufficient for him to move on. Perhaps you can help each other."

He left them there at the entrance to the chapel. Cedar looked inside. It was tiny, with only room for a simple altar and three wooden benches. A man sat on one of them, his back toward them, his shoulders shaking. Cedar walked in slowly, but he didn't seem to notice her. She cleared her throat, and he turned around and saw her, his tear-stained face creasing in confusion. Then he looked behind her and took in the others in the doorway and let out a gasp. He fell to his knees and crossed himself. "The gods of old," he whispered. "Have you come to take me away for my sins?"

"No!" Cedar said quickly, with a horrified glance at Finn. "We're just looking for something. The abbot—um, Abbot Abercrombie—said you might be able to help."

Still on his knees, he drew back, as though afraid she might strike him. "I know what you're looking for," he said, his voice quavering. "It's not here, it's not here," he moaned.

"It's okay," Cedar said, trying to sound soothing. "It's Thomas, right? We just want to know where it is. The Stone of Destiny," she added, in case he was referring to something else entirely. "Is it . . . hidden somewhere?"

The man began to weep uncontrollably. "I was the keeper of the stone when they came. I would have died to save it, but they stole it from us, may they be ever cursed!"

"The English?" Cedar asked. "King Edward?"

The ghostly man spat on the floor and began tearing at his hair. "It's my fault that Scotland was lost. If I had only protected the stone, the English would not have been able to conquer us!"

Cedar stared at the wretched man at her feet, and tried to think of something to say. "I'm no historian, but I think the English just had a bigger army. Besides, it was technically Ireland's stone, not Scotland's. It's not even Ireland's, really—it belongs in Tír na nÓg with the Tuatha Dé Danann. So Scotland couldn't have been cursed when taken. It never belonged to Scotland in the first place."

He looked up at her incredulously. "How is this possible?"

"The stone you were protecting came from Falias, one of the Four Cities, the original homeland of the Tuatha Dé Danann. It's in another world," she explained. "The Danann loaned it to the Irish kings, and one of them then loaned it to his brother Fergus, King of Scotland. *That's* how it came to be here. We have come to take it to Tír na nÓg. That's where it belongs."

The man stopped crying. "Do you speak the truth?" he said.

She nodded fervently and got down on her knees beside him, taking his shaking hands in her own. "Thomas? I know I probably look human to you, but I'm really one of them, one of the Tuatha

Dé Danann. And believe me when I tell you that it wasn't your fault that Scotland was defeated."

Cedar felt a soft wind sweep through the room. The man on the floor stood up, straightened his clothes, and smiled at her. "Thank you," he said softly. "I do not know where it is, except that it is no longer here. May you find your Stone of Destiny." Then he glowed slightly, becoming increasingly translucent until she could no longer see him at all.

"That was incredible." Finn walked into the chapel and helped her to her feet. "You gave him the peace he's been waiting for for more than seven hundred years."

"And now we know that the stone that was here really *was* taken by the English," Cedar said. "So maybe the one in Edinburgh Castle is the real one after all."

"You guys? You might want to come see this." Jane was looking out of a narrow window in the hallway outside the chapel. Felix hoisted Eden into his arms and was at the window in two long strides. Finn was right behind him.

"What is it?" Cedar said, rushing over to join the others. Eden let out a whimper and buried her face in Felix's neck.

"Druids," Finn said, his eyes narrowing. A dozen figures wearing long dark cloaks had gathered outside of the abbey. Apparently unable to see the ghostly building, they were slowly wandering the grounds, their faces obscured by hoods.

"Druids?" Cedar repeated, moving closer to the window. "What are they doing here?"

"Two options," Felix answered. "Either looking for the Lia Fáil . . . or looking for us."

"Do you think Nuala sent them here? How would they know where we were?" Cedar asked. She placed her hand on Eden's back and rubbed it soothingly, but she couldn't keep the worry out of her voice.

"I don't know," Felix answered. "Perhaps someone overheard us at the pub. Or it could just be a coincidence. Or, if the druids truly are in league with Nuala, it wouldn't surprise me if they're searching for the Lia Fáil to keep us from finding it."

"Well, they won't find it here," Cedar said. "But we should probably leave. It doesn't look like they can see us, but the abbot might let them in."

"I can assure you, he will not," came a voice behind them. Abbot Abercrombie had joined them, and his eyes were trained on the figures who were roaming around beneath his halls. "There is little love between your druids and the men of this abbey. They have tried to find us before. But they hunger for power, not knowledge. We are not faultless ourselves, of course—our continued existence in this place bears evidence to that fact. But no druid will cross this threshold while I am abbot here." Then he smiled at Felix and gave another of his strange little bows. "You, of course, are always welcome here, my lords and ladies. We are at your service."

"Thank you. It doesn't seem like *they* are anymore," Finn muttered. He took Eden from Felix and turned to face the abbot. "We need to leave without being noticed. I'd like to avoid a fight if we can. We need a door—a real one."

"You will find no real doors here," the abbot said, ignoring the strangeness of the request. "The closest is in the stone chapel on the hill. It has fared slightly better than this noble hall."

"What if they see us?" Eden asked in a small voice, her face pressed against Finn's chest.

"They *will* see you once you leave this place," the abbot said. "But perhaps my brothers and I can provide enough of a distraction for you to reach the chapel safely. Give me but a moment." He faded away, and Cedar turned back to watch the druids mill around the grounds of the Palace. They moved slowly, as though waiting for something to happen.

Well, something is about to happen, Cedar thought. She just wasn't sure what.

They headed to the front of the abbey, near the door, and after a few moments, the abbot reappeared beside them. "I have roused my brothers. But you will need to move quickly. Are you ready?"

Finn tightened his grip on Eden. "Felix, you'll make sure Cedar and Jane get out safely?"

Felix nodded. "You and Eden lead the way and open the sidh, the ladies will follow you, and then I'll come through last."

The abbot folded his hands and closed his eyes, as though in prayer. "It is time," he said. Then he disappeared, and the ghost door in front of them swung open.

Cedar grabbed Jane's hand and together they followed Finn and Eden out of the abbey. The fresh air of the material world filled her lungs as they sprinted toward the stone chapel. The druids were still there, but a ghost had appeared beside each one of them. Based on the druids' terrified reactions, the ghosts were very much visible. Cedar tried to ignore them and ran as fast as she could. Finn and Eden had just reached the chapel when she heard a voice cry out, "There they are!"

"Just keep going!" Felix said from behind them as they dodged the replica Lia Fáil and hurtled toward the chapel door. She heard a loud crack and a yell, and then they ran through the shimmering air of the sidh, tumbling onto the floor of Cedar's apartment in Halifax. Finn slammed the sidh shut the second Felix was through. There was a thump as something hard fell to the floor. A severed arm draped in a long black sleeve lay bleeding on the carpet in front of them. It had clearly been amputated by the closing of the sidh. Cedar stared at it, horrified.

"Oh . . . gross . . . ," Jane said from beside her, scooting away.

"Good timing," Felix said to Finn as Eden inched toward the arm, her eyes wide.

"Don't even think about touching that," Cedar told her, getting to her feet. She led her daughter away from the gruesome sight, shuddering as she thought about what the arm's owner must be going through back in Scone. "Why don't I make you some hot chocolate?"

"Mum, who were those guys? Why were they chasing us?" Eden asked as she sat down at the table and watched Cedar bustle around the kitchen.

"They're called druids," Cedar told her. She never knew exactly how much to tell Eden, but it was probably better for her to know what they were up against. "I think they are looking for the Lia Fáil as well." It didn't seem necessary to say that the druids could have been looking for *them*.

"Gran was a druid," Eden said.

"She was," Cedar agreed. "And so is Liam, the man who was here yesterday. But there are good druids and bad ones. So we just have to keep our eyes open and try to stay away from the bad ones, okay?" She placed a mug of hot chocolate in front of Eden and tossed in a handful of mini-marshmallows.

"Got it. Stay away from bad druids," Eden said as she slurped down a marshmallow. Cedar smiled. The innocence of childhood must be making it easier for her to accept all of the astonishing experiences they'd had over the past few weeks. She seemed to be taking it all in stride. *She was born to be a fairy princess,* Cedar thought.

They wrapped the arm in several black garbage bags and tossed it through a sidh Eden made to the middle of the Atlantic Ocean. A couple of hours later, after a gourmet meal of frozen pizza and potato chips, they decided it was time for their heist to begin. Cedar's stomach twisted with nerves as they all gathered in her bedroom. She wished she was the one going instead of Finn, but he was the only one who could alter his appearance on a moment's notice. Besides, she would never be able to lift the stone, even if she could break through the glass case.

Finn snapped his fingers and hurried out of the room, reemerging a few moments later with a black bed sheet. "Something to hide under until I transform," he said. "Assuming you don't have a balaclava."

She shook her head. "What are you going to transform into?" she asked. "A bear?" She was trying to imagine what animal could be strong enough to break through the glass—and possibly steel—that held the stone.

"Mmm, something like that," he answered noncommittally.

Felix checked the time. "All right," he said. "It's the middle of the night in Edinburgh. Off you go, Finn. We'll be watching from this side."

Finn leaned down and kissed Cedar. "Good luck," she whispered, then gently nudged Eden. "It's time, honey." Eden nodded and walked over to the door. "Remember, the Crown Room, where the stone was," Cedar said.

"I know," Eden said, and opened the door.

Finn threw the black sheet over his body and stepped through the sidh. They all crowded around the doorway to watch him. The room was completely dark and Cedar could barely see anything. All she could make out was the rippling of the sheet as Finn's body started to twitch and grow. Then she saw something huge obscuring the doorway. The faint, shimmering light of the sidh reflected off what appeared to be . . . scales. Then a large, horned head appeared through the doorway and a golden eye as big as her fist winked back at them.

"Did he . . . ?" she said, taking a step back in surprise. "Did he just turn into a . . . ?"

Felix was laughing. "A dragon! I haven't seen one of those in centuries! Well, it will do the trick, no doubt."

Cedar wished she could hear what was happening on the other side, but sound never traveled through the sidhe. She wondered if alarms were going off and wished that Finn would hurry. The glass case had been covered with steel blinds, and Finn was slashing them to ribbons with his claws. For a moment, the sidh was concealed by blackness and she couldn't see him at all anymore, but then a blast of dragon-fire enrobed the case, illuminating the throne room.

"Cedar, fire!" she heard Jane yell.

"I know!" she said, unable to take her eyes off the sidh.

"Not there—here!" Jane said, grabbing her arm and shaking it. Cedar looked around. In an instant the room had filled with fire and smoke. Cedar glanced back through the sidh—had Finn's fire gotten out of control? But there were no flames around the door; this was something different. Cedar grabbed Eden and ran to the window, but a blast of flames burst out in front of them. In an utter panic, Eden broke away from her and ran for the sidh. Cedar grabbed her before she could bolt headlong into Finn's dragon fire, which was still lighting up the Crown Room. Eden screamed as the door to the sidh slammed shut and immediately burst into flames. The smoke and heat in the room were so intense that Cedar knew they wouldn't be able to bear it much longer. She put her lips close to Eden's ear and yelled, "We need to get out! Use the bathroom door! Get us out of here!"

She guided Eden, who was coughing and choking, through the smoke and toward the en suite door, which was still untouched by the flames. Eden flung it open and Cedar pulled her through, hoping that Felix and Jane would follow.

◌◯

Cedar was splayed on the ground, coughing and sucking in fresh air. She reached for Eden. Her face was covered in soot and her hair singed, but she looked unharmed.

"Are you okay? Can you breathe?" Cedar asked, her voice hoarse. Eden nodded. Cedar propped herself up and looked around to see where Eden's sidh had taken them. It was dark, but she could

make out tall stone towers all around them, and she could feel—
and see—the cobblestones beneath them. They were back in the
square courtyard of Edinburgh Castle. And they were not alone.

She heard Felix curse. Distant dark figures surrounded them
on all sides. As in Scone, they were wearing long robes, their faces
obscured by hoods. Cedar could barely see them in the dim glow
of the city lights.

And then Eden started screaming again. But this time it wasn't
out of her terror of being burned alive. She had the same wild-eyed
stare as the night before, when she'd opened the sidh to Nuala's
home. She was clutching her head, and when Cedar tried to grab
her, she twisted away. "Jane!" Cedar cried, hoping her friend could
help her hold Eden. "Jane!"

Cedar looked around. Jane wasn't with them. "Felix, where's
Jane?" she cried. The doorway leading to Cedar's blazing apartment still gaped open, and Cedar looked at it in horror.

"I thought she was with you!" Felix yelled. He was circling
Cedar and Eden, his eyes fixed on the dark figures who were slowly
starting to move in on them.

"She's still in there!" Cedar yelled.

Felix swiveled around, his eyes searching for Jane in the courtyard. "I can't leave you here!" he yelled, his face twisted in anguish.

"Go!" she cried. "Quickly!" He cast one last tormented gaze at
her and Eden before plunging back into the burning sidh.

Eden had collapsed onto the ground and was still clutching her
head and screaming as she writhed and thrashed on the cobblestones.

"Eden, hang on, baby," Cedar pleaded. "Come on, stay with
me, I'm right here."

Seconds later, with a sudden burst of light, Felix emerged
through the sidh, a figure clasped his arms. Then Eden went
limp and fell silent, and the sidh disappeared. Felix laid Jane's
body down beside Cedar, who stared aghast at the unrecognizable figure.

The tall Danann whirled to face the druids, his face contorted with rage. "Is this what she has you doing?" he roared. "Burning people alive? Torturing children?" He circled around Cedar and her two charges. Cedar held Eden's limp body, praying for a miracle.

And then Finn came, growing bigger in size as he escaped the confines of the Crown Room. There was a sound like an explosion, and large chunks of stone started to fall from the castle walls. The druids yelled and scattered, their arms held up to protect their heads. One of them wasn't fast enough, and there was a sickening crunch as his bones shattered under the weight of a great hunk of stone. Cedar looked up, and for a moment the stars were obscured by the spread of dark wings above her. He landed so that his feet were straddling her, though he was now so huge that she would have needed to stand to touch the smooth leather of this stomach. The Stone of Destiny was clutched in one of his talons. He breathed in and then a burst of bright blue flame shot out of his jaws, sweeping in a circle around them. Felix reached under Finn's great belly and pulled Cedar out, and then went back for Eden and Jane, slinging one over each shoulder.

"Get on his back," he said.

Cedar knew better than to argue. She scrambled up the scales as best as she could, feeling the heat of fire through Finn's thick hide. She found a spot where she could hold on to the two horns that were jutting from his neck and then took Eden from Felix. Holding her daughter between her arms, she grasped Finn's horns in her hands. Felix climbed up behind her, Jane still slung over his shoulder. After a moment, she felt a swoop in her stomach as they took off, flying higher and higher, Finn's great leathery wings beating the air on either side of her. She squeezed her eyes shut and then opened them and looked down to see the courtyard in ruins, faint blue flames still flickering in places. She closed her eyes again and concentrated on hanging on to her daughter as they soared out over the open sea.

CHAPTER 8

They had been in the air for only a few minutes when they began their descent. Cedar saw the blinking beam of a lighthouse up ahead, and then Finn landed with a jolt. She climbed down, Eden clutched in her arms. Felix had already carried Jane to the ground and was leaning over her. As soon as everyone was off, Finn transformed back into himself. "What happened?" he asked, his face stricken. "The sidh to the apartment disappeared. I knew I had to get out—I looked out the window to see if anyone was coming, and that's when I saw you in the courtyard."

Cedar didn't answer him for a moment. Cradling Eden in her arms, she felt for a pulse, experiencing a wave of relief as she sensed a slow, steady beat beneath her fingers. "She has a pulse, Felix," she said haltingly, turning toward him. "Is Jane . . . ?"

"She's alive," he said. "But barely."

Cedar looked down at her friend and muffled a sob. Jane's hair and clothes had burned away, leaving only red raw tissue underneath. It was as though her skin had melted and then cooled in all the wrong places. Felix had taken off his jacket and shirt and was wrapping her up in it. Finn did the same.

She heard faint sirens in the distance and could see the lights of Edinburgh twinkling at them from across the water. They must have landed on a small island.

"There was a fire in the apartment, I think the druids started it—" Cedar started to tell Finn, but Felix interrupted her.

"We don't have time," he said. "I can save them both, but I need supplies and a place to work."

"But Eden can't open a sidh," Cedar said. "Where can we go?"

Felix looked at Finn. "Can you get us to Logheryman's house? He'll have everything I need."

Finn nodded. Then Cedar noticed the stone lying at his feet for the first time. "You got it," she said, her voice hollow.

"Yes, but . . ." He knelt down and touched it. "It's not warm," he said. Cedar touched it too. It was cool, rough, and perfectly ordinary. "Felix, you try," she said. Still holding Jane, he reached over and placed his hand on it, then shook his head.

"Stand on it," Finn said, and she did, Eden in her arms. The stone stayed silent.

For a moment the three of them just stood there, the horror of what had happened settling on them like the dense fog that drifted over the island. The relative safety of the apartment was gone; they couldn't go back there. Eden was unconscious, and Cedar had no idea what was wrong or what the druids had done to her. And Jane . . .

"It's a fake," Felix said. "Leave it here. We have to go. Jane doesn't have much time."

ॐ

In seconds the great dragon was before them again, and they scrambled up on his back, carrying their unconscious companions. This flight was longer, and Cedar closed her eyes and listened to the beat of Finn's wings as they soared across the ocean toward Ireland. So far their quest had been fruitless, and had cost far more than she'd expected. She held Eden tighter and told herself that Felix could wake her, that he could save Jane's life. He was the god of healing, after all—surely he could save them. She couldn't allow herself to consider the alternative.

She glanced behind her at Felix, though the motion made her head swim with dizziness. He was crouched over Jane's body, his lips moving rapidly. She wondered if he was trying to work his healing magic even as they flew . . . or if his ministrations were the only thing keeping Jane alive for the voyage to the leprechaun's house. She turned back around and saw the lights of a city below them. Belfast, she assumed, and felt Finn bank and turn to avoid flying directly over the city. Not that it really mattered. Unless the druids had disabled the castle's security system, she was pretty sure that their whole escape from the courtyard was even now being studied by Scotland Yard or uploaded to YouTube.

A few minutes later they made a rugged landing in a small clearing in what appeared to be a forest. It was completely dark, and Cedar could barely make out Finn's hulking outline as Felix helped her climb down. Then she heard a ripping sound and Felix's voice saying, "Here, light this before you transform." There was a blast of blue flame, and the clearing around them suddenly sprung into view. Felix was holding Jane in one arm and a burning branch in the other. Finn transformed and took Eden from Cedar, and they immediately started through the trees.

The area was only partially cleared, and there were several stumps that looked as though the trees had been ripped right off rather than neatly sawed or chopped. Cedar remembered then how Murdoch had taken out his grief and anger over his son Oscar's death on the trees surrounding Logheryman's house. She hoped that she wouldn't have another death on her hands tonight.

They walked silently through the trees to the cottage that had welcomed them only a few weeks ago. The windows were dark, and the torch cast eerie shadows around them. Finn rapped loudly on the door, but there was no answer.

"Logheryman!" Finn yelled. He tried the knob—it was unlocked—and the door swung open with a long creak. Wordlessly,

Finn shifted Eden into Cedar's arms. He cautiously eased himself through the door, and moments later Cedar could see the light of the torch flickering through the windows. Then the windows all went bright, and Finn stepped back outside and extinguished the torch. "It's empty," he said. "There's no one here."

Felix and Cedar carried Jane and Eden inside. Felix laid Jane on the sofa, and Cedar sat in an armchair and cradled Eden in her lap. She wondered where the leprechaun was, and her stomach twisted nervously. But they couldn't move Jane, not now. She sat silently as Felix unwrapped Jane's body from the shirts and jackets and barked instructions at Finn, who went down into Logheryman's cellar in search of supplies. Felix was muttering to himself—or to Jane. Cedar couldn't make out what he was saying.

When Finn came back into the room, his arms were full of jars and small linen bags filled with what Cedar took to be herbs and various potion ingredients.

Felix groaned in relief. "Thank you," he said, starting to sniff the contents of the jars and bags.

"Will those help you heal her?" Cedar asked.

"Yes," he answered. "She is past the point where I could heal her by touch alone. My grandfather knew the power of every herb in existence. He is the one who taught herb-lore to the druids, though I daresay they probably retained it better than I did. I could heal with a touch, why did I need to know the properties of so many plants? Still, I did not forget everything I learned. At least . . . I hope not."

Cedar watched as he continued to examine the herbs that Finn had gathered for him. Then he called out to Finn again. "I need clean linens. Do not under any circumstances use the ones from Logheryman's bed. Hot water, whiskey, and several bowls. In fact—is there a bath?"

Finn ran off to check and came back nodding, his arms full of more supplies.

"Good," Felix said. "Find something to sterilize it with—use the whiskey if you have to. Then fill it with hot water, as hot as you can make it."

While Finn was doing this, Felix measured and poured several of the herbs and powders into a large cracked bowl. Then he yanked out a handful of his own hair and stirred it into the mixture.

"Your hair?" Cedar asked.

Felix nodded. "I need to be in contact with her at all times, it's what's keeping her alive. I'm going to submerge her in the hot water with these herbs; they will amplify my power and speed her healing. But I'm not taking any chances. If we are attacked again and I break contact with her, she may die. Having part of my body in the water with her might keep her alive until I can get back to her."

Cedar shivered at the thought of another attack. But if the druids could find them at Scone, at Halifax, and then at Edinburgh, they could surely find them here.

"How is Eden?" Felix asked, taking his eyes off Jane for a second to look at Cedar. "Any change?"

"No," Cedar said. "But her pulse is still steady, and her breathing seems normal."

"Then I do not think she is in any immediate danger," Felix said. "Forgive me, Cedar, but I must tend to Jane first."

"I know," Cedar agreed. "Please, do. She needs you the most right now."

Finn came back into the room and reported that the bath was ready. Gently, Felix lifted Jane into his arms and left the room. Cedar struggled to her feet, still holding Eden, and followed. She watched as Felix gave the bowl to Finn and instructed him to dissolve the mixture in the water. The water in the bath bubbled and hissed, and lavender-colored steam rose from the surface. Without losing contact with her for even a moment, Felix laid Jane down into the water and then followed her in. He was still wearing the khaki pants Jane had so despised upon first meeting him, but his shirt was on the floor of the front room now, covered in her blood. He cradled her in his arms, then pulled her under the water with him.

"Will it work?" Cedar asked Finn as he reached for Eden. She rubbed the burning muscles in her arms, feeling exhaustion set in as the adrenaline in her system started to fade.

"She's very far gone," Finn said. "But I've known Felix all my life, and there's never been an injury he wasn't been able to heal if he got there in time." Cedar thought of her mother Kier, who had died of her injuries in Maeve's arms, and wondered how her own life might have turned out differently if Felix had been there to save her. But her thoughts were interrupted by a splash. Felix was lifting Jane's head out of the water, and Cedar cried out in relief when she saw Jane's mouth open to take a gulp of air. She started to rush forward but Felix stopped her with a look. "Not yet," he said, and then submerged her once more. Three times he repeated this process, and three times Jane gulped for air. Cedar slowly moved to the side of the bath and knelt down. She watched in amazement as Jane's tortured skin start to knit itself together. Where it had been red, even black, it became a milky white, like the color of a newborn baby. Cedar watched as her friend's broken body became whole again.

"You did it," she said to Felix the next time he emerged from the water. He nodded, his wet hair falling in his eyes.

"She will survive," he said, cradling her head. "Although I'm afraid there is nothing I can do about her hair. It will have to grow back naturally." Just then Jane's eyes flickered open. She opened her mouth and tried to speak, but nothing came out, only a wheeze. Then she closed her eyes again.

"Is she okay?" Cedar asked.

"Her body is still healing on the inside," Felix said. "Finn, hand me that bottle, there." He pointed to a tiny glass bottle that he had brought into the bathroom.

Finn handed it to him, and Felix poured a few drops of a clear liquid between Jane's lips. "She will sleep for several hours now, while her body finishes healing. But I think it's safe to remove her from the bath and from my touch."

Cedar helped Felix lift Jane out of the water and wrap her in towels, and then he carried her back to the sofa and gently laid her down. Cedar blushed as he stripped out of his soaking pants and wrapped himself in a towel, setting himself down on the floor in front of the sofa.

"You look exhausted," Cedar said. "Can I get you anything?" Felix leaned his head back against Jane.

"Healing takes its toll," he said. "But I will be fine," he repeated. "I'll look at Eden now."

Finn laid the limp form of their daughter in Felix's lap. He examined her closely, frowning. "The best guess I have is that she is protecting herself. I think she has disappeared deep inside herself to protect her mind from the druids. They must be affecting her somehow—maybe that's why she opened the sidh to Nuala last night and why she brought us to the courtyard and closed off all our escape routes. I don't think they're controlling her mind . . . it's more like they know they're influencing her movements by terrifying her. The power of suggestion, perhaps."

"Well, we got lucky in one regard. . . . I don't think the druids were expecting to see a dragon," Cedar said to Finn. "They scattered as soon as you arrived."

"Most of the druids who are alive today have never experienced the creatures of the old world," Finn said. "You're right—I think I took them by surprise."

"Still," Felix said. "If you hadn't arrived, I'm not sure if I would have been able to defeat them all before they got to Cedar or Eden, or whoever they were after. There must have been a dozen of them."

Finn started pacing the room, casting nervous glances out the window. "This won't do," he said. "We cannot find the Lia Fáil *and* fight an army of druids. And where the hell is Logheryman? He should be here. *Nothing* feels right about this."

"We need Liam," Cedar said suddenly. "He knows how the druids work. He can help us fight them. He said he wanted to help."

Felix and Finn glanced at each other. "*Druids* just attacked us," Felix said. "And you've only just met him. How do you know we can trust him?"

"*He* wasn't one of the druids who attacked us," she protested. "And he hates Nuala, remember? We need his help. If she's sending her druids after us, the best way to fight them is to have one on our side. He can help us figure out how they think and what they might do next."

"He tells a good story," Finn said. "But how do you *know* he's on our side? We can't afford to take any chances. We only have six days left. . . ."

"If he was in league with Nuala, he would have killed me the first time I met him and spared her all this trouble. She'd be queen now and well on her way to destroying humanity."

"Druids can be unstable—," Felix started to say, but Cedar stopped him with a huff of exasperation.

"Seriously? You want to paint them all with the same brush? You still can't get the master-and-servant mentality out of your heads, can you? Not all druids are bad, just like not all of the Tuatha Dé Danann are good."

Finn and Felix were quiet for a long moment, both of them looking slightly abashed. "You're right," Finn finally said. "And we do need help."

Felix nodded and looked down at the child in his arms. "And perhaps he'll know what to do for Eden. My skill is with healing, but she's not injured. I think she might just be afraid to wake up."

Cedar was wearing the same jeans she's had on the day before, and when she reached into her back pocket, Liam's card was still there. She breathed out a deep sigh of relief as she examined it. *Trinity College, Dublin.* He'd told her that he was flying home that morning, so at least he was in the same country. She went to use the phone in Logheryman's kitchen. All of their cell phones and laptops had been in her apartment, and had—in all likelihood—been burned to a crisp. She dialed his cell phone number and then realized it was the middle of the night. He picked up on the first ring. She gave him a brief rundown of what had happened and where they were.

"I can be there in two hours," he said.

After hanging up, she came back into the living room.

"You should sleep," Finn said. "There's nothing we can do until he gets here."

"We should have a plan," Cedar said, but her thoughts were sluggish and her body ached with exhaustion.

"Later," he said, guiding her into the reclining armchair and covering her with a soft blanket. "Sleep now. We have no idea what tomorrow will bring."

❧

Cedar awoke a few hours later to the sound of muffled voices. She opened her eyes and winced at the crick in her neck. The voices were coming from the kitchen, and she stood stiffly and headed toward them. Liam, Felix, and Finn, who was holding Eden, were sitting around Logheryman's rickety kitchen table. "Hey," Cedar said groggily. Liam stood at once and pulled out a chair for her.

"Are you all right?" he asked.

"Um . . . I guess so," she said, still trying to clear the cobwebs from her brain. "As well as can be expected, I suppose. What time is it?" In truth, she felt like she'd been hit by a train, but of the three females in the house, she certainly had the least reason to complain.

"Three a.m. I've looked at Eden, and though I'm no doctor, I'd say that Felix is right. She's hiding in there," he said in his soft lilt.

"So how do we convince her to come out?" Cedar said.

"Well, there is one thing that could work. . . . It's a fairly advanced spell," he said. "In fact, it's one of the last things I taught Maeve. She was just starting to get the hang of it when—well, when we lost touch."

Cedar wondered why he and Maeve had lost touch so completely when they had obviously been very close. She added it to her mental list of things to ask him when they had more time.

Liam continued. "I can create a potion that will allow you to enter Eden's mind. She's dreaming, you see, and this potion will allow you to join her in that dream. When she sees you, she'll feel safe, and you can guide her out."

"How will I do that?" Cedar asked.

"You are firmly tethered to this world, this reality," he said. "I think it should be fairly easy for you to gently, and safely, bring her out of her own mind and back into the waking world. You *want* to come back, you *need* to come back. And if you're with her, she'll want to come back too."

Cedar looked over at Finn and Felix. "What do you think?" she asked.

"I've heard of such a potion before," Felix asked. "But I've never seen it used. I can't say how it will work."

"Can *I* do it?" Finn asked. "Instead of Cedar?"

Liam nodded thoughtfully. "You could, theoretically. But forgive me for saying that in this case the bond between mother and daughter is perhaps a bit stronger."

Finn flushed but said nothing. He was well aware that he'd missed most of Eden's life.

"Okay," Cedar said. "Let's do it. How long will it take?"

"That I cannot say," Liam said. "But make sure she feels confident and relaxed before you suggest leaving the safe place she has created. Is there somewhere you can both lie down?"

"The bedroom," Finn said.

"I'll watch him prepare it," Felix said.

"Of course," Liam replied calmly, ignoring the implied suspicion. "I brought all the necessary ingredients, plus some extras in case you need them in the future." The two of them headed into the kitchen, and Finn carried Eden into the bedroom. Cedar followed them. The room was plain, with chipped beige walls and musty blue curtains. The bed was unmade.

"Where do you think he is?" Cedar asked, pulling up the covers. She'd been so preoccupied with Jane and Eden that she'd barely spared a thought for the leprechaun. The last time she'd seen him, he had helped them—for a price. She hoped he was okay.

"I don't know," Finn said as he laid Eden down, resting her head against the pillow. "But from what I know of Logheryman, he can take care of himself. He may just be traveling."

She looked down at the still, small figure on the bed, and smoothed Eden's forehead with her hand. "It's okay, baby," she whispered. "Mummy's coming to get you."

There was a knock on the open door, and Liam came in carrying a tray with two mugs. Felix followed, and nodded at Finn and Cedar.

"This is going to work, right?" Cedar asked Liam nervously.

"There's no reason why it shouldn't," Liam said. "And if it doesn't, it just means she's not ready yet. It won't harm either of you. Are you ready?"

Cedar nodded, and Liam propped Eden up a little so he could pour some of the potion between her lips. She swallowed reflexively, and then he eased her back down onto the pillows. "Now hold her hand, or put your arms around her," he said. "The two of you need to be in constant physical contact." Cedar gathered Eden into her arms, and then accepted the mug he handed her with one hand. She looked over the rim as she took a sip, and met Finn's eyes, which were filled with worry.

"I'll be back soo . . . ," she started to say, and then everything went black.

CHAPTER 9

When Cedar opened her eyes, her first thought was that she had gone through a sidh . . . or back in time. She was standing on the veranda of Maeve's house in the country, the house where she'd grown up. The sky was a bright blue, brighter than she'd ever seen it, and the smell of the ocean was so crisp and strong it made her eyes water. Was this the inside of Eden's mind? She hadn't thought it would feel so real.

She looked around for Eden, expecting her to be close by. When she didn't see her, she turned to look inside the house. Then her ears picked up a faint scraping sound, and she stopped to listen. *Scrape, scrape, scrape.* It sounded like digging. She stepped off the veranda and turned toward the sound. That was when she saw her.

Eden was kneeling in the fresh soil of Maeve's grave. Her arms were covered in dirt up to her elbows, and there were muddy smears on her cheeks and forehead. She was digging in the grave with her bare hands, making a small mound of dirt beside her. Eden was crying, and saying, "I want Baby Bunny, I want Baby Bunny . . ." in a small, plaintive voice.

Cedar rushed over to her daughter. "Eden!" she called, and then she slowed down, remembering Liam's warning not to frighten her. But Eden acted as if she didn't hear her. She kept right on digging. "Eden, it's Mummy!" Cedar said, clearly but softly. Then she noticed another figure lying in the yard.

"Mum," Cedar whispered. Maeve's body was lying in the gravel where Nuala had shot her. Her white blouse and bright yellow skirt were covered in dirt and blood. Cedar rushed forward, her eyes fixed on her mother. She knelt down, tears welling in her eyes. She reached out to brush the blood-matted hair off Maeve's face, and then screamed and jumped back. Instead of Maeve lying dead on the ground, Cedar was now staring at her own lifeless body. Her green eyes were open and sightless, though they looked right at her. Her mouth was the most disturbing thing of all; it was wide open in a tortured, silent scream.

"What's the matter, Cedar? Scared of your own mortality?"

Cedar ripped her eyes away from her gruesome doppelgänger and saw Nuala standing next to her. She scrambled to her feet. "What are *you* doing here? Are you part of Eden's dream?"

Nuala paced around Cedar in a circle, like a lioness sizing up her next meal. "I am," she said. "As much as you are. It seems as though we both share a bond with little Eden now, doesn't it?"

Cedar grew cold. "What are you talking about?"

"Didn't she tell you? Eden and I have dream-walked together before."

"But you're not with us now, not in real life," Cedar protested, wondering if Nuala had somehow overpowered Felix, Finn, and Liam and was now lying on Logheryman's bed with her and Eden.

"I don't need to be," Nuala said. "But I am glad that you're here. The Council is being very . . . stubborn, shall we say. They insist on giving you a chance. Of course, if you don't return from your little escapade, they'll hardly be able to blame me. I've been in Tír na nÓg all this time, busy making friends."

"I'm not afraid of you," Cedar said. She could tell that Nuala's power wasn't having an effect on her, not here in Eden's mind. There wasn't any of the usual fogginess she felt when the other woman spoke to her. "You can't hurt us here."

"Mmm, maybe . . . but then again, maybe not." She snapped her head around to face Eden, who was still digging in the grave. "Eden!" she called.

This time, Eden heard. She looked up, her eyes widening in horror when she saw Nuala. She jumped to her feet and started backing away. "No, not you," she whimpered. "Leave me alone, please!"

"Eden?" Cedar said. "Can you hear me now?"

Eden stopped backing away and looked at Cedar. "Mummy?" she said in a small, hopeful voice. Then she noticed the body on the ground, and her face crumpled. She ran toward it, looking back and forth between Cedar and the body in confusion.

"It's okay, honey," Nuala said, walking slowly toward the child. "Your mother is dead, see. But you'll be okay. I'm going to look after you now."

"Don't listen to her," Cedar snapped. "I'm right here, Eden. I'm not dead."

"That's just what your mind wants you to believe," Nuala said, kneeling down to Eden's level. "I'm so sorry, sweetheart. But don't worry. I'll take care of you."

"You killed my mum?" Eden asked, her eyes wide.

"No, of course not, my dear. She did this to herself. She was reckless, dragging you all over the world looking for the Lia Fáil. It's her own fault. She left you alone. But I'm here now. You can trust me."

Slowly, Eden knelt down beside the body on the ground. Cedar put her hand on her daughter's shoulder and said, "Eden, it's okay, I'm right here. This is just a dream. I'm not dead, and I've come to get you." Eden looked at her, but didn't seem to register what she was saying; her eyes were still fixed on the dead Cedar. Then she stood up, and Cedar jumped back.

Her six-year-old daughter had morphed into someone she had never seen before. This woman had Eden's wavy brown hair and olive skin, but was taller than Cedar. Holding her head up high, she slowly turned to face Nuala.

"You!" Nuala hissed. The woman tilted her head slightly.

"Did you miss me?" she asked in a teasing voice. "The Morrigan has not yet claimed you, I see."

"That was just a dream," Nuala said through her teeth. "*This* is just a dream."

"Is it? I think we both know that's not quite true," the woman said.

Cedar stared at her. She looked a bit like her daughter, or how her daughter might look in twenty years . . . could it be? "Eden?" she asked tentatively. The woman swiveled around.

"Mum," she said, her voice suddenly stern. "You're not safe here. You should go."

"What are you talking about? I came to get you, to wake you up. I'm not leaving without you."

Eden nudged Cedar's body on the ground with her toe. "Let's get rid of this," she said, and the body dissolved into nothing. "Now seriously, Mum, you should go. I'll be right behind you."

Cedar stood her ground. "I don't care how old you look, I am not leaving you alone here with *her*."

"Oh, you don't have to worry about me. I can take care of her," Eden said.

"Is that what you think?" Nuala's voice came out in a snarl. "When you fled deep into your own mind to save yourself? You're not even safe here. You're not safe anywhere. I will always be able to find you."

Suddenly Nuala wrapped her hands around Cedar's throat. Eden let out a snarl and advanced on them, but Nuala sent her sprawling in the dirt with a fierce kick. Cedar gasped for air, but nothing could get through. She clawed at Nuala's arms, but they were like steel. "Forget about the Lia Fáil. Forget about becoming queen." She dropped Cedar to the ground and stood over her.

"No," Cedar gasped through shallow and ragged breaths.

"What?" Nuala snapped.

Cedar struggled to her feet. "I will never stop fighting you," she said, her eyes locked with Nuala's. "*You* should be the one who's afraid. When I find the Lia Fáil and prove that I am the true queen, you're going to wish you had never messed with my family."

Nuala laughed derisively. "What are you going to do, human me to death?" she said. "You've already used that trick once, and it won't work on me."

She wrapped her hands around Cedar's neck again and squeezed. Already weakened by the first attack, Cedar was powerless to stop her. "I gave you a chance," Nuala said. "But you just don't learn, do you? Don't worry, you won't die alone. I'll kill them all; everyone you love. In fact, I think I'll start with your friends here in Tír na nÓg. They're being rounded up as we speak. Such a pity you weren't there to save them this time."

Cedar could feel her mind shutting down. Great black patches swam in front of her eyes, obscuring her vision. She looked around for Eden, but everything was an indiscriminate blur. And then she was on the ground again, pulling in desperate, painful breaths. As her vision started to clear, she could make out someone standing in front of her. The hem of a black lace gown drifted by like smoke. It was Eden, or rather the woman Eden would become. Her voice was deep, dark, and filled with power.

"Someday, Fionnghuala, we will meet in the waking world, when I have come into my full power. You had better hope you are dead by then."

Then Cedar felt herself being picked up. The next thing she knew, she was staring at the ceiling of Logheryman's bedroom. The first rays of dawn were struggling to make it through the grime on the room's only window. There was shouting, and when she turned her head, she saw that Finn had pressed Liam up against the wall, his hands at the other man's throat.

"Stop," she croaked.

Finn dropped the druid and rushed to her side, his eyes half-mad with worry. Felix was there too, she noticed now. He was kneeling at the bedside, his shirtsleeves rolled to his elbows.

"Mummy?" Eden said, looking around groggily, her hair a sweaty mess on her forehead.

Finn fell onto them both. "Ow," Cedar said, and he quickly shifted to give her more space.

"You're okay," he said, holding her hands tightly in his, like he would never let them go. "You did it."

Cedar shook her head gingerly and then winced. She took one of her hands from Finn's grasp, and ran her fingers over her throat. Her neck felt bruised and raw, just as it had in the dreamworld. "Yes," she said. "It wasn't as easy as I thought." She looked over at Liam, who had stood up and was hovering in the corner. "What's going on? Why were you shouting?"

"We thought you were dying," Finn said, with a glare at Liam. "We couldn't wake you up, but you were having trouble breathing. It was like someone was choking you."

"Someone *was* choking me," she said. "But it wasn't Liam's fault." She told them what had happened. Eden's jaw dropped when Cedar told them the part about seeing Eden's older self, and how she had saved Cedar from Nuala.

"I don't remember that part at all," Eden said. "I just remember looking for Baby Bunny and being scared. And then . . . then I saw you on the ground." Her lip trembled, and she looked like she was on the verge of tears.

Cedar hugged her close. "It's okay now," she said. "We're both okay." She looked at the others. "From what Nuala said, I could tell that she and Eden had shared dreams before." She turned to Eden. "Honey, do you remember anything like that?"

Eden thought for a moment. "I think so," she said. "Gran gave us each something to drink, and it was supposed to help me figure out what Tír na nÓg looked like so I could open the sidh for Nuala. But it didn't work."

Cedar stared at her. *"Gran?"* Right before her death, Maeve had told Cedar that she'd tried to help Nuala get to Tír na nÓg in the hopes of saving Eden from all the Tuatha Dé Danann. But she had only mentioned using the starstones, not this.

Liam was pale. "I'm so sorry, Cedar. If I had known . . ."

"Is that why Nuala's been able to mess with Eden's mind? Because she did this dream-thing with her?" Cedar asked.

"It makes sense," Liam said. "She's not working alone. This is powerful druid magic. But yes, that dream-share would have created a bond between them that would make Eden more susceptible—"

"How can we stop her?" Cedar interrupted. "What can we do to block her out of Eden's head?"

"I . . . I don't know," Liam said. "I'll need to do some research, and maybe some tests. It's possible, though, especially since Eden is a sidh-closer. Perhaps we can amplify her power or teach her to block Nuala."

"There's something else," Cedar said, looking anxiously at Finn and Felix. "Nuala said that the others back in Tír na nÓg are being rounded up. She said she's going to kill them."

Finn and Felix exchanged worried glances.

"Do you think she was telling the truth?" Felix said tentatively. "Maybe she was just trying to scare you so that we'll stop looking for the Lia Fáil."

"Can we really take that chance?" Cedar said. "Our starstones were in my apartment—in the fire. We have no way of getting in touch with the others. We'll have to go back."

A silence fell on the room. After a few long moments, Finn said, "It might be a trap."

"Even if it is, we can't do nothing," Cedar protested. "We need to make sure they're okay. And while we're there I think we should talk to Nevan. She once told me that people can learn how to block her telepathic ability. Maybe she can teach Eden how to keep her mind closed to Nuala."

Finn frowned. "That's the thing—Eden should *already* be able to block Nuala. She's a closer—there's no way Nuala should be able to get into her head like this."

There was another heavy moment of silence, and then Liam cleared his throat and said, "Maybe it's not her, it's her druids. Closers like you and your daughter are immune to the abilities of the other Danann. But druid magic works differently. If Maeve really did use this spell to link Eden and Nuala, it may have created a bond that's stronger than Eden's natural resistance to Nuala's ability, making her more susceptible to Nuala . . . and her druids."

"Whatever it is, we need to check on the others and talk to Nevan," Cedar said. "We can't afford to stop looking for the Lia Fáil for long, but if she comes with us, she might be able to teach Eden how to block Nuala out. And I think we should all go—we can't afford to split up if the druids are still after us. How is Jane?" she asked Felix.

"She's doing very well," he said. "She's still sleeping on the sofa, and her healing is almost complete. But I don't want to move her yet. I should stay here with her."

"I'll stay with her," Liam said. "And I'll put some defensive spells around the house, just in case. But I don't think she'll be in any danger. She's not their target."

"I think we should wait," Finn said firmly. "Just for a few hours. You and Eden have both been through an ordeal. And you've hardly slept."

"But—" Cedar started to protest. Finn cut her off.

"You can't go without food and sleep all day and all night," he said. "And neither can Eden. Just sleep for a few hours. Let your body recover. That's all I ask."

Cedar wanted to argue, but Finn had that look on his face that told her he wouldn't back down lightly. "Fine," she said. "*Then we'll go.*"

Felix and Liam excused themselves from the room, and Cedar settled back into the pillows. Eden snuggled into her on one side, and Finn on the other. Cedar stared at the ceiling. Her body was exhausted, but her mind was reeling. How could she sleep when Nuala might be rounding up her friends at this very moment and plotting her next attack on Eden's mind? And they were still no closer to finding the Lia Fáil. She lay there for several minutes before sitting up and sliding out of bed.

"Where are you going?" Finn asked sleepily.

"I'm going to make a cup of tea," Cedar said. "It might help my mind stop whirring." She tiptoed into the kitchen, where she found Liam sitting alone at the table, his long fingers wrapped around a steaming mug. Next to it was an empty mug and a full teapot.

"I was hoping you'd come," he said in an undertone.

"You were?" Cedar asked, confused.

"You need to sleep," Liam said. "But I also know that there's a lot weighing on your mind. Just as there is on mine."

"Yes," Cedar agreed. "I just keep thinking . . . what if we don't find it?"

"You'll find it," Liam said. "You're just like your mother— Maeve, that is. When she set her mind to something, there was no stopping her."

Cedar sat down across from him, and he poured her a cup of tea. She fingered the charm bracelet on her wrist, the one that had belonged to Maeve. She wondered what the charms had meant to her adoptive mother, if there was a story behind each one. "I feel like I hardly knew her at all," Cedar said. "I know she loved me, and I loved her, but we never really . . . clicked, you know? We were never close."

"I'm not surprised," he said. "She did love you, I'm sure of it. Otherwise she would have handed you over to Rohan when he and the others first came through the sidh, searching for Kier. But you look a lot like your father. I think you brought up a lot of complicated emotions for her."

Cedar stared down into her tea. She had felt the same way about Eden at times, before Finn had returned. She loved Eden more than anything, but there had been times when her daughter would get a look in her eye or an expression on her face that reminded her so much of Finn she had to turn away. Now that he was back, she delighted in discovering all the things he and Eden had in common. But it hadn't always been that way. And Eden was her own child . . . she couldn't imagine what it would have been like to raise the daughter of a rival.

"Will you tell me about her?" she asked. "I'd like to hear about the Maeve *you* knew."

Liam smiled sadly. "All right," he said and paused for a moment. "She was a feisty thing. Very eager to learn, but insistent on doing things her way, which is definitely not the norm for druids, I must admit. She was only my second pupil, but the other one I'd had was a breeze compared to her."

"Why did Brogan ask you to teach her?" Cedar wondered. "Did you know him?"

"I did not," Liam answered. "I knew who he was, of course, but we had never met. Up until now, the druids and the Tuatha Dé Danann haven't had much to do with each other for a very long time. We were happy with our lives on Earth, and the Danann rarely left Tír na nÓg anymore. When he came into my office at the university and told me who he was, I had a hard time believing him. Not that I doubted the existence of the Tuatha Dé Danann; rather, I wasn't sure what he could want from me."

"Wait a minute . . . how old are you?" Cedar asked. "That must have been almost forty years ago. You were already at the university then?"

Liam smiled, the skin around his eyes crinkling. "Let's just say that I'm older than I look."

"Are you immortal? Like the Tuatha Dé Danann?"

"No, no, nothing like that. Druids usually live longer than most humans, but no more than an additional human life span. There are certain spells and potions that can lengthen our lives."

"Huh . . . I'm sorry for interrupting you. Please, continue."

"Brogan told me he had a young friend, a human who was exceptionally bright and keen to study the druidic arts. I was intrigued by his offer, and once we had worked out the details, I took a leave from my job and went to live in an apartment in Halifax. He was quite adamant that I was never to stay at Maeve's house," he said with a wry smile.

"He didn't trust you?"

"No, though he had no cause for worry. It was obvious that she loved him more than life." Liam shook his head, lost in sad memories. "It was wrong, the way she loved him—it was an obsession. He enjoyed her, and treated her well, at least from what I could tell. But he never loved her the way she loved him."

They sat in silence for a moment. Cedar swirled her spoon around in her half-empty cup. Liam's was empty, but he didn't seem to notice.

"I don't know what his plans were for her," he said, looking bewildered even after all these years. "She believed he would take her to Tír na nÓg once her training was complete. But I don't know if he told her that or if it was just something he let her believe. I don't think it was ever what he intended. He enjoyed having her here, away from his people, as his own escape from reality. But then why train her to be a druid? I asked him that question myself, but he always just said, 'I have my reasons.'" Liam snorted in derision. "I was a blind fool then, but his reasons seem pretty clear to me now. He didn't want her to have a normal life, lest she meet a human man and fall in love with him instead."

Cedar put a comforting hand on his forearm. He looked up at her sharply, as if suddenly remembering her presence. He covered her hand with his own and smiled. "I'm sorry," he said. "Sometimes I forget that it's your father I'm talking about. As you can tell, we had our differences. I'm sure these aren't the stories you were hoping to hear. There was much happiness during the years I knew her. I know that's what I should be remembering."

He laughed unexpectedly. "Such a soft heart, she had! When it came time to give her a lesson on divination using cat entrails, she refused to do it. I had brought a stray cat with me that I'd captured in an alley in Halifax. But she took the poor thing in and gave it food and water. She wouldn't let me come near it. In the end we had to drive to the animal shelter to steal the body of a cat that had been put down. I told her it wouldn't work as well, that a living animal always gives the clearest readings, but she would have none of it." He smiled at the look on Cedar's face. "I know it must seem barbaric, but these are the ways of the druids that have been passed down for centuries. It's time-honored magic, even if it doesn't fit so well with today's mores."

"I guess . . . ," Cedar said uncertainly. She filled up their mugs with more tea. "Was she funny at all?" she asked. "I just . . . I have such a hard time picturing her young and carefree."

"Oh, I don't think she was ever completely carefree, at least not after she met Brogan. She was always obsessing about when he would come to visit her next. She begged me to teach her how to stay young forever, but there is a certain order to these things, and it wasn't yet time for me to share those secrets with her. But yes, she was funny. She had a wicked sense of humor and never seemed to take her lessons quite as seriously as I hoped she would. But she was so intensely curious—it was never enough to tell her to do something. She'd also want to know why I was asking her to do it, what she should expect, and all the various historical events that had led up to my request. She was like a sponge, always asking, always questioning, always learning. If she had continued her studies, I'm sure she would have become the greatest druid of us all."

"Why did she stop?"

"Because he left, and it nearly killed her. And then you came along. Even if she'd wanted to keep learning, the druid training is very intensive, and there was no way she could keep it up with a newborn to care for, especially not alone. I offered to help, but . . . she wasn't interested." The look on his face suggested that it wasn't just the training Maeve had rejected.

Liam squeezed Cedar's hand, misinterpreting her troubled expression. "Don't feel bad. You brought great joy to her. You and Eden both."

After a few minutes Cedar excused herself to go back to bed. She could have listened to Liam's stories all morning, but her eyelids were becoming unbearably heavy. She paused at the door of the kitchen and looked back at the man who was huddled over his cup of cold tea. She opened her mouth to ask a question but paused, not wanting to be rude.

"Yes," he said with a slight smile.

"Yes?"

"Yes, I loved her. I know you've been wanting to ask. I love her still. It doesn't stop with death."

Cedar wished she had some words of comfort to offer him. She wished she could tell him that she was sure Maeve had loved him back in some way . . . but Maeve had never mentioned having a teacher or a friend or anyone at all in her life who fit Liam's description. Even when Maeve had confessed the truth about Cedar's background, she had never so much as mentioned Liam. The thought made Cedar sad. She had known Liam for only a short while, but she was growing very fond of him. She wondered what her life would have been like if Maeve had loved him in return. On impulse, she walked back to the table and wrapped her arms around Liam's slumped shoulders.

"I think you would have made a wonderful father," she said, kissing the top of his head. Then she turned and padded slowly down the hall and into the room where Finn and Eden slept and crawled in between them, thinking of family.

◦◦◦

A few short hours later they were ready to go to Tír na nÓg. Cedar's heart pounded nervously. "We should go in and out as secretly as possible," she said. "Hopefully Nuala and the Council will never even know we were there." It was already midmorning, and she was anxious to get moving, although nervous about what they might find there. She cast an anxious glance at Jane, who was still in a deep sleep on the sofa.

"Go," Liam urged her. "I'll look after her, don't worry. Just make sure your friends are safe."

Eden grabbed the knob on the closet door. "Where to?" she asked.

"How about your room in Tír na nÓg?" Cedar said. Eden's eyes lit up, and she swung the door open. Felix went through first and paused for a moment, glancing around, before motioning for the others to follow. Cedar and Eden came through, with Finn right behind them. They were at the very top of Eden's bedroom tree, beside the blue cushion that served as her bed. The sky above was a pale blue, with cotton candy clouds rimmed with pink and orange. For a moment, there was total silence. Then a voice ripped through Cedar's mind with such force that she dropped to her knees. It was Nevan, and she was terrified.

CHAPTER 10

What is it?" Finn asked, grabbing Cedar's arm and helping her to her feet.

"Nevan," she gasped. "Something's wrong." She looked at Felix, who was frozen in place, every muscle in his body tense. "Can you hear it too?" He nodded tersely.

"What's she saying? What's wrong?" Finn asked. "Damn it, I *hate* not being able to hear her."

"She's not saying anything," Cedar said. "She's just . . . crying. How do we find her?" She headed toward the spiral staircase in the tree's thick trunk. Then she stopped. Nevan was speaking to her.

Cedar? I know you can hear me, so that must mean you're here. Go back to Ériu! It's not safe here. They'll be looking for you too.

Cedar turned and repeated Nevan's words to Finn. Felix was still listening. Cedar assumed that Nevan must be talking to him as well. Then she heard the voice again.

They've taken him. They've taken Sam . . . they've taken everyone, and I don't know where they are. I'm hidden, but I don't know what's happening with the others.

Cedar relayed this to Finn and watched his face grow red. "This is madness," he said. "How can Nuala get away with this?"

"It might not be Nuala," Felix answered. "It might be the Council."

Cedar awaited some further communication from Nevan, but there was only silence. "Is she saying anything else to you?" she asked Felix.

He shook his head. "No. There's nothing."

"If only she had told us where she's hiding—" Cedar said.

"I'll go look for her," Finn said. "The rest of you stay here."

"I should come with you," Cedar said, ignoring his frown. "You can't hear her, but I can. I can tell you what she's saying. How else would you find her?"

"No. It's too dangerous," Finn said. "I'll be back as soon as I know anything." With that, he gently moved Cedar aside and disappeared down the spiral stairs.

Cedar ignored him. "Eden, stay here with Felix," she said. "I'll be back soon." She followed Finn down the twisting staircase, almost tripping in her hurry to catch up with him. When she reached the golden door that opened onto the willow-lined courtyard, she shoved it open. He was already on the far side of the courtyard. "Finn, wait!" she called.

"I told you to stay there," he said.

"Yeah, well, I'm not very good at doing what I'm told. How do you expect to find her? She could be anywhere."

"Not anywhere. I spent most of my childhood on the run, remember? I know all the good hiding spots." His voice was laced with bitterness, and Cedar realized once again how little she knew of his childhood here in Tír na nÓg.

"I'm coming with you," she said softly. "Nevan might tell me where she is."

"Cedar, you know what happened the last time you ran into Nuala. And that was just in a dream. I know her, and she doesn't like being backed into a corner. She plays dirty."

Cedar didn't like being reminded of how well Finn and Nuala knew each other. All of Finn's friends and relatives had expected him to end up with Nuala someday, because he was the only available male who could never be influenced by her ability. She wondered, but had never dared to ask, how far they had gone down the road of courtship before he'd realized he could never love her.

"Maybe Felix was right—maybe she's just trying to distract us from finding the Lia Fáil, and there's no real danger." She hoped it was true.

"She must have bewitched the whole damn Council," he said quietly.

"I don't think there was any need," Cedar said. "Most of them seemed pretty agreeable to her plan for Ériu. The only one who didn't seem tempted by it was Gorman. I think it's like you said before—it wasn't just Lorcan who thought the way he did. The poison runs deeper than we'd thought." She started pacing, trying to figure out how they could find the others without risking capture themselves. They were standing in front of the door that led to the common area. Finn pulled it open a crack, and then pushed it shut tightly. He nodded to himself without speaking.

"What—" Cedar started to say, but he motioned for her to be silent.

"I'm not letting you come with me. If I don't come back," he mouthed, so quietly she could barely hear him, "go back through the sidh. Find the Lia Fáil. It may be the only thing that can save us now."

Cedar opened her mouth to protest, but it was too late. He was through the door in a second . . . and he slammed it behind him. Cedar ran to the door and banged her body against it, but it wouldn't move. Its magic had saved it from Lorcan's forces during the civil war, and it was certainly strong enough to withstand her.

"Finn!" she yelled, banging her fists against the door. "Finn!" she yelled again, pushing and pulling it and trying to wrench it open. But it remained stubbornly closed. She stood there glaring at the door so intently that she wondered if she might be able to burn through it with her eyes. She cast it one more venomous look and then sprinted back through the courtyard and into Eden's bedroom. She took the stairs two at a time up the tree trunk.

"What happened?" Felix asked, jumping to his feet as soon as he saw her. Eden was out on a far tree limb, balancing on one leg.

"He's gone off on his own," she growled. "He shut the door right in my face. Stupid, heroic, I-can-do-everything-myself-I-don't-need-any-help . . . god!"

"Give him a break," Felix said. "He's just trying to keep you safe."

"Yeah, but who's going to keep *him* safe while he's traipsing around Tír na nÓg with the whole Council after him?"

"Well, they're not exactly after him, since they don't know that he's here," Felix pointed out. Cedar felt like punching him. He grinned at her, which was infuriating. "You know that stubborn pigheadedness is exactly what he admires in you, right?"

"Ha ha ha," Cedar said, narrowing her eyes at him. "It just so happens that I have a better idea for finding Nevan than running pell-mell around Tír na nÓg with no idea where to look."

"Oh?"

"Eden!" she called, and Eden started wobbling her way back along the branch. "We don't have to go through the sidhe to see what's on the other side," she explained to Felix. "We can look in all kinds of places without sticking our necks out, so to speak."

"But only places that Eden has seen before," Felix said.

"Yes, there is that," Cedar admitted. "I wish I had taken her on a bit of a tour before we left. . . ."

"Nevan showed me around while you and Daddy were at the meeting," Eden said, hopping up and down in place. "I know lots of places. I bet I even know where she's hiding."

"Really?" Cedar asked.

"Uh huh. She showed me some of her favorite places," Eden said.

Cedar was moved. She was so used to being the only person to care for Eden besides Maeve, who was now dead. To know that Eden was loved by so many people was a strange and wonderful thing.

"Where did she take you?" she asked her daughter.

"Lots of places," Eden said. "Um . . . there was one that used to be an orchard, with tons of trees, but there was no fruit on them anymore. And then we went to this big rocky place, but the rocks were all red and purple. It was really pretty. But I think my favorite place was the cave."

"The cave?" Felix asked sharply.

Eden nodded. "It was amazing! It was this underwater cave, but there's no water in it now. She carried me so that I wouldn't get my shoes all muddy. It's hard to see the entrance, but once you're inside it's totally cool. All different colors and sparkly. And there are these little tunnels you can follow."

Cedar looked at Felix. "Do you know what she's talking about?"

"Yes," he said. "I've been there, but only once, back when we were still fighting Lorcan. He had just imprisoned Nevan's family and was looking for her. We hid there for three days. I wouldn't be surprised if that's where she is now."

"Okay," Cedar said. "Let's find out. Eden, try and open the sidh inside the cave, away from the opening."

"I *know*, Mum," Eden said, rolling her eyes. She placed her hand on the tree truck. Through the shimmering cloud of the sidh there was darkness, but Cedar could make out the glittering pink and yellow and orange of the cave's walls.

"Stay here with Felix," Cedar told Eden. "But if I make this symbol"—she made her hands into fists and crossed them in the air—"close the sidh immediately, do you understand?" Eden nodded.

"Wait just a minute, weren't you just complaining about Finn leaving you behind as he rushed into danger?" Felix protested, grabbing her arm.

"Yes, but someone needs to stay here to protect Eden, and we both know that you're better equipped to do that than I am. *And*

Finn doesn't have a sidh he can escape through," Cedar said, yanking her arm away. "So the situations are totally different. I'll be right back, hopefully with Nevan."

She stepped through the doorway and felt the cool, damp air of the cave hit her skin. She stood still for a moment, waiting for her eyes to adjust to the darkness. The cave was larger than she'd expected. She could stand comfortably, and the glittering walls lent the place a peaceful, magical feeling. She could make out dark shapes toward the back of the cave, which must be the entrances to the tunnels Eden had mentioned. She looked behind her and could just barely make out the dim light of the entrance. Eden had placed the sidh well.

Suddenly she heard a voice in her head. *Cedar? Is that you?*

"Are you here? It's just me, you can come out," Cedar said softly. She didn't hear any footsteps, but Nevan's figure became more and more distinct as she slowly approached Cedar from the back of the cave.

"Come on, let's get you out of here," Cedar said, reaching for Nevan's hand.

"I can't. I can't leave," Nevan said out loud as she got closer. Cedar frowned. Nevan's eyes were red, and her usually bright smile had been replaced by a grim line.

"Why not?" Cedar asked. "Are you okay?"

"Because once the others have been released, they'll come looking for me. I've sent them messages to meet here when they can. If I'm gone, they'll think I've been taken."

"Can't you just send them another message telling them you've gone somewhere safe?"

"This *is* safe—" Nevan said, though her eyes were filled with fear.

Her words were cut short by a rustling sound near the front of the cave. Cedar looked back at the sidh in alarm, ready to push

Nevan through at the first sign of trouble. Felix and Eden were on the other side, looking at her. She shook her head slightly. Not yet. Cedar grabbed Nevan's hand and held still. Another rustle . . . like the sound of wings. Then two tiny birds swooped in over their heads. Nevan screamed and gripped Cedar's hand tighter. A second later, Finn and Riona were standing beside them.

"How did you get here?" Finn demanded, staring at Cedar. She glared at him and then indicated the sidh, as though the answer should be obvious. He looked momentarily stunned. "Ahh . . . ," he said. "I hadn't thought about that."

Riona pulled Nevan in for a tight hug. "Are you all right, dear? We've been getting your messages, and you sounded so afraid."

"I *am* afraid," Nevan said. She was shaking. "I don't know what's going on, but it all seems like . . . like last time."

"Oh, my dear, it's very different," Riona said soothingly. "At least, for now. No one is being harmed; they just wanted to ask us some questions about our time on Ériu. You'll have to talk to them too, or else they'll assume the worst."

"What kind of questions?" Cedar asked. "And why?" She told Riona and Nevan about what Nuala had said in the dream about rounding them up.

Riona pursed her lips in disapproval. "Well, I don't know how much Nuala has to do with it. I think she was just trying to scare you. We're all right, as you can see. It's ridiculous, if you ask me. But Rohan thinks we should play along, and I suppose he's right. If the Council doesn't trust us, they won't trust you either. So we've done our best to cooperate. They have it in their heads that we were 'consorting' with humans. We told them how strict we were about that while we were on Ériu. But Nuala has already told them about all the humans she had to, er, deal with, which is sadly somewhat true. But she's also fed them complete lies about secret meetings with government officials, and now they're worried that *we* were the ones who planned on waging war with Tír na nÓg once we had found the sidh-opener.

"Well, I won't deny that the thought crossed our minds, but only as a way to get rid of Lorcan. Anyone with sense could see that we had nothing but the best intentions for our land and our people."

"So Sam is . . . he's okay?" Nevan asked in a trembling voice.

"Yes, my dear, he's fine. I had no idea you were so upset. He's more worried about *you* than anything. I mean, we're all a bit shaken up." She turned to Cedar. "Finn told me all about what happened. I'm so sorry, Cedar. I wish there was some way we could come with you. But if any of us leaves now it would prove to them that we have something to hide, some hidden agenda."

"I understand," Cedar said, but she felt a wave of disappointment crash over her. Yet another setback. She had been so excited about a starting a new life in Tír na nÓg with Finn and Eden, but nothing had gone right, and now Eden was in more danger than ever. *Maybe I should have taken Liam's advice the first time I met him*, she thought. *Maybe we should have stayed.* But then Nuala would have had her way, and they would have faced the same horrible fate as everyone else on Earth. Besides, it was too late now—the wheels had been set in motion, and there was no safe place left for them. Only by finding the Lia Fáil could she stop this madness. She looked sadly at Nevan.

"We had hoped that you'd be able to come with us and teach Eden how to close her mind to Nuala," Cedar explained. "Somehow she's able to find her way into Eden's dreams. We think it might have something to do with the druids working with her, but we're not sure. I understand if you need to stay, though. I don't want to put any of you in danger."

Nevan looked back and forth between Cedar and Riona, frowning. "It *must* be the druids, not Nuala. Her ability shouldn't allow her into Eden's mind. I'm sorry, Cedar. I wish there was something I could do, but it would take me months to teach Eden how to close her mind. It's really hard to learn, especially for kids. Even then it might not work. It might just be something she won't be able to do until she's older."

Cedar nodded grimly. "Okay," she said. "Thanks. In that case, we should get back and figure out what we're going to do next."

"I wish we could come with you," Riona said. Then she turned to Nevan. "We're meeting at Gorman and Seisyll's. I saw Sam with one of the Council members—he should be free soon, then he'll meet us back there. Let's go. Good luck, Cedar."

Cedar hugged them and wished them luck in return, then walked back through the sidh without looking at Finn.

CHAPTER 11

"Where's Nevan? I saw her, isn't she coming?" Eden asked as soon as Cedar stepped through the sidh into her daughter's tree house bedroom. Finn followed her and closed it behind him.

"She couldn't come," Cedar answered tersely. "Let's go back to Logheryman's house." With wide eyes, Eden opened the sidh, and a moment later they were back in the leprechaun's living room. Jane was sitting up on the sofa and sipping a mug of tea, wrapped in one of Logheryman's old robes. Liam was pacing the floor behind her.

"Hey!" Jane exclaimed, standing up when she saw them. "You made it back, thank God! I'm so glad."

"*You're* glad? I'm so happy that you're alive!" Cedar exclaimed, pulling her friend in for a gentle hug. "How are you feeling?"

"Besides totally bald and badass? Fine," Jane laughed. She looked at Felix, her cheeks reddening slightly. He was standing stock-still behind Cedar, his eyes fixed on Jane. "Thank you, Felix," Jane said. "You saved my life."

Cedar hadn't thought it was possible, but she was certain that Felix was blushing. He looked down at the floor. "It's nothing," he said. "I'm glad you're okay."

"Liam's brought me up to speed. He told me all about the dream. Holy shit, Ceeds. But is everyone okay? And why didn't Nevan come?"

Cedar quickly explained what Nevan and Riona had told them. "I think they're okay—for now. But if Nuala becomes queen,

I have a feeling she's going to settle a lot of old scores." Before they could ask her any more questions, she said, "Could you excuse us for a moment? Finn and I need to have a chat." Grabbing Finn by the arm, she pulled him into Logheryman's bedroom.

"What the hell was that?" she asked, rounding on him as soon as she had shoved the door closed behind them. Finn's lips were pressed together, and his fists were clenched. He was looking at the wall behind her, avoiding her gaze. Cedar glared at him, her eyebrows raised, clearly expecting an answer. He continued to look around the room—anywhere but at her. She could hear the others talking in the hallway and hoped Eden wasn't listening at the door.

"Cedar, I—" Finn finally began, but by then Cedar had decided she didn't actually want to hear his excuses. She cut him off.

"You treated me like a child back there!" she burst out. "I may not have any of your superpowers, but I am *not* helpless. We are both adults, Finn. We're partners. You can't just slam a door in my face and expect me to deal with it."

Finn was staring at the ground now, his arms crossed, and she thought she heard him mutter something like "reckless." She took a deep breath and forced herself to calm down, to try to consider things from his perspective.

"Listen," she said. "I know that you care about me. I know that you're worried about losing me. At least, that's what I'm hoping this was all about, and that you don't just think I'm incompetent. But you don't get to make decisions like that for me, and you can't keep me safe by keeping me locked up. I won't live that way, and it's certainly not going to help us find the Lia Fáil."

Rather than waiting for a response, she marched back into the living room. Felix was sitting on the sofa beside Jane, who was hugging Logheryman's robe tightly around her.

Jane's tense face relaxed as soon as she saw Cedar. "Everything okay?"

"Yeah, except for the obvious—no stone yet," Cedar said. "Aren't you cold, Jane?" She gestured toward the flimsy robe. "Can I get you a blanket?"

"Nah," Jane answered. "Unless it has a computer attached. I feel naked without my tech. I mean, I suppose I technically am naked under this robe, but you know what I mean. . . ." She closed her eyes and trailed off, her cheeks burning. Cedar suppressed a grin. Jane was usually impossible to rattle, but something about being brought back from the brink of death by a devastatingly gorgeous mythical being had messed with her composure. Jane opened her eyes again and said, "Hey, I wonder if Eden could sidh me in and out of a shop?" She looked at Eden, clearly intrigued by this new possibility.

Cedar laughed and said, "Yes, I suppose she could, if we could manage it without you getting caught, which is unlikely. We'll think of a way to get you some clothes, don't worry." She snapped her fingers. "I should have brought some from my closet in Tír na nÓg. You could have worn them to your next medieval festival."

Jane's laugh was interrupted by the sound of the front door opening. Silence fell upon them at once, and Cedar's heart jumped into her throat. Then she exhaled loudly. "Logheryman."

The leprechaun was standing in his doorway, staring in surprise at the group gathered in his living room. He looked as old and ornery as ever, but there was a bright bruise on his left cheek and scrapes down the side of his neck. His sharp eyes took them all in, lingering for a split second on Jane and Liam. Slowly, and without saying a word, he closed the door behind him and then turned back to face his visitors.

"They told me you would come," he said, "I must say I had my doubts."

"Who told you? Are you okay?" Cedar asked, staring at the bruise. "What happened to you?"

"Lovely to see you, too, Miss McLeod," he said. He ignored her questions and walked right past them and into the kitchen, where he poured himself a large glass of whiskey. After taking a rather sizable gulp, he came back into the living room and once again regarded the group. "I should ask the same of you. What brings you back to my humble abode so soon?"

Cedar hesitated, not sure how much to tell him. "Eden and Jane were badly hurt," she said. "We needed a safe place to stay while Felix healed them."

Logheryman took another long swallow and then nodded slowly. "Long has my house been a safe haven for the Tuatha Dé Danann," he said. "It is perfectly understandable why you would come here. But it is not a safe place now. They suspected you would come here. That's why they took me."

"Who took you? The druids?" Cedar asked.

"Indeed," Logheryman said. "Fortunately, keeping me is not as easy as taking me. Escape is my specialty, you might say."

"What did they want with you?" Felix asked, moving closer to look at the bruising on Logheryman's cheek. The leprechaun brushed him away with a wave of his hand.

"Nothing I can't look after," he said. "They wanted information about a roving band of Dananns. They seemed quite . . . motivated."

"How much did they offer you?" Felix said, a faint look of disgust on his face.

"Well, that's between them and me, now, isn't it?" Logheryman said. "Oh, don't worry, child, I'm not going to turn you over for a mere thirty pieces of silver. And I doubt I could detain you even if I had a mind to."

Felix raised his eyebrows. "Detain us? I'd like to see you try," he said.

"Oh, spare me the testosterone, Toirdhealbhach. I see you've regained your usual form. I suppose the ladies prefer it." Logheryman looked with interest at Jane. "It's not every day that I find a bald and naked woman wrapped in one of my robes. Who might you be, my dear?"

"This is Jane," Cedar answered, stepping in front of her friend. "She's a friend of ours. And this is Liam. He's also a friend—and a druid."

Logheryman's expression darkened instantly. "Have you lost control of your senses?"

Finn, who had been silent up until now, stepped forward. "He's not with them," he protested. "He's been helping us." Cedar wondered if this defense of Liam was his way of making up for leaving her behind, or if he was actually starting to trust the druid.

"Helping you?" Logheryman sneered. "Why, pray tell, would a druid want to help the Tuatha Dé Danann? Perhaps *he* is the one who has lost control of his senses."

Liam bristled visibly. "I can assure you, I have nothing to do with your assailants. Cedar called me because they needed help."

"And what kind of help do you provide, exactly? Did she need someone kidnapped and threatened? It seems to be your kind's area of specialty."

"We don't have time for this," Cedar snapped. "He's with us, and that's it. We came here for help. Eden and Jane are better, but now we need information."

"What you need, my dear, is to remove your little band of troublemakers from my house. I did not sign up to become involved in a dispute between the Danann and the druids."

Cedar looked at him incredulously. "That's it? We come to you for help and you're just throwing us out without even listening? You have no idea what's at stake."

"Oh, I'm sure it's something cataclysmic," he said in a bored tone. "I appreciate that you think so highly of me, but I'm sure that whatever the current crisis is, you can handle it on your own." He walked over to the door and held it open.

No one made any move to leave. Cedar continued to glare at Logheryman, then crossed the room and slammed the door closed.

"You think that pretending to be neutral is going to help you?" she said, swiveling so that they were face-to-face. "They already know that you've helped us in the past. And they'll find out that we were here and that you let us go. Does that sound very neutral to you?"

Logheryman looked down his nose at her. "Would you rather I *not* let you go?" he asked.

"I'd *rather* you do the right thing and help us!" she said, taking a step back. "I don't know what lies they told you, but they are working for someone who wants to destroy the world and everyone in it."

Logheryman rolled his eyes. "Unlike you, my dear, I've known the Tuatha Dé Danann for more than five minutes. They tend to be, mmm, melodramatic, shall we say? I'm sure that whatever merry chase they've led you on this time, it's not as bad as you think."

Cedar gaped at him. "Are you serious?" She pulled Jane forward. "They tried to burn my best friend alive—and would have succeeded if it hadn't been for Felix. And they trapped Eden in a nightmare in her own mind—and it was Liam who helped bring her out. They're serious. If Nuala succeeds, she'll create a war on Earth that will wipe out everyone. That isn't melodrama. And you can't just go back to your normal life and pretend that nothing is happening."

She took a deep breath. "Listen, I know you don't want to get involved. I get that. But it's too late now. If we don't find what we're looking for, everyone on Earth will die. You're *already* involved. Help us stop her."

Logheryman considered her for a long moment, then sighed. "I might be able to offer you some assistance, but there is the matter of payment, of course . . . ," he began.

"Damn the payment!" Cedar said. "Have you never in your life done something just because it's the right thing to do? Help us, and you'll save millions of lives. Refuse to help us, and all the gold in the world won't save you."

There was another long pause. "And what exactly are you look-ing for?" he asked.

"The Lia Fáil," she replied. "The Stone of Destiny. It's been lost for centuries. We have less than a week. Once we find it, it will prove that I'm the rightful queen of Tír na nÓg, not Nuala. Then she won't be able to move forward with her plan."

Logheryman raised his gray eyebrows. "*You* will be queen? Are you sure your motives here are entirely pure?"

Cedar silenced him with a glance. "I don't *want* to be queen, but it's the only way. Do you know anything about the Lia Fáil or not?"

Logheryman pursed his lips as he looked around at each of them in the room. Cedar held her breath. Finally, he spoke. "I don't. But I know someone who might, and at any rate it's best for us not to stay here. Follow me, if you will."

He turned and walked through the kitchen and out the back door. After a moment's hesitation, Cedar grabbed Eden's hand and followed him. The others filed behind her. She heard Felix whisper to Finn and Liam, "Stay sharp. I've never known Logheryman to do anything just because it was the right thing to do."

The leprechaun led them past the clearing where Finn had landed as a dragon and onto a narrow path that headed into the woods.

"Where are we going?" Cedar asked. She glanced behind her to see how Jane was faring. She was walking at the back of the group, still clutching the robe around her and stumbling along in a pair of Logheryman's thin slippers. Liam had his arm around her shoulders and was helping her along.

"I am not entirely solitary," Logheryman replied. "We are going to the house of a friend. It's not far."

After a few minutes they emerged from the woods into a clear-ing, in the center of which stood a small, whitewashed cottage. It was about the same size as Logheryman's house, but much more well kept. Bright flowers spilled from painted window boxes, and

Cedar could see a neat, orderly garden on the side of the house. It was midmorning, and an elderly woman with long white hair that fell to her waist was crouched among the pole beans, a pile of weeds beside her.

"Maggie," Logheryman said as they approached. The woman raised her head but didn't turn around as she fussed with the ties on one of the poles.

"You've made some friends, Martin," she said. Cedar raised her eyebrows. *Martin?*

Maggie stood up and brushed the dirt off her knees. She turned around and took in the group standing behind Loghery-man. "Well," she said, "I'd better put the kettle on." They followed her through the front door and into a cozy sitting room. "Have a seat, have a seat," she said. "Tea first, then introductions." She disappeared into the kitchen, and Cedar could hear the rattle of cups and saucers being pulled out of the cupboard.

"Who is she?" Finn asked Logheryman. Eden was sitting on her father's lap in a faded armchair draped with a hand-knit afghan. Felix stood by the door, and Liam and Jane had taken seats beside Logheryman on the sofa near the fireplace. Cedar paced the floor, her eyes fixed on Logheryman.

"Maggie O'Daly. An old friend," he said. "I've known Maggie since she was a wee girl. She's one of the few people left who believe in the old ways. You can trust her."

"You think she can help us?" Cedar asked.

"If it's knowledge you're after, then yes," he said. "She's a file."

Cedar saw Finn, Felix, and Liam make signs of acknowledgment, but she had no idea what a file was. "What's that?" she asked.

"They call us seanachai these days," Maggie said, coming back into the room with a tray laden with cups and saucers and a large pot of steaming tea. "Storytellers, bards, that sort of thing. But the fili used to be the most important role in Irish society. This was centuries ago, of course. We were the lawmakers, philosophers, poets, historians, and sorcerers all rolled into one. After a time, the roles were split up: The brehons became the judges and lawmakers, the druids became the priests and magicians, and the fili became the poets and storytellers—which was the same things as being a historian in those days. There are still some of us kicking about, though precious few, I'm sure. My grandfather was one. In fact, the O'Dalys were fili to the High Kings of Ireland even before Saint Patrick arrived, and long before that, I'd wager."

Logheryman brought out more chairs from the kitchen, and Cedar sat down beside Finn and Eden and accepted a cup of tea from Maggie. She sighed audibly as the hot liquid ran down her throat and gratefully took a cookie from the plate that was being passed around. She watched Eden wolf hers down and felt a pang of guilt. Logheryman's cupboards had been bare; all Eden had eaten for breakfast was a packet of chips.

Cedar gazed at Maggie, who was sipping her tea and seemingly unperturbed by the group of strangers in her living room. The old woman looked kindly at Jane. "What happened to your clothes, dear?" she asked.

"Um . . . they got burned," Jane said, blushing and pulling the robe more tightly around her. "There was a fire."

Maggie pursed her lips and looked disapprovingly at Logheryman. "Getting into mischief again, Martin?"

"You flatter me, but I'm afraid I can't take credit for this one," he answered with a smirk. "My, er, friends seem to have landed themselves in a fair amount of trouble all on their own. Also, I fear I must trespass on your hospitality for a while, dear Maggie. My home has been compromised for the time being."

"Again?" Maggie said, her eyebrows raised, and Cedar wondered how often Logheryman found himself at odds with the world.

"It will all blow over soon, I'm sure," he said, "And I'll admit that I had another motivation for this visit. I'm afraid I can't go into details, but do your vast stores of knowledge include anything about the Lia Fáil? My companions here are very interested in its whereabouts, and I am sadly unable to help them in that regard. They shan't be here for long; once they have their information, they'll be on their way."

"The Lia Fáil? Aye, now there's an interesting subject." She nodded slowly. "There are many stories about the Stone of Destiny."

"We know about Murtagh mac Erc loaning it to his brother," Cedar blurted out. "But the Stone of Scone at Edinburgh Castle is a fake. It was taken from Scone by the English, but we don't know where it is now."

Finn shot her an exasperated look, but Cedar didn't care. They didn't have time to beat around the bush.

"So it's not just stories you want, then," Maggie said, eyeing Cedar keenly. "You want the truth. Well, there is truth to be found in stories, that's for certain."

"Not all stories are true," Eden piped up from her father's lap.

"They're always true about something, little one," Maggie said, passing Eden another cookie. "If not about what actually happened, then maybe about the person telling the story—or about the person hearing it. I've been telling stories for more than seventy years, and listening to them for even longer, and I call tell you there is always some truth to be found. And it is truth you are after, am I right?"

Cedar nodded.

"Then I have a story for you. Do with it what you will."

৩১৯

Maggie cleared her throat and then began. "Many years ago there was young man named Donald O'Brien, living just outside a wee village near the banks of the River Boyne. He had a kind heart and handsome face. Everyone who knew him spoke well of him, for he was a hard worker, and yet he always took the time for a friendly chat or to offer a helping hand. Even the wild beasts took a shine to him, for it was he who would take food from his own plate to feed a stray cat, and he never forgot to leave seed outside for the birds and wee creatures of the forest during the long winter months. As a child, he used to play with the daughter of the man who tended sheep just over the hill. She was called Utain, and she was a homely little thing, all elbows and knees and wispy brown hair. She used to cut her hair short to try to make it grow fuller, which made her look more like a scarecrow than a young maiden. But she was a sweet girl, and she and Donald were fast friends, even as they grew and approached adulthood. Then one day Utain went missing on her way into the village. Donald looked everywhere for her, as did half the village, for her family was well loved. But she was nowhere to be found. Her family grieved for her, but many girls in the village were secretly glad she had disappeared because of her close friendship with Donald.

"One of these girls was called Marsha. Her father was a wealthy merchant, and she had everything a girl in those days could dream of. She was also the prettiest girl in the village, with bouncing brown curls and a rosy complexion. But on the inside she was vain and petty, and she had often taunted Utain for her plain looks. Marsha made no secret of her plans to win Donald as a husband. In fact, to hear her talk of it, they had already published the bans and would be married in a fortnight! But if Donald ever felt any affection for her or harbored the same ambition, he never let on. He treated her courteously, as he did all the young ladies who crossed his path. But Marsha's vanity was such that she led herself to believe he could not possibly find another wife as desirable as her, and she convinced herself that he truly did love her.

"Then one day there was a visitor from the city. A young woman by the name of Aiofe was traveling with her aunt to visit their relatives several villages away. But when they passed by Donald's family's farm, their horse grew lame. And so they begged hospitality from Donald's family in the hopes that the horse would recover with time. Being kind-hearted, Donald's mother welcomed them in and offered them food and a place to stay. Well, when Donald first saw Aiofe, he felt desire as he had never known before. For she was more beautiful than any woman he had ever seen. Her chestnut hair fell to her waist in thick, glossy waves. She was tall and strong, with curving hips and a full bosom. When she smiled, which was often, her eyes sparkled like stars in the night sky.

"But not only was she beautiful, Aiofe had a vibrant spirit. She would not be waited on and insisted on helping Donald's mother serve the evening meal and prepare the guest beds. Her aunt said little, and so it was Aiofe who chatted merrily about life in the city and asked many questions about the surrounding countryside.

"The next day their horse was still lame, and Donald said that he would tend to it, if they would do them the honor of staying a little longer. Aiofe's aunt agreed. By then, word had spread of the beautiful city dweller lodging at the O'Brien farm, who seemed to have finally captured young Donald's attention. Well, upon hearing this, Marsha flew into a right rage. Early the next morning, before first light, she set out for the O'Brien farm, determined to see this rival for herself and find a way to get rid of her.

"The sun was rising when Marsha approached the farm. She tiptoed around to the back of the house, where she knew the guests would be sleeping. But before she could get to the window, the back door opened. Marsha quickly hid herself behind the hedge. Out of the door crept a young woman, but it was not the beautiful girl from the city. Why, it was none other than Utain, small and ugly as ever, though of course a few years older than the last time Marsha had seen her. Marsha stood there in shock, wondering what Utain was doing in Donald's house and why no one had spoken of her return.

"The scrawny girl looked around, a shawl wrapped over her bony shoulders. She wore only a thin shift, but in her arms she carried a fine dress of deep blue silk. Marsha followed the girl down to the river as quietly as she could. It was midsummer, but the water was cold in the early morning, and Utain shivered as she removed her shift and placed it and the dress on the dry bank, entering the water naked. When she was waist deep in the water, she started chanting words in a strange language. Then she bent backward and submerged herself completely. When she rose up out of the water, she was no longer the small, ugly girl from the farm next door. She was a glowing vision of perfection, more beautiful than any woman Marsha had ever seen, like a bright flower growing in the midst of a swamp. Utain gazed at her reflection in the water for a moment and smiled. Then she climbed out onto the bank, clothed herself in the blue dress, and headed back toward the house.

"Well, Marsha had seen enough. Utain had to be a witch—there was no other explanation for it. She dared not confront her directly, but she knew that something had to be done. She returned home and told no one what she had witnessed. The next day, when it was announced that Donald and Aiofe were to be married, Marsha knew that she needed to find some way to expose Utain for who she was and end the engagement before it was too late.

"So Marsha stole some coins from her father's purse and went to Old Nat, the eldest woman in the village. Some said Nat herself was a witch, others claimed that she had druid blood in her, or was a changeling, switched as a baby for one of the fairy folk. Marsha had never believed these tales, putting no stock in the old ways—until now. She told Old Nat what she had seen and asked for a way to expose Utain's deception without putting herself in harm's way. After Marsha gave her some of her father's gold, Old Nat told her of the existence of a magic stone that was said to remove enchantments. If Aiofe really was Utain in disguise, she said, the spell would melt away as soon as she stepped on the stone, and Donald would see her for the homely farm girl she was.

"Marsha returned home to continue her scheming. Then she sent a message to Donald and Aiofe with her congratulations, saying that she would like to give them a new mare as a wedding gift and that they could choose the horse themselves. To do this, they would need to come to a certain hill, where Marsha and her grooms would be waiting with several mares for them to choose from.

"Thrilled with Marsha's kind offer, Donald and Aiofe accepted, and promised to meet her there on the arranged day. When that day arrived, Marsha set out early, with neither groom nor horses, and followed the directions given to her by Old Nat. Nat had told her where the stone could be found, on the hill they called Tara.

"Marsha worried that Nat's plan might not work, but she had no choice but to go through with it. When Donald and Aiofe arrived, Marsha greeted them warmly. 'My grooms are bringing the horses now,' she told them. Then she led Aiofe over to the stone. 'If you'll just stand up here, you'll be able to see them as they crest the hill.' Aiofe stepped up onto the stone, and then it happened. Her glossy tresses withered and shortened until they were like bits of straw that had been blown about a courtyard. The plumpness of her breasts and hips shrunk until her dress hung loosely on her lank figure. Her cheeks paled and her eyes grew dull. She looked down at herself in dismay and covered her face in her hands. Marsha stood there watching, waiting for Donald's horrified reaction.

"But it never came. He was surprised, even shocked, to be sure. He stared open-mouthed at the girl before him. But then he rushed to her and crushed her in his arms, saying her name over and over again. 'Utain, Utain, Utain.' Needless to say, this was not the reaction Marsha had been expecting.

"'She's a witch!' she cried. 'I saw her down at the river, using sorcery to make herself beautiful. She should be hanged!'

"'Is it true?' Donald asked Utain. 'Are you a witch?'

"'No,' Utain sobbed. 'But I went to see one. I loved you so much, you see, but I knew you deserved better. You deserved someone beautiful. I knew . . . at least, I thought I knew . . . that I would never be more to you than a friend. And I couldn't bear it. I couldn't live without you. I ran away; I thought if I didn't see you every day, I would forget about you. But I didn't. I nearly drove myself mad with longing. So I went to a witch, and she gave me a spell to perform each morning in the river that would make me beautiful. I thought . . . I thought maybe then you'd love me. And you did . . . as Aiofe, not Utain.'

"'You're wrong,' Donald said then, taking her into his arms again. 'I did love you as Utain. I only loved Aiofe because she was kind, clever, and strong in heart—she reminded me of you, and I thought I had lost you forever. I don't care about the rest of it, Utain. You are back, and you love me, and that is all that matters.'

"So they went back to their homes, and were very happy together."

Maggie sat back, a satisfied look on her face. Cedar blinked. She had become so engrossed in the story that it was a surprise to realize that it was over. Finn reached over and squeezed her hand and then leaned over and whispered in to her ear, "I'm sorry. About leaving you behind."

She looked up into his golden eyes and squeezed his hand back. "Thank you," she whispered back. "I love you."

"What happened to Marsha?" Eden asked.

"She returned to the village, where her father had discovered that she had stolen money from him. He decided that he had been far too lax with her. So he sent her to work in the kitchen of his inn until she could pay back the money she'd stolen—plus interest. She tried to tell him about Utain and Aiofe, but he just laughed at her. 'You're as crazy as Old Nat,' he said. 'Aiofe has gone back to the city; it seems as though country life wasn't to her liking after all. But don't feel too sorry for young Donald. I heard Utain is back, and the boy seems happier with her than he ever did with that pretty girl. Fickle lad, if you ask me, but that's young people for you.'"

Jane laughed, and Eden said, "I like that story. Can you tell us another one?"

"Maybe another time, dear," Maggie said. "But I believe you were leaving shortly, is that not so?"

"Wait," Cedar said. "So you're saying that the magic stone in this story is the Lia Fáil, and that it's still at Tara?"

"I have no way of knowing for certain," Maggie answered, holding up her hands. "But it is an old story, one I learned from my grandfather, and he from his. As I said before, there is a germ of truth to be found in even the most outlandish stories. Was there really a young woman who could change her appearance by baptizing herself in the River Boyne? Was there really a stone that could reveal one's true self? Impossible to tell for sure, but I'd say it's at least as likely as the existence of leprechauns," she said with a wink.

"But the Lia Fáil just roars," said Jane with a puzzled expression on her face. "It doesn't 'reveal one's true self,' does it?"

"Maybe . . . I mean, if one's true self is the king or queen, it would reveal that, right?" Cedar said uncertainly. She glanced over at Finn, whose brow was furrowed. Liam had stood up and started pacing, glancing every now and again out the window.

"Well, it's the most recent account we've heard of the Lia Fáil," Finn said. "Or at least of a stone with magical properties. The fact that it's in Tara makes it even more likely. We know it's not the standing stone at Tara that they call the Lia Fáil for the tourists—I've been there and touched it. Not even the human scholars believe it is the stone of legend. But it could be somewhere else; Tara is a huge place. Perhaps Murtagh sent a fake to Fergus, and the one they were protecting for so long at Scone Abbey wasn't the real thing after all."

The thought made Cedar strangely sad. She remembered the grief of the abbot whose job it had been to guard the stone. He had spent centuries in anguished purgatory for nothing. She was glad that he was finally free. She got to her feet. "Does the story say exactly where it is on this hill?"

"As this young man says, Tara is vast—both in geography and history," Maggie said. "The story only says that the magic stone was at Tara, nothing else."

"Well, it's the best lead we've got," Cedar said. She looked at Eden nervously. "I'm just worried that they'll manage to get into Eden's head again, or attack us. But we're vulnerable to them no matter where we are."

"You're right. If they knew we were going to be at the castle, surely they'll think we'll head to Tara sooner rather than later, right?" Jane asked. "I mean, if it's not at Edinburgh and not at Scone, it's the most obvious place to look, isn't it? It's the only place we know for sure had the stone at some point in history. Didn't you guys—I mean, the Tuatha Dé Danann," she glanced nervously at Maggie as she corrected herself, "have a kingdom and castles and all that jazz there?"

Felix smiled. "Something like that. Tara is a very old, very special place," he said. "And it's fine to let our gracious host in on our secret. When we lived at Tara, it was the royal seat of our High King, and the place where the Council would meet and debate. Not a stone of those buildings has survived, of course. This was several millennia ago. But Tara has been a sacred place since before humans started recording time. It was the center of everything. Now . . . well, you'll see once we go there, which should be soon."

"I know," Cedar said. Her head was starting to pound, and she pinched the bridge of her nose as she thought. "We have to go . . . but we also have to assume that they'll be waiting for us there. If we could figure out exactly where the stone was, maybe I could just slip in and grab it."

"You can't just 'grab' the Lia Fáil," Felix said. "It would be far too heavy for you to lift."

"And we're not splitting up anymore, remember?" Finn said. Cedar opened her mouth to argue but closed it again. He was right; if they were anywhere near the druids, it would take both Finn and Felix to protect them.

"What about Brighid?" Felix said softly.

Brighid. Of course. Cedar kicked herself for not thinking of her sooner. She was still upset that Brighid had helped Nuala, but Cedar could hardly blame someone else for falling under the redhead's spell. After all, she had done so herself. But she had to wonder if Brighid's self-absorption wasn't partly to blame for how easily she'd provided Nuala with the information she wanted. But there was no point fretting about that now. Brighid had been on Ériu for more than fifteen hundred years. If anyone knew the true whereabouts of the Lia Fáil, it would be her.

"Of course!" Cedar exclaimed. "We should have gone to see her first. I'm sure she knows exactly where the Lia Fáil is."

"I wouldn't be so sure about that," Felix said, and Cedar's smile faltered. "She's quite intentionally ignored anything to do with our people for some time. I don't think she would have kept track of the Lia Fáil."

"I figured we could use the backup. We managed to escape the druids last time, but Finn can't keep turning into a dragon every five minutes if we want to keep a low profile. And we almost lost Eden and Jane."

"As flighty as she might seem, Brighid is more powerful than all of us. If she doesn't know the exact location of the stone, maybe she'll agree to come to Tara with us. She could at least help us fight the druids."

"Yeah . . ." Finn said slowly. "Brid's kind of gone underground since she found out about what happened with Nuala. She doesn't deal very well with . . . well, failure. When she found out that Nuala tricked her into helping her find that painting of Tír na nÓg, and made her forget about it . . . well, it wasn't pretty. She's off sulking somewhere, and she's sworn to have nothing to do with the Danann."

"Can't you at least ask her?" Cedar said. "She adores you, and now she owes us one for the whole Nuala thing."

"I'll give her a call," Finn said. "If she hasn't changed her number on me. Maggie, may I use your phone? I'm afraid we lost all of ours."

"Of course, my dear," she answered, nodding. "It's on the counter in the kitchen."

"I'd like to come with you," Liam said to Cedar. He had been very quiet since they had arrived at Maggie's, and it had crossed her mind that he'd probably prefer to be back in the university library in Dublin.

"Of course," she said, pleasantly surprised.

"I may not be as powerful as Brighid, but I know how to fight my own kind, if it comes to that," he said. "I'd like to help keep you safe, if I may. And Eden, too, of course."

Cedar smiled at him. "You have been very kind," she said. "Thanks for coming all this way and for all the help you've given us already. Eden might still be trapped in that dream if it weren't for you."

He blushed and apologized again for what had happened between her and Nuala in the dream.

"You had no way of knowing that Maeve had given Nuala and Eden the same potion," she told him, "or what the result would be."

Just then Finn returned to the room. "Well?" Cedar asked. "What did she say?"

"She says she hates phones," Finn said, a wry expression on his face. "She wants to see all of us in person."

Cedar sighed. "She wants to see *you,* you mean."

Finn grinned at Felix. "Actually, I think she's more interested in Felix this time," he said. "She became quite adamant about the visit *after* I told her he was with us, and that he's ditched his fisherman disguise."

Cedar looked at the clock. The day was getting on, and she was bone tired. But they had less than a week. There wasn't time to lose. "Okay, let's go," she said. "Is she still in New York?"

"No," Finn said. "She's, uh, well, she has her own island."

Somehow, this did not surprise Cedar one bit. "Of course she does."

"Uh, guys?" Jane said. "How are we going to get there? Via dragon? 'Cause I'm assuming Eden doesn't know what Brighid's island looks like, and all my tech is toast."

"Brighid said she'd send over some pictures of the beach beside her place," Finn said. "Apparently she has protections on the house so that we can't just show up in her bedroom." He gave Felix a sly grin. "She said she'd make an exception for you." Felix rolled his eyes. Jane scowled and hunched further down into her robe, running her fingers self-consciously over her scalp.

Cedar turned to Logheryman. "Where's the closest town? We need to get to a library or an Internet café."

Maggie answered for him. "It's not far," she said. "But if it's technology you need, why don't you just borrow mine?" She reached into a drawer in the desk in the corner and pulled out a tablet computer. "I use it for reading, mostly, and for the games. I wouldn't have expected folk like you to need such a thing."

Jane grinned at her. "This is my kind of magic," she said, taking the tablet from her. "And you are one very hip old lady." Maggie laughed at this and took up some knitting from a basket on the floor while Jane, Finn, and Eden hunched over the screen.

"There they are," Finn said, reaching across Jane to slide a photo across the screen. "See that, Eden? Think you can take us there?"

"Yeah, that place looks awesome!" Eden said. "Let's go!"

"Hold on a second!" Cedar called before Eden could reach the nearest door. She turned back to Maggie. "Thank you very much for your help."

The old woman bowed her head slightly at Cedar. "It's been my pleasure," she said. "I'm here to help you anytime you need me."

Cedar turned to Logheryman. "Did the druids tell you what they were planning on doing next? Did they say anything about Eden—how they can get inside her head?"

"They were looking for information, not offering it," he answered with a roll of his eyes.

"Well . . . thanks anyway," she said. "For deciding to help us."

Logheryman merely nodded. Cedar walked over and stood beside Eden. "Okay," she said. "Let's go."

"Thanks for the story!" Eden called, and then she reached out for the door and yanked it open.

CHAPTER 12

W ait, Eden!" Cedar called, racing through the door after her daughter. Eden was sprinting along a dark beach under the glow of the moon, the light reflecting off the puffs of sand she was kicking up with her feet. She slowed to a walk, but didn't turn around. Cedar stopped to take in her surroundings.

Leave it to Brighid to have a home in such a breathtaking, exotic place. They were on a small island off the coast of Thailand under a glowing full moon and a skyful of stars that were brighter than any Cedar had ever seen before. The moon was so large and incandescent that she could actually see the enormous dome-shaped mountains rising out of the water. It had been early afternoon at Logheryman's house in Ireland, but it was evening here, and the only lights were the celestial bodies and a scattering of tiki torches that lined the beach. A bird sang in a nearby palm tree, and Cedar felt her body start to relax. The warm air felt amazing, and she peeled off her light jacket and bent down to take off her shoes and socks. She almost laughed when her toes sank into the sand.

"Wow. Just . . . wow," Jane said, coming up behind her. "Can we stay here forever?"

Cedar grinned and followed Eden's footprints along the beach. "It's like we're in another world," she said, and Finn snorted at the irony.

"Brighid does have a flair for the exotic," he said. He took her hand, and together they walked down the beach. She allowed herself to pretend for a moment that everything was normal, that they were just a normal couple walking hand in hand down a pristine white beach, watching their daughter play in the sand. Someday, she thought, this will all be over. She squeezed his hand and looked up to meet his eyes.

"It's almost perfect, isn't it?" he said.

"It is," she said with a smile. "Almost enough to make me forget that we're on the run from an angry horde of druids who want to kill us while we look for a stone that could be anywhere on the planet."

"Yes, there is that . . . ," he said. Then he called out to Eden, and she ran back to join them. "This way, I think," he said, and the rest of the group followed him up a narrow, torch-lined path that led off the beach and over a small incline that was covered with large, leafy trees and a tangle of vines and exotic grasses.

When they emerged on the other side, Cedar couldn't help but break out into a grin. Brighid's "house" was enormous, and built like a modern version of a medieval castle, complete with a moat and drawbridge. But instead of rough bricks and stones, the entire thing was smooth and white, and more than half of the building was paned in sheer glass. Cedar couldn't see any spotlights, but the building was completely lit up, as though glowing from within.

They walked around to what seemed to be the front, where two large white pillars stood, a single sheet of solid glass between them. A silver button started to pulse on one of the white pillars, and Finn walked over and pressed it. A voice came out of thin air. "Come in, please. She is expecting you." Immediately the glass retracted into the ground and a delicate white bridge rose up out of the moat, which was filled with water so smooth it looked like a mirror, perfectly reflecting the moon and stars above it. Cedar joined hands with Eden and Finn, and together they crossed the bridge toward the castle. Felix and Jane followed, and Liam walked a pace or two behind them. The massive front doors, made entirely of glass, swung open to admit them. Then they heard her.

"My dears!" Brighid said, holding out her arms as she descended a large, curving white staircase, dressed in a flowing white pantsuit. She looked as though she would have been equally at home in the yoga studio and at an evening ball. Her hair was loose and cascading around her shoulders, softening the striking features of her face. They waited for her at the bottom. Cedar glanced over at Finn, who nudged Felix forward with his shoulder, an amused grin on his face.

"Well, look at you, Toirdhealbhach," Brighid exclaimed, reaching for Felix first. "Aren't you a sight for sore eyes?" She cupped his face in her hands and kissed him enthusiastically on both cheeks. "You are *very* welcome in my home," she said, with a look that clearly said he'd be very welcome in her bed as well. Cedar heard a soft huff from Jane behind her.

Brighid didn't notice, because now she was oohing and aahing over Finn and how dreadful his fight with Lorcan must have been and was he absolutely sure he didn't need to stay with her for a while to recover? Finn demurred politely and brought Eden forward. "I don't know if you remember meeting her," he said. "But this is our daughter, Eden."

To Cedar's surprise, Brighid's face softened and she knelt down so that she was at Eden's level. She shook Eden's hand softly. "It's a pleasure to meet you, Eden," she said. "I understand that we've met before. I'm sorry to say I do not remember it."

Eden smiled and said, "It's okay. Nuala does that to people. I like your house."

Brighid stood up and beamed. "Why, aren't you sweet? It's my own private retreat, although I'm always thrilled to have guests, of course. And now tell me about these humans you brought with you," she said.

"This is my friend Jane," Cedar said. Brighid looked Jane up and down, her dark eyebrows raised in question.

"I was in a fire," Jane said. "Felix healed me. Couldn't do any-thing about the clothes or the hair, though."

"Did he now?" Brighid gave Felix an admiring look. "Well done, darling." Then she turned back to Jane. "We'll get you all fixed up, don't you worry," she said. "And you've brought a druid, I see."

Liam stepped forward and bowed slightly. "This is our new friend Liam," Cedar said.

"Mmm," Brighid said, running her eyes over Liam. "Well, they're dead useful to have around, that's for sure. I had one for ages and ages, but then he went and died, which I suppose they all do, eventually. I meant to get a new one but then decided I pre-ferred to travel alone. Still, good for you for acquiring one so soon. You didn't waste any time after finding out who you really were, did you, Cedar?"

Cedar gaped at her. "He's our friend, not our servant!" she said, indignant.

"Really? How interesting," Brighid said in a tone that indi-cated she was already bored of the subject. "Well, let's not stand here in the foyer gabbing. Come in, come in, humans, gods, and druids, all." She turned and swooped out of the room and onto an expansive balcony that overlooked the ocean.

"We came to ask—" Cedar began, following her onto the balcony.

"For my help, I know," Brighid said. "No one ever comes to see me just for the company. But that can wait. Look at yourself, dear. Your friend Jane isn't the only one who has seen better days. I've instructed my people to prepare baths for you, and some light re-freshments. Then you will rest, then we will feast, and *then* you will tell me about all of your troubles. I insist."

"Thank you, but we really don't have time," Cedar said.

"There is always enough time, darling," Brighid said dismis-sively. "Now off you go, ladies. Vanessa will show you the way." She pointed to a tall, muscular woman who was wearing a dress of soft white leather that barely came down to her upper thighs. She was standing so perfectly still that Cedar hadn't even noticed her when they'd come out onto the balcony. "And gentlemen, follow me, if you please," Brighid said. "Your druid may come as well, if you wish."

Finn gave Cedar a small smile. "It won't take long," he said, leaning down to whisper in her ear. "And if we accept her hospitality, she'll be in a much better mood. Besides," he said with a sniff, "you do need a bath." She rolled her eyes and swatted him away.

"Be good!" Brighid said with a wink, then Cedar, Jane, and Eden turned to follow Vanessa, who led them back through the expansive foyer down a narrow hallway lined with erotic black-and-white photographs of the naked human form. At the end of the hallway she opened a door, and stepped back so that they could enter. It was, without a doubt, the most incredible spa Cedar had ever seen.

"Oh wow," Jane breathed. Vanessa, who had yet to speak, closed the door behind them, leaving them alone.

How many worlds will we enter here? Cedar wondered. It was as if they'd entered a secret glade hidden deep within the rain forest. The ground beneath their feet was the softest moss, cool and refreshing. Sunshine glimmered like liquid diamonds through the glass ceiling, which was hung with vines and huge bright pink flowers. Steam rose from a half dozen pools, and an intoxicating scent of something less tangible than any one spice or perfume filled the air. Peace, maybe, or laughter. They walked around the room, trying to take it all in. A waterfall flowed out of a wall of glittering rocks and into a large pool. One wall was lined with rows of thick robes and towels and several shelves of delicate glass bottles filled with different soaps and lotions.

"Can I go in, Mummy?" Eden asked, pointing to one of the small pools near the lotions.

"Of course," Cedar said. They stripped off their clothes and gently submerged themselves in the warm water.

"Oooooh, it smells like bubble gum!" Eden exclaimed. Small pink bubbles began to form on the surface of the water all around her, and she laughed in delight.

"Really?" Cedar said. "I smell mint, and . . . rosemary." The water around her was a dark green, and she could feel her skin tingling with pleasure. She leaned closer to Eden, but still couldn't smell the bubble gum.

"I know!" Eden said. "I bet it smells different to each person!"

Cedar nodded. "I think you're probably right," she said. "Hey, Jane, come over here and tell us what you smell." Jane was still standing by the rows of bottles, examining the labels. She knelt down and ran her hand through the water in the pool where Cedar and Eden were bathing.

"I smell . . . patchouli," she said. "Mmm. I'm going to try one of these other pools, and some of these bottles." She grabbed an armful of bottles off the shelf and eased herself into a pool that was completely surrounded by magnolia trees in full bloom.

Cedar watched as Eden gathered handfuls of bubbles and threw them into the air. They floated down slowly, some landing on her head and one on her nose. Feeling a sudden rush of affection, Cedar reached over and pulled her close. "Mum, you're squishing my bubbles," Eden said. Cedar laughed and released her. "Sorry, baby. I just needed to hug you. Are you doing okay? You know, with everything that's going on? You're being so brave."

Eden nodded and pushed a pink bubble around the surface of the water with her finger. "Yeah," she answered. "Sometimes I get scared, but . . . well, don't laugh. I feel like I have a friend living inside me. It's kind of like she *is* me, but she's older, and she's not scared of anything."

Cedar remembered the older Eden who saved her life in the dream with Nuala. "I'm glad you have her," she said. "I think . . . I think she *is* you, or the woman who you'll become. But it's okay to be scared. I'm scared too sometimes. We just have to keep going. It's good that we have people who can help us—on the inside and on the outside."

Eden nodded. "I'm so glad we found Daddy," she said.

"Me too," Cedar said with a smile, stroking Eden's hair.

Eden squirmed and said, "Can we try some of the other pools?" They climbed out and wrapped themselves in thick, fluffy robes that warmed at their touch. They slipped their hands into the water of several of the other pools, and settled on one that smelled like freshly baked cinnamon rolls to Eden and vanilla and honey to Cedar. Once they were in the water, thick foam began to form over their skin, and bubbles appeared in their hair. Eden squealed, "I think it's telling us we need to wash our hair!" and reached up to scrub her scalp. Once they were clean, the bubbles melted away and the water became clear again. After a while Eden inspected her fingers. "I'm turning into a raisin." She scampered out of the water.

"Mmm?" Cedar mumbled. She had almost fallen asleep in the warm, soothing water. She looked around for Eden, who had pulled on her robe and was eating small orange fruits out of a glass bowl. Cedar got out too and noticed for the first time that there was a long white table in the corner of the room, about waist-high and contoured like a massage table. She wrapped her robe around her body and climbed onto it, wondering if it would magically ease the remaining knots in her muscles. The bed was warm and welcoming, and it seemed to shift slightly to accommodate her. Then she felt hands on her back and lifted her head to see who it was. Vanessa had reappeared, seemingly out of nowhere, and started to knead the muscles between her shoulder blades. She sighed and relaxed, making a mental note to thank Brighid for insisting they come down here. In fact, she was having a hard time remembering why she'd objected to the idea in the first place.

The next thing she knew, someone was calling her name. She looked around, disoriented, and realized that she was in a large bed, the glow of a nearby lamp glinting off the white sheets. She was dressed in a soft white T-shirt and lounge pants. Eden was sleeping beside her, her brown hair spread across the pillow, smelling of bubble gum and cinnamon.

Jane stood at the foot of the bed, grinning.

"You have hair!" Cedar said.

"Yep. One of those bottles was labeled 'hair renewal,' so I dumped the whole thing into one of those pools and came out with this." Jane reached up and ran her hand through a short pixie cut of dark blonde hair. Her eyebrows and eyelashes had grown in too.

"So that's what your natural hair color is," Cedar said with a laugh. "But how did I get here?"

"You fell asleep on the massage table," Jane answered. "Vanessa carried you over here and put pajamas on you. That girl is strong! Then Eden crawled in next to you and was asleep in about two seconds. How do you feel?"

"Amazing," Cedar said. "But how long was I asleep?" She suddenly remembered the reason for their visit to Brighid and kicked herself for giving in to distraction.

Jane shrugged. "A few hours, at least. I slept too. Should we go find the boys?"

Cedar swung her legs off the bed. "Yes." She paused. "I'd like to let Eden keep sleeping, but I don't want to leave her here alone."

"We won't be far; I think they're just through that door," Jane said, pointing to a large sliding door a few feet away. "Listen, you can hear their voices."

Jane was right; she could hear the deep timbre of male voices and a feminine voice that could only belong to Brighid.

"Where'd you get those clothes?" she asked, noticing for the first time that Jane was dressed in a red sundress. It was a drastic change from the ripped jeans and black T-shirts she usually wore, but Cedar had to admit it looked great on her.

"Oh, this?" Jane said, looking down at the shiny silver belt and pleated skirt. "It was on the foot of my bed when I woke up. I figured it was better than putting back on Logheryman's old robe. I feel kind of girly, though. Look, you've got one too." On a chair near Cedar's bed was a pale yellow sundress with a wide blue belt. She changed into it, and was delighted to find that it fit her perfectly, as did the delicate white sandals sitting beside the chair.

"What happened to my old clothes?" Cedar asked.

Jane shrugged again. "Dunno. Brighid probably tossed them." She hesitated for a moment, then, glancing at the sliding door, asked, "Do you think I look weird? You know, with the hair and this dress?"

Cedar smiled. Leave it to Jane to be cool as a cucumber when she was bald and wearing an old robe and to be self-conscious about looking fresh and pretty. "You look fabulous," Cedar told her. "I'm sure he'll think so too," she added with a wink.

Jane scowled at her. "That's not what I meant," she said, but she straightened her dress and ran her hands through her hair again. Cedar smiled broadly and pushed a button beside the sliding door.

As Jane had said, the others were gathered just outside the door, on a sprawling balcony that overlooked the strange, mountain-like forms rising out of the ocean. Finn and Felix were sitting on either side of Brighid, leaning in to her and speaking in soft voices. Liam stood off to one side, looking out over the ocean as the moon rose in the sky, his brow creased and his hands clenched on the railing. They were all dressed in new, clean clothes, and were sipping a pale peach drink from crystal goblets. Several tables on the deck were laden with trays of food, and Cedar's stomach rumbled loudly. It felt like a long time since she'd had tea and a cookie back at Maggie's house.

"Well, *there* you are!" Brighid exclaimed, rising to her feet. "We thought you were going to sleep all night. Did you enjoy the spa?"

"Yes, thank you," Cedar answered politely. "But now we—"

"Don't they look lovely?" Brighid asked Finn and Felix, waving her arms at Jane and Cedar's dresses. "They clean up rather well, if I do say so myself. Come, eat and drink with us. We were just getting started."

"Thank you, but we really should be going soon," Cedar said with a pointed look at Finn. Felix was watching Jane with a bemused expression on his face. Blushing, she started to load a plate with braised lamb.

"Yes, yes, I know all about your little adventure," Brighid said. "Fionnbharr has been telling me all about it. I remember the Lia Fáil well, of course. It's about this size," she said, holding out her arms to measure out about two feet. "Or at least it was, before Cúchulainn smashed it into two in one of his fits. He was always so temperamental, that one. Anyway, I really don't know why they want it back so bad. It probably doesn't even work the way it used to anymore. As you sure you really need to find it?"

"Yes," Cedar said emphatically. "If we don't, Nuala will become queen and start another world war here on Earth. We *have* to find the stone."

"Well, if you must, I wish you luck," Brighid said. "But I'm afraid there's really nothing I can do to help you. I have no idea where it is now, and I'm not about to go traipsing around Ireland with you on some hero's quest."

"Don't you care about what happens to the world?"

"Oh, I'm sure it's not as bad as you think, dear," Brighid answered. "My people are always wrapped up in some drama or another, and it usually comes to naught. I told myself a long time ago that I was done getting involved in their affairs. No, no, I appreciate your visit, of course, but this is something that doesn't really concern me anymore."

Cedar stared at Brighid incredulously, feeling a burning in the pit of her stomach. They had wasted almost an entire day here in the hopes that Brighid would either know where the Lia Fáil was or help them deal with Nuala's army of druids. Now it seemed as though all they were going to get for their troubles was a nap and a polite dismissal.

"Fine," Cedar snapped. "We'll do it ourselves. We might get killed, but at least *we* will have tried."

"Oh, come now, don't be like that," Brighid said, raising an eyebrow. "You won't be leaving empty-handed. I've been working on a little something since my last unfortunate run-in with my own kind—not you, of course," she said, tossing her lustrous waves of hair in Finn's direction.

She walked over to a small pedestal that stood on the corner of the balcony. On it was a small crystal bottle the shape of a teardrop. Brighid picked it up and handed it to Cedar. "I think you'll find this very useful."

Cedar fingered the delicate bottle. "What is it?" she asked.

Brighid regarded her carefully. "Fionnghuala, or Nuala as you call her, is the great-great-grandniece of a friend of mine, who also had this strange ability of persuasion. We were quite close, for a while, until she went mad and killed herself. Her power was very great—greater than Nuala's, I'd say—and when she was young, she would play cruel jokes on those she called friends, revealing their deepest secrets and forcing them to act against their will. It was foolish of her, of course, and when she grew older she regretted all the pain she had caused. But by then it was too late. She was shunned by almost everyone. I was one of her only friends. I believed her repentance was sincere and—to my knowledge—she had never used her ability to cause me harm. When I decided to leave Tír na nÓg and settle on Ériu for good, I may have been the only friend she had left. I heard years later that she had killed herself—whether out of remorse or loneliness I do not know. But there is no doubt that her ability was more curse than gift. Only a handful have possessed it, and almost all of them met with some sort of tragic end. Nuala's own mother, who also had the gift, was killed by Nuala's father."

Cedar felt an unexpected stirring of sympathy for Nuala. Riona had once told her that she would never wish Nuala's gift on anyone, and Cedar could understand why. But she was still the enemy, and they still needed to defeat her. "So what's in this bottle?" she asked.

"Before she killed herself, my friend put a great deal of effort into trying to overcome her ability, or negate it somehow. And in a way, she succeeded. She created a potion that would make others immune to her ability for a short while. It worked—she tested it on me, and was unable to persuade me of anything after I had consumed only a drop. Unfortunately, it was very difficult to create, and she couldn't exactly dump it into the drinking water, so to speak, so it didn't help her as much as she had hoped in the end. But that is what I have been working on. My memories are not as crystal clear as they used to be—this was more than a thousand years ago—but I have tried to re-create this potion to the best of my ability. I believe I have succeeded. I have made enough so that I will be invulnerable to Nuala's power should she come calling anytime in the next few hundred years—just like Finn and Eden are naturally. This bottle should be more than enough for you all. A single drop is all you need."

Cedar clutched the bottle tightly in her hand. "Thank you," she said. She still wished Brighid would come with them, but at least this was something that would be useful *if* they made it back to Tír na nÓg. She turned to go, but Brighid spoke again.

"And I happen to know someone who might help you with your quest. He hates druids more than anyone, and he's very powerful. They would think twice before attacking you if he was part of your company. Personally, I'm sure Fionnbharr and Toirdhealbhach are all the protection you need. But, since you seem to think otherwise, you might want to enlist his help. And besides . . . if you wake him, he should be able to lead you directly to the Lia Fáil."

This made Cedar stop in her tracks. She whirled around to face Brighid. "Who is he?" she asked.

"His name is Abhartach," Brighid said.

The reaction was immediate. Finn and Felix both sprang to their feet with cries of protest. Liam, who had been staring out at the ocean, spun around so quickly he almost lost his balance. A look of horror marred his face, as though Brighid had suggested waking the devil.

"Brid, you've got to be kidding," Finn said.

"Oh, come now," Brighid said, a pout playing on her lips. "Surely you are not afraid of a mortal being."

"That's the problem," Felix said, his voice laced with disgust. "He *isn't* mortal, but he should be. We should leave him buried in the ground where he belongs."

"You don't believe those silly stories about him, do you? He was a great magician, that's all. No different from your kind, Liam."

"He is nothing like my kind," Liam snapped. Cedar looked at the men in the room in confusion. Who *was* this Abhartach?

Brighid waved her hand lazily in the air. "What, pray tell, is the difference?"

"Abhartach is a demon," Liam spit out. "He has used some sort of evil sorcery to give himself power."

"Some might say that the power of the druids is not altogether . . . natural," Brighid pointed out.

"Um, can I interrupt here? For those of us who aren't a billion years old, who the hell is Abhartach?" Jane asked.

Finn answered. "Abhartach was a chieftain in Ireland many years ago. The stories say he was not kind to his people."

"A gross understatement," Liam muttered.

Finn shot him a silencing look, then continued. "So the people persuaded another chieftain to come and kill him, because they were too afraid to do so themselves. The chieftain slew Abhartach and buried him upright in the ground, as was the custom for Gaelic nobility."

"How's he going to help us if he's dead?" Jane asked.

"He's not dead," Felix answered. "Or at least, not completely."

"The story goes that the next day the people saw Abhartach walking around, alive again, and, well . . ." Finn trailed off.

"Demanding sacrifices of blood to keep himself alive," Liam supplied. "The people were terrified, naturally, and let him drink their blood lest he kill them with dark magic. The neighboring chieftain slew him again, with the same result. Finally, the chieftain had the sense to consult with a druid about what could be done. The druid, by his craft, determined that Abhartach could not be truly killed because he was one of the undead, a neamh-mairbh. But he could be defeated by running him through with a sword made of yew, burying him upside down, raising a dolmen over his grave, and then sprinkling thorns in a circle around the area."

"Did it have to be done at midnight on a full moon with the toenails of a black cat too?" Jane muttered under her breath.

"This is no laughing matter," Felix snapped. "What the druid says is the truth. Or do I need to post it online before you'll believe it?"

Jane flinched. "Forgive me if I find it hard to accept the idea of an Irish vampire-zombie coming out of retirement to help us find . . . well, it's all sounding a little crazy."

"As crazy as a child who can open doors to other worlds?" Felix asked.

"Knock it off, you two," Cedar said sharply before turning back to Liam. "What happened? Did the druid's plan work?"

"We believe so," he answered. "Abhartach has been neither seen nor heard from since."

"Well, it's all nonsense, if you ask me," Brighid said. "Abhartach demanding blood sacrifices and all that. The one thing I know for sure about him is that he's drawn to magic like rain is drawn to the earth."

"He's . . . what?" Cedar asked. The men still looked mutinous, but Cedar was open to anything at this point.

"He has—or had—an uncanny ability to find magic. People, artifacts, whatever. He was famous for it, back in the day. Personally, I think what *really* happened to Abhartach is that certain druids didn't like having someone more powerful than them around," she said with a sly look at Liam.

"That's insane," Liam protested hotly, straightening up and looking Brighid in the eye. "There is a code of honesty and integrity among druids. We would never stoop so low as to destroy a rival magician. Our work and abilities stand for themselves."

"Whatever you say," she said dismissively. "Cedar, darling, you asked for my help, but the choice is yours. Abhartach is one of the most powerful wielders of magic that ever existed. He alone will be able to lead you to the exact location of the stone. The fact that he strikes terror into the heart of the druids can only work to your advantage. If you want to wake him, all you need to do is remove the stones over his grave. They call it Slaghtaverty Dolmen, or, more colloquially, the Giant's Grave, which, as you'll see, is rather ironic. Tell him I sent you. I'm sure he'll remember me."

Cedar turned to Finn and Felix. "What do you think?"

They both looked hesitant. "It's a bit of a wild card," Finn said. "I don't know, Cedar. I think we should take our chances without him. Let's at least go to Tara and check it out."

"We don't have that luxury," she said. "What if the druids attack us while we're wandering around, touching every stone in the place? What if Eden gets locked in her own mind again? It's too much of a risk. They knew where to find us in Scone and Edinburgh, and they'll almost certainly be waiting for us at Tara. I say we go get Abhartach first and *then* go find the Lia Fáil. We'll be quicker *and* stronger with him."

"No," Liam said quietly. He was standing slightly behind them, still near the railing of the balcony.

"Sorry?" Cedar asked.

"I won't do it," he said. "If you insist on this foolhardy plan, you'll have to do it without me. I won't be part of it."

"Liam, this isn't about some old grudge between Abhartach and the druids—it's about stopping Nuala from destroying the world. Look at the bigger picture! If Brighid is right, he can help us."

"No. You don't understand, Cedar—you think that all the magical creatures in the world are as noble as Finn and Felix here. But there are demons like Abhartach who exist only to cause suffering and pain. I know you well enough by now to know I can't stop you from doing what you want. You're too much like Maeve that way. But I won't help you do this, no matter what the reason."

"Mummy?"

Eden was standing by the sliding door, her hair mussed from sleep and her mouth open in a wide yawn. Finn walked over and picked her up, spinning her around. She squealed and clung to him. Cedar turned back to Liam. "Fine," she said, her voice tight. "Where will you go?"

"If Eden could return me to Logheryman's house from here, I'll pick up my car and drive back to the university."

"Of course," Cedar said. She walked over to Eden, who was still in Finn's arms, and said, "I'll explain where we're going next in a minute, but first, can you open a sidh back to Mr. Logheryman's house? Liam is going to go back there instead of coming with us."

"How come?" Eden asked as Finn set her back on the balcony.

Cedar looked at Liam, who was pacing back and forth near the railing. "He has other things he needs to do," she said.

"Okay," Eden said with a shrug, and then she grabbed the sliding door and pulled it open. Through the shimmering air they could see the front of Logheryman's house, and Liam's brown car parked in the driveway. After shaking hands with Felix and Finn, Liam exchanged a long glance with Cedar.

"Will you not rethink this madness?" he asked, his eyes pleading. She shook her head.

"I'm sorry you won't come with us," she said. "But I hope we'll see each other again soon."

"I hope so too," he said with a lingering gaze, before turning and walking through the door. They watched as he got into his car, and then drove out of their line of vision. Eden pulled the door closed.

"Well now!" Brighid exclaimed, clapping her hands together. "I think you made a good decision, Cedar. Druids can be such naysayers at times. They take their jobs *far* too seriously, if you ask me. Toirdhealbhach and I were just reminiscing about—"

"I think I should go, too," Jane interrupted.

"What? Why?" Cedar asked, surprised.

"I want to help, I really do," Jane said. "But honestly, I'm more of a hindrance than anything. I'm just someone else you have to worry about. Look what happened back at the apartment. There's nothing I can do that the rest of you can't. I think it would be better if I just stayed out of the way."

Cedar knelt down beside Jane, who was sitting on one of the lounge chairs with an empty plate in her lap. "You're not in the way, Jane," Cedar said. "If you don't want to come along, I totally understand. It's dangerous, and I should probably be forcing you to stay somewhere safe. But please don't think that you're useless, just because you're not Tuatha Dé Danann. If you look at it that way, I'm useless too. You're smart and encouraging and brave, and if you want to come with us the rest of the way, I'd love that. But it's your call—I'm not going to force you into it."

Jane looked at the ground, silent for a moment. It was Felix who spoke next. "I won't let anything else happen to you, Jane," he said softly. "If you come with us, you will be safe. I promise."

Jane was still looking at the floor, but Cedar could see that her cheeks were beginning to redden. Cedar tried to hide a smile. "Well . . . okay," Jane said. "If you're sure."

Cedar stood. "We're sure." Turning his back to Brighid, Felix reached out his hand to help Jane up. She took it, and didn't let go.

"I suppose you need to know where you're going," Brighid said. She pressed a button on the wall, and a panel slid back to reveal a wide computer screen. "Show us the Slaghtaverty Dolmen."

◦◦◦

Nuala was feeling very pleased with herself. She sat in the drawing room of Councilwoman Sorcha's home, an emerald haven deep in the forest. The walls glittered with lush green leaves studded with jewels, and they drank wine out of delicate crystal goblets. It was an illusion, of course, as were all the places of beauty on Tír na nÓg these days. Outside the glittering walls of her host, Tír na nÓg was as bleak and barren as when Nuala had first arrived with Eden. Nothing had changed since Lorcan's death. Not a single flower had bloomed, nor had the water resumed its path down the mountains. The sky was the same dull, choking gray, and Nuala found herself coughing, something that had previously only happened to her on Ériu. Earlier this evening she had coughed into a white handkerchief that Sorcha had handed her and had been dismayed to see black specks on the previously pristine cloth. It was the same everywhere, Sorcha told her, tossing her thin blonde hair behind her shoulder.

"In some places the trees have turned black, as though they are covered with soot," she told Nuala, leaning forward conspiratorially even though they were only two in the room. "And mothers will not let their children go outside for more than a few minutes, if at all. We are becoming prisoners in our own homes."

"Then the sooner we can go back to Ériu, the better," Nuala said. "Our people will not survive if we stay here, unless the druids come at once and are able to heal the land."

Sorcha nodded enthusiastically. "I've said it before, but in my opinion your return is the best thing that could have happened to us."

Nuala smiled and tried to look modest, but inside she crowed triumphantly. Finn and Cedar had done her an enormous favor by killing Lorcan, and she had wasted no time in taking advantage of it. She had started planning as soon as they'd disappeared back to Ériu. She had spent many years observing the politics and power struggles of her people, and she knew how to play the game. She began revealing herself one by one to the major players—those from the oldest families, those with the most influence, and—most important—those who craved power almost as much as she did. She had told them all the same story, letting them believe that she was confiding in them and them alone.

She told them that Rohan had played a part in King Brogan's death and had lied to cover it up before fleeing to Ériu to escape justice. She fabricated tales of secret meetings with human government officials and how he had allowed his small crew of rebels to reveal themselves to humans and to fraternize freely with them. She told them of the vast numbers of human soldiers and the weapons of mass destruction that even they, the Tuatha Dé Danann, would not be able to fight against. With her every word she had created confusion, suspicion, and fear, while with the same breath fervently declaring that she was—and had always been—thinking only of her people and their land.

Of course, Lorcan had laid much of the groundwork for her with his years of antihuman propaganda. Most of the Danann agreed that Lorcan had been too harsh, but they still regarded humans with resentment and were more than happy to hear of Nuala's experiences among them. Many of them had never met a human, or if they had it had been centuries ago. So they believed her when she described their pettiness, their greed, their corruption. She told them how bloodthirsty humans were and described in detail their willingness to slaughter each other for no reason other than the joy of killing. The humans were weak-minded, she said, but they possessed powerful weapons. Lorcan was wrong to think of engaging them in war. But it was only a matter of time before the humans engaged with the Danann—especially if Rohan and his fellow rebels had their way.

Secretly, Nuala was glad the land had not renewed itself after Lorcan's death, as they'd believed it would. No one was happy living in this desolate wasteland anymore, and they all wanted a reason to leave, to find a land of beauty and warmth to call their own again. Perhaps the druids would be able to help . . . perhaps not. The Tuatha Dé Danann needed Ériu, which meant they needed her. And, remarkably, they trusted her. The long years she had resisted using her ability in Tír na nÓg were paying off. Now, her ability was seen as the very thing that might save their race. Her words and her ideas made sense, so of course they did not suspect her of bewitching them, of reinforcing their fears and hopes and prejudices with subtle suggestions and stories that sounded very much like the truth.

Now that the Council had decided to give Cedar the opportunity to prove herself, Nuala had been forced to turn her ability up a notch. She was certain Cedar would not succeed . . . but she couldn't afford to take any chances. She had started exerting her power more strongly over the members of the Council so that no matter the outcome of Cedar's quest, *she* would be the one in control.

She did her best to appear humble, to flatter those with influence, to listen to their ideas and their complaints, and to make sure they knew that she only wanted to use her ability for the good of her beloved people. She was no threat to anyone; she was just a beautiful woman who offered wisdom, hope, and a peaceful return to the land they had once claimed as their own.

Her promises about the druids were not false. While Rohan and Riona and their friends had tried to blend in with human society, Nuala had used her time on Ériu to find as many of the expelled druids as she could. Rohan had been unaware, and for good reason—he would have expressly forbidden it, out of fear that one of them would report back to Lorcan. But Nuala knew better. The druids hated Lorcan, who viewed all creatures who were not Tuatha Dé Danann as inferior. But she was different. As soon as she realized that humans were not as wonderful as she'd been led to expect, she had started finding and befriending the druids—except for Maeve, the mother of the whelp who had stolen Finn from her. She had long respected—even envied—the power of the druids, and she knew they'd be invaluable allies somedays.

She smiled again at Sorcha and accepted another glass of wine. "I am so glad that you are on the Council," Nuala told her. "I just hate to think of what would happen to our people if sentiment won out over reason."

Sorcha nodded. "I know exactly what you mean," she said. "Brogan was loved by many, and in some ways he was a great king. But in my opinion he was too soft. He cared nothing for the advancement of our people. If he were still king I'm sure he would do nothing to ease our suffering, not if it meant taking up arms against his precious humans."

If he were still king, the land probably wouldn't be suffering, Nuala mused, but she kept that thought to herself. Some blamed Tír na nÓg's decline on Brogan, saying that he was responsible for the land's decay because he'd started the war with Lorcan. Nuala encouraged this belief as much as she could, but it was because it suited her, not because she believed it.

Sorcha leaned forward again. "I heard that Brogan took a human as his lover," she whispered. "And that Cedar is the result of their union, and that she's not Kier's daughter after all. They say that Cedar's real mother killed Kier and her baby so she could pass off her own child as one of us. Of course, others say that she *must* be one of us since she returned to life after Lorcan's death, but I wonder if she was truly dead. Maybe she killed Lorcan by some dark druidic curse she learned from her mother."

Nuala made a noncommittal sound and tried to look concerned. She knew very well that Cedar was indeed the child of Brogan and Kier, but the more confusion and doubt there was about Cedar's parentage, the better. "I wouldn't be surprised, but with both Brogan and Kier dead, it is impossible to know for sure," Nuala said. Cedar's return to life—and to Tír na nÓg—had been unexpected. Cedar had more fire in her than Nuala had realized.

Sorcha was prattling on about how wonderful it would be to have the druids with them once again. Nuala kept silent, resisting the urge to tell Sorcha that she had promised the druids full equality. They would no longer be the servants that Sorcha remembered. But she would deal with that when she was queen. In the meantime, her faithful druids were doing everything they could to make that happen.

CHAPTER 13

"Are you sure this is the right place?" Jane asked. They were standing in the middle of a lush green field. The sun was shining brightly even though it was late afternoon, and the sky was a vast expanse of blue. It was a rare cloudless day in Northern Ireland, and for once the sidh that shimmered in the air behind them didn't seem out of place. Cedar stepped away from it and soaked in the surroundings. A green-gabled farmhouse stood sentry in the distance, and a scattered herd of bulls wandered aimlessly through the surrounding fields. There was no breeze. The world around them was still and quiet, as though they had entered the inner sanctuary of a cathedral.

"I suppose that's it," Cedar said, pointing. In the middle of the field was a solitary hawthorn tree, raising its leafy arms toward the late summer sun. It grew out of a circle of red mud that was exactly the same diameter as the tree above it. No grass grew beneath the tree. In the mud lay the three stones that were called Slaghtaverty Dolmen—or, as Brighid had said, the Giant's Grave. The dolmen was made up of a large stone and two smaller stones. They weren't in any particular order now, but it seemed as though the larger stone had once rested on top of the smaller ones, a mini-Stonehenge in the middle of nowhere. Cedar took a step toward it.

"Be careful, okay?" Jane said, consulting the tablet that Brighid had given her. Her delight at being reunited with technology was palpable. They each carried a small backpack of food and supplies that Brighid had insisted on giving them, and Cedar and Jane had changed out of their sundresses into what Jane called "normal clothes," aka jeans and T-shirts. "It says here that they tried to chop the tree down a few years ago, and all three of the chainsaws broke even though they were brand-new. Oh, gross, one of the saws actually chopped off someone's hand. And later, a researcher came here and almost broke his neck."

Cedar gave Jane an uneasy look and then glanced up at the sky, which was darkening rapidly under a layer of thick clouds that seemed to have sprung up out of nowhere. Finn and Felix also had their eyes trained on the sky, their faces grim. The formerly picturesque setting was growing more ominous by the second. She felt the hair rise on her arms, and wondered if she should send Eden back through the sidh. But when she turned around, it was no longer there. Where once there'd been a doorway back to Brighid's house, there was now only grass, and beyond that, a long fence. "Where'd the sidh go?" she asked.

"Oops," Eden said, looking sheepish. "I kinda closed it. I thought we were always supposed to do that so no one could follow us. Is that bad?"

Cedar's heartbeat quickened slightly. "It's okay," she said, but she didn't like it. Liam's warnings about Abhartach had seemed less threatening back in the opulence of Brighid's sunny home. The silence here was too unnatural, and now they had no sidh to escape through if it turned out that he was right. She glanced at the farmhouse in the distance. Their closest exit wouldn't be close enough if Abhartach chose to attack them.

Cedar started walking toward the tree. Finn was beside her, carrying a spade he had borrowed from Brighid. Eden followed them, flanked by Felix and Jane. The wind had picked up, and it was unusually chilly for late August—Cedar thought she could actually smell winter on the air. She shivered. She was starting to feel strangely unwelcome in this haunted field.

When they reached the tree, they discovered that they were no longer alone. Three bulls had wandered over and were standing on the other side of it, gazing at them with baleful eyes. Two of the bulls were black, and their eyes were as dark as opals. The other was pure white, with no spots or markings anywhere on its expansive hide. Its eyes were a reddish-brown, the color of the mud beneath the tree, and the three of looked at Cedar without blinking.

"Shoo," she said to them, but they just stood there, watching. "Do you think they're dangerous?" she asked Finn.

"Nah, they're just regular bulls," he said. "Felix, give me a hand with these stones, will you?"

As Felix and Finn heaved the stones off the ground and set them outside the dirt circle, Cedar put her hand on the tree's trunk, feeling the rough bark beneath her fingers. Suddenly, she felt a sharp pain lace through her palm. "Ouch!" she cried, yanking her hand away from the tree. Immediately, Finn was at her side, examining the bleeding palm.

"It's like . . . it bit me," she said. Blood seeped out of a jagged wound that ran across her palm like a knife slash. A smear of blood marked the spot where her hand had been resting on the tree. As they watched, it disappeared, seeping into the bark like water poured on a sponge. Cedar clenched the fist tightly.

"Let Felix look at that," Finn said, but Cedar shook her head.

"It's fine," she said. "We can take care of it later."

"You two might want to back up," Felix said. He was standing a few feet away, on the grass where they'd moved the three stones. They hadn't even started to dig beneath the tree yet, but the ground was trembling. She could feel it through the soles of her feet, a deep rumble in the earth that reminded her of the quakes she had occasionally felt while living on the west coast. But she knew this was no earthquake. Tiny pebbles on the ground began to shake, making the ground beneath the tree look like it was vibrating. The bulls snorted and stamped their feet and then turned and stampeded toward the other end of the field. The other bulls who had been grazing nearby followed them, tearing up the ground beneath their hooves as they thundered away.

Cedar and Finn stepped back to join the others, and Cedar held on tight to Eden with her uninjured hand. As they watched, the tree began to sway violently, its branches snapping through the air like a whip. And then, with a sharp crack that rang through the air, it broke in two, as though a giant had snapped it over his knee. The ground stopped shaking, and a swirl of dust arose from the ground—a small, self-contained tornado of red dirt and pebbles. And then, as suddenly as it had started, it was over, and a man stood before them.

Only, he was not quite a man. He stood only a few inches taller than Eden. His beard fell to his knees in a tangle of gray hair and clumps of dirt, with a few bits of tree root sticking out at haphazard angles. He was wearing what appeared to be animal hides, roughly sewn together by thick strands of leather. His skin was the most remarkable thing of all. Through the dirt, Cedar could see that every inch of it was covered in dark markings, like tattoos. They stood there staring at him for a moment, and he at them.

Then he spoke words Cedar did not understand in a deep, grating voice. Felix took at step forward, and addressed the man in the same strange language. "What are they saying?" she whispered to Finn.

"I don't know," he answered. "I haven't learned this language."

They stood still and listened to Felix and the dwarf rally back and forth with their words. They spoke rapidly, and occasionally one of their voices would grow loud and angry. After a few moments they stopped speaking entirely, and stood glaring at each other. Felix was breathing heavily, but the dwarf looked untroubled, though his eyes were dark.

Felix stepped to the side so that he could speak with the others without turning his back on the dwarf. "This is Abhartach," he said. "He is grateful that we have freed him from the curse of the druids."

"Will he help us?" Cedar asked, stepping forward. Felix flung his hand out to stop her.

"Don't get too close," he said. "I told him about Liam's concerns and the stories about his cruelty and his death. He is unimpressed, to say the least. Before he decides whether to help us, he wants to tell you his story, so that the world can know the truth about him."

"Can't it wait?" Cedar asked. "Ask him if he'll come to Tara with us and show us where the Lia Fáil is . . . then we can hear his story."

"Already tried that," Felix said, shaking his head. "He's quite insistent. I had no idea he was a dwarf. They're even more stubborn than you are."

Cedar made a face at him and said, "Okay, fine, let's hear the story. But then we *really* have to go." She looked around nervously, wondering if an army of druids would suddenly appear around them.

Felix said a few words to Abhartach, who was still standing remarkably still. Cedar supposed it was a skill he'd had occasion to learn over the last several centuries. "I'll translate as best as I can," Felix said. Abhartach started speaking in the same strange, guttural language, pausing every few seconds so that Felix could translate.

"I was a simple peddler with a wife and two sons," Felix began. "The dwarves were a proud and ancient race, but we kept to ourselves. Most of them, that is, but not I. Ever since I was a young child I had longed to see other parts of the world. Being a peddler was not the noblest of professions, but I had little skill in craftsmanship, and it allowed me to travel as far as my feet could take me, and to meet other races and beings. I sold fine carvings and tools made by my fellow dwarves, plus whatever interesting trinkets I picked up along the way. Whenever I entered a new village, I always found myself drawn to whatever magic could be found there. Sometimes it was the local druid, sometimes a sacred tree or the place where sacrifices were made. Wherever there was magic,

I would find it. I could go into crowded markets and point out magic wielders or selkies in their human disguise. As I traveled, I could identify the sidhe of the Tuatha Dé Danann in what looked like ordinary hills and trees to other people. I had always been fascinated with magic, but it was rare for a dwarf to have any gifts in that area, and even then it was usually limited to the shaping of stone and wood.

"And so I began testing myself. I found that I had some rudimentary skills, but I needed a teacher. So I approached the chief druid near my home and offered myself as his apprentice. He merely laughed, saying that dwarves did not possess the necessary intelligence and skill to master the druidic arts. But I did not give up. There were many other beings that were skilled in magic, and I was able to find them all. They were not as haughty as the old druid was and were glad to share their knowledge with me. In return, they sent me on quests to find ancient magical artifacts or to determine the best place to perform certain rituals. I traveled far— across the sea and into strange lands—to learn all I could from every creature I could find. Every day, my power grew.

"But it was not enough. I wanted more. I tried various substances to enhance my powers and my affinity with the magical world. Mushrooms, herbs, potions of my own creation . . . human blood."

At this, Felix stopped translating and said a few harsh words to Abhartach, who shrugged and kept talking. When he paused, waiting for his words to be translated, Felix exhaled loudly and then turned back to the others.

"It was remarkable. When I drank human blood I could see the world of magic more clearly than ever, and I could see far—not just with my eyes, but with my mind. Word of my power spread, and magic-seekers began coming from all over the world to learn from me. They would freely offer their blood as payment. In my travels I had acquired a great deal of wealth, and was now chieftain.

I was never cruel, as your druid has said. No people were better protected than mine, as no enemy would dare cross me.

"Now the druid who had rejected me as his apprentice had gone mad with hatred and jealousy. He would watch as the travelers would pass his house to come to mine, for my skills exceeded his in all things. He thought I was a demon and started spreading lies about the origins of my power. Twice he sent a great warrior to kill me, and twice I dispatched the attacker with ease. He would not fight me himself, of course, because he knew he could not overcome me.

"But though I was powerful beyond measure, I had never been permitted to study the druidic arts. Parts of their lore were still a mystery to me. The last person the druid sent to slay me was not a great warrior, nor a powerful magician or rival chieftain. It was my own son, who was still a young man.

"My son believed, as others did, that I was immune to death. He believed it more strongly than most. He was a foolish child, too eager to please others and too proud of our family's high standing. The druid told him that I could be killed with a sword of yew. My son, of course, denied it. He said that there was nothing in this world that could kill his father. And so the druid bet him a very large sum that he was wrong, which my idiot son thought would be an easy way to become rich in his own right. So that night he plunged a simple sword of yew into my heart. The druid was wrong: I did not die. But I was trapped inside my mind, unable to work my body or use any magic. To the world, I appeared dead. I heard my son's wails and my wife's keening. I heard the druid tell the villagers that I would terrify them no longer if only they would do as he commanded. They buried me upside down, because the druid told them that only human chieftains should be buried in the traditional way, standing up straight and proud. He said I was an evil spirit and that the only way to keep me from haunting them was to sprinkle thorns around the grave and to raise a dolmen over my feet. But I have been alive these many years, waiting for someone to free me from my prison at long last."

When Felix stopped speaking, there was silence. Finally, Cedar spoke. "Please tell him that we are grateful for his story and that we will do what we can to redeem his name among the Tuatha Dé Danann and among the other magical beings of the world." She waited as Felix translated this for Abhartach, who nodded gravely. "Have you told him why we need his help?" she asked.

"Yes," Felix said. "I will ask him if he has decided."

Cedar squeezed Eden's hand while they listened to Felix and Abhartach converse. She knelt down to her daughter's level. "There, now you can say that you've seen a real live dwarf," she said softly.

Eden smiled. "I didn't think he'd be so dirty." Cedar laughed, but the smile slid off her face when she took note of Felix's stormy expression.

"He says we ask too much," Felix said. "He has been in the ground for more than fifteen hundred years and has no desire to return there. He will exact his revenge on the druids, but not in open combat."

Cedar stared at him incredulously. "But we freed him!" she said. "And he won't help us?" Her face was flushed, and she glared at the dwarf, who stood there impassively.

Felix held up a hand. "He won't come with us to retrieve the stone," he said. "He says he's not at his full strength, obviously, and he fears that he might not be able to defeat an army of druids. But he *will* help us find the stone."

"How?" Cedar asked. "How can he do that if he won't come with us?"

Felix rubbed the back of his neck. He was staring at the ground, silent. Then he looked directly at Jane. "You heard the story," he said softly. "He needs blood. Human blood."

All eyes were now on Jane, whose face had gone ashen.

"No!" Cedar said quickly. "I'm human, he can use me."

Felix shook his head. "It is Danann blood that runs through your veins. Jane is the only true human among us."

Jane stepped forward. Her chin was held high, but she couldn't disguise her trembling. "Okay," she said. "It's okay." She grabbed Cedar's hands tightly, trying to force a smile.

"Jane, no," Cedar said. "I won't let you. There's got to be another way."

Jane shook her head. "But there isn't, is there?" she said. "This is so much bigger than any of us. It's *my* world that's in danger, and I'm glad I can finally do something to help." She looked at Felix. "Does he need . . . all of my blood?" she asked.

Felix translated her question to Abhartach, who answered in a couple of terse sentences.

"He says he can tell you are very dear to us and that he'll try to take only what he needs. He says . . . there is a risk, but he cannot see the stone without the blood."

Jane took a deep breath and squeezed Cedar's hands again. "I haven't talked to my mum in ages," she said. "If it . . . doesn't go well, tell her . . . tell her I ran off with some nice guy and that I'm very happy," she said with a teary smile. "Nah, don't tell her that, she won't believe you. Just make something up. But tell her I love her."

"No, you're going to be fine. She's going to be fine, right?" Cedar looked imploringly at Felix.

"Yes," Felix said, his face like stone. "I'll make sure she is."

"So, how do we do this?" Jane asked. Felix held her gaze for several heartbeats before turning back to Abhartach.

"He says a bowl and a knife is the traditional way. In my opinion, it's also the safest. I say that we go up to that farmhouse and see if we can't find the proper supplies there. Then we can open a sidh to get the hell out of here once he tells us where the stone is."

Finn nodded. "We'll have to go to the farmhouse to make a sidh anyway," he said. "Let's go." Cedar grabbed Eden's hand and started walking, but stopped when she heard Abhartach's angry voice behind her. "What is it?" she asked Felix, who looked grim.

"He thinks we'll try to escape," he said.

"Why would we do that? We need his help," she said.

"He wants to do it here," Felix said. "He says he is too weak."

"Fine," Jane said in a loud, clear voice. "Let's do it here. Finn, can't you transform into a scalpel or something?"

He shook his head. "No, but . . ."

"One of the big cats should work," Felix interrupted. He sat Jane down on the grass and held out her arm. "Just make it as clean as you can." He beckoned for Abhartach to come closer, and spoke to him quietly. "I've told him that I will control the flow of the blood, and that he may collect it in his hands and drink from there. Under no circumstances is he allowed to drink directly from your body. I want you to tell me if you are feeling weak or light-headed."

Finn frowned in concentration for a moment, and then Eden squealed. "Watson!" she cried. A housecat that was identical to her neighbor's pet climbed up onto Jane's lap, and Jane stroked it, laughing.

Felix smiled. "I told you one of the *big* cats," he said, flicking one of the cat's pointed ears. "But this will do. Give me a claw."

Finn obliged, holding out his paw and extending his claws. Felix told Jane to relax and then deftly swept the claw in a small, neat line up her forearm. Cedar turned Eden toward her and hugged her close. Immediately, bright red blood began running down Jane's arm and dripping off her wrist. Abhartach, who was kneeling beside her, held out his muddy hands to catch the drips then lapped at them like a dog.

"Never fancied myself a cutter before," Jane said, smiling weakly. The cat gave her one last purr and licked her arm, then jumped down onto the grass and transformed back into Finn. Cedar reached out to him, and he put his arms around her.

"This isn't right," Cedar whispered, her voice muffled by his chest. "I should be the one doing this, not Jane."

"You don't always have to be the one making the sacrifices," he told her. "We all want to see Nuala defeated. You were the only one who could destroy Lorcan . . . and Jane is the only one who can help us here. She's going to be fine. And I think she'll be more than fine if Felix has anything to say about it."

Cedar grinned despite her worry. "They seem like such an odd couple . . . but perfect for each other at the same time. Do you think they'll stop fighting for long enough to see it?"

"I think they already see it . . . and it scares the hell out of both of them," he answered.

"Interesting choice of cat," Cedar said. "And it made me think: When I first found out that Eden was missing, Watson stayed with me for the whole night. It was so strange; usually he doesn't visit for more than a few minutes. Was it you?"

Finn shook his head. "No, I was still on my way back to Halifax," he said. "But it wasn't Watson. It was my mother. She told me about it later. She was worried that you'd be angry because she had invaded your privacy, but she couldn't bear the thought of you spending that night all alone."

Cedar was speechless for a few heartbeats. She remembered that horrible night and how much comfort that small bundle of fur had brought her. She felt her eyes well up at the memory. "I'm not angry at all," she said. "It was very thoughtful of her. She hardly knew me at the time."

Just then a roar of rage from Felix brought them back to the present. Abhartach was no longer lapping up Jane's blood from his hands—he had his mouth firmly planted against the open wound on her arm. Felix had grabbed him and tried to tear him off, but he stopped at Jane's wail of pain. "You're ripping my arm off!" she screamed.

"He's going to drain her!" Felix yelled. "Finn, help me!"

"Stay back!" Finn yelled at Cedar and Eden as he ran forward. Felix was saying something in the dwarf's language, but Abhartach seemed oblivious to everything but Jane's forearm. Felix held Jane's body down while Finn tried to loosen the dwarf's grip, but after a moment he fell back, panting.

"I can't loosen it," he said. "I've never seen such a strong hold."

Jane was lying limp on the grass, her eyelids fluttering. She was quickly losing color.

"He's using some sort of magic," Felix said. "Damn it, where is that druid when we need him?"

Finn looked around frantically. "I need a yew tree . . . he said that's what killed him."

"Just knock his head off!" Felix yelled.

"Right," Finn said, and Cedar held Eden close as he transformed into his dragon form and let out a great roar. He took one lunge toward Abhartach, his jaws opening wide to reveal rows of sharp teeth the length of Cedar's forearm. But before he could close them around Abhartach's head, the dwarf finally lifted his mouth from Jane and flung out one hand. Finn froze, immediately immobilized.

Felix immediately gathered Jane into his arms and pressed his lips to her forehead. "She's still alive," he said to Cedar, and then said some things to Abhartach that required no translation. The dwarf raised his bushy eyebrows and said something back.

"What's he saying?" Cedar asked. She was pressing Eden's face into her stomach so that she wouldn't be able to take in the gruesome scene. Abhartach's beard was rust-colored with Jane's blood, and Jane was as white as a corpse. Eden squirmed and tried to break free. "Mum, I can't breathe," she said. Cedar loosened her grip but didn't let go.

"He says it was taking too long. And that you should call off your dragon. Then he will tell us where the Lia Fáil is," Felix said.

He pressed his forehead to Jane's and started singing softly, so low Cedar could barely hear him.

"Finn," Cedar said softly, "Don't attack him."

Abhartach nodded at her, then waved his hand again. The dragon gave one last snort, and then Finn was beside her, glaring at the dwarf with undisguised venom.

"Mummy?" Eden asked. "What's happening?"

"The dwarf took too much of Jane's blood," Cedar explained. "But Felix thinks she'll be okay . . . right?" She looked at Felix and breathed out a sigh of relief when he nodded, though he didn't take his eyes off Jane. He pulled a roll of white cloth out of one of the backpacks and wrapped it around Jane's arm, then opened a jar of herbs and placed a small gray leaf on her tongue. "Tell him he got what he wanted," Cedar told Felix. "Where is the Lia Fáil?"

Felix translated, and Abhartach walked a few paces away and then sat down. He put his hands on the ground and closed his eyes, breathing steadily and deeply.

After several minutes, Abhartach opened his eyes and stood. He spoke to Felix, and then, without another word, spun around once and disappeared.

"Did he tell you?" Cedar demanded.

Felix nodded. "Maggie was right. It *is* in Tara . . . inside the Mound of Hostages."

❦

"I'm fine . . . ," Jane mumbled as Felix carried her up the hill toward the farmhouse. "Want to go with you . . ."

"Absolutely not," he answered firmly.

"Jane, you can't even walk," Cedar said.

Jane opened her eyes and gave Felix a look that was probably intended to be flirty. She was so weak it looked more like she was drunk. "Aren't you going to fix me again?" she said.

Felix grinned down at her. "Most definitely," he said. "I just need to make a list of all the things that are wrong with you. Your taste in music, for example. And the fact that you watch *Doctor Who.*"

Jane tried to laugh, but it came out as a snort. Felix hoisted her more securely in his arms and said, "I've already fixed you; your body just needs to regain some energy. But I think we're done taking chances with you. Brighid is an excellent healer. She'll watch over you while you finish recovering and try to keep you out of trouble—if she can."

Cedar looked at him sharply. "She's a healer? I didn't know that."

He nodded. "There's not a whole lot Brighid can't do. She's not limited to one or two specific abilities like the rest of us. Music, poetry, healing, growing things . . . you name it, and she's mastered it."

"Yeah, but can she turn into a dragon and a housecat on the same day?" Finn asked. He was walking beside them, Eden riding happily on his back.

"You've got her beat there," Felix laughed.

"Listen, I've been thinking," Cedar said, examining the bandage Felix had wrapped around her injured hand. He had healed the wound with a few words but Finn had insisted she wrap it up for good measure. "Brighid's place is probably the safest place we're going to find. I definitely think Jane should go back to Brighid, but I also think Eden should go there too. She can open the sidh to Tara from there."

"Mummy, no . . . ," Eden started complaining. "I want to be with you and Daddy."

"It's too dangerous, baby," Cedar said. "I wish you could stay with us too, but I think you'll be safest with Brighid and Jane. I should have made you stay there in the first place."

They had reached the farmhouse, and Finn motioned for them to be quiet as he slipped Eden off his back and crept toward a small shed with her. There was a padlock on it, but Finn snapped it off easily with one hand. "Back to Brighid's, okay?" he whispered to Eden. "Let's go straight inside, to the foyer with the big staircase." Eden nodded and pulled open the door. But instead of Brighid's imposing entryway, all they saw was the inside of the shed, complete with a few shovels, an empty barrel, and a rusty lawnmower. Cedar frowned.

"Why didn't it work?" she asked.

"I forgot. Brighid has protections on her place that make it impossible to create a sidh into the house." He reached out and closed the door, looking over his shoulder to make sure they were still alone. "Let's try it again; the beach this time." Eden opened the door again, and again they all stared into the musty darkness of the shed. Cedar looked around nervously.

"I don't like this," she said. Finn pulled a phone out of the backpack Cedar was wearing and dialed a number. Then he shook his head and hung up.

"If she's there, she's not answering," he said. "It might be nothing. Maybe she just decided to increase her security after we left. She might be worried that the druids will come looking for us. Or . . . maybe she's just in the shower. Brighid is impossible to predict."

"But she must have known that there was a chance that we'd need to come back!" Cedar exclaimed.

"Maybe," he said, but he looked uncertain. "But one of the reasons she's survived this long is that she always puts her own needs first." He looked sadly at Cedar. "I don't like it either. But there's nothing we can do right now if the sidh won't open. We have no choice but to go on to Tara. All of us."

Cedar took a deep breath and tried to calm the panic that licked at the edge of her nerves like a flame. "Okay," she said. "Eden, stay close to Daddy. Remember the spot we looked at—the one with the big ditch."

They had looked at photos of Tara at Brighid's house while they had access to her several large computer screens. Finn had pointed out a secluded area on the south end of the expansive hill where they could appear without attracting attention from any tourists visiting the ancient site.

When Eden pulled the door open this time, they were greeted by the telltale shimmering air of a sidh. "Cool!" she said, taking a big step toward the sidh before Finn grabbed her, yanking her back to his side.

"Wait," he said sternly. "I'll go through first."

He walked through the doorway. Cedar watched him as he looked around furtively and then turned and beckoned for the rest of them to follow. As she walked through the sidh, Eden's hand clasped tightly in hers, Cedar could hear Jane mumbling, "You can put me down. . . ." But Felix held her tightly to him as he followed them.

They were standing in a deep ditch in a wide, open field. The ground beneath Cedar's feet was covered in thin, scraggly grass. It was slightly muddy, as though it had just rained. "This part of Tara is called Rath Laoghaire," Felix told them as they climbed up the steep embankment. He set Jane down but kept an arm protectively around her waist. "King Laoghaire was the High King of Ireland who was converted to Christianity by Saint Patrick. They say the king is buried here." He snorted. "I never liked Patrick much, though some of the monks were all right."

"Jesus, Felix, how old *are* you?" Jane sputtered.

"Older than Jesus," he said with a smile. "What, you think I should act my age?"

"Ugh. No, thanks. You're fine just the way you are," Jane said quickly.

They had reached the top of the embankment, and Cedar gazed around them in open wonder. Finn hadn't been exaggerating when he'd said Tara was huge. The hilltop seemed to go on forever, a vast expanse of green rippled with deep furrows that she knew looked like giant rings from the air. She turned slowly in a circle, taking in the view. The sun was hanging low in the sky, and the few trees on the hilltop cast long shadows that lent an eerie feel to the ancient hilltop. Around them, the Irish countryside opened up for miles and miles, hills and valleys and forests and church spires decorating the landscape as far as she could see. Finn followed her gaze. "They say you can see almost a third of the island from here on a clear day," he said. "It's no wonder this site was the seat of the High King."

"Sheep!" Eden yelled, the strong wind whipping her hair in her face. A flock of sheep were grazing on the other side of the embankment they had just climbed. Eden started to run toward them, but Finn reached out and caught her arm.

"You have to stay close," he warned her. Cedar shook herself. This wasn't the time to be taking in the view—the druids could be upon them at any moment.

"Where's the Mound of Hostages?" she asked.

"That way," Finn answered, pointing to the north. They pulled their jackets close against the wind and headed in that direction.

"Is that the fake Lia Fáil you mentioned?" Cedar asked, indicating a large phallic-shaped standing stone on top of a mound in the distance.

"It is," Finn answered, though he was only half paying attention to her. His gaze was sharp as he constantly swept the area around them with his eyes. "The Mound of Hostages is just beyond it."

"Mum, I just stepped in sheep poo," Eden complained, trying to wriggle her hand out of Cedar's grasp.

"Shh, baby, we're almost there," Cedar said in what she hoped was a soothing voice even as she tightened her grip. They had yet to see anyone else on the hill, which struck Cedar as odd. A chill ran up her spine that had nothing to do with the biting wind. "Isn't Tara kind of a tourist attraction?" she asked. "I'm just surprised we seem to be the only ones around."

"Well, it *is* getting close to dark," Jane said hesitantly.

"Cedar's right," Felix said, frowning. "It shouldn't be this empty. I don't like it." They were nearing the deep ditches that ringed the large standing stone Cedar had seen in the distance.

Eden wrenched her hand from Cedar's and sprinted down into the ditch and then up on the other side, whooping triumphantly when she reached the top. Puffing with the effort, Cedar caught up with her. She was about to start reprimanding her daughter when she noticed Finn suddenly stand up stock straight, the muscles in his neck straining.

"What is it?" she asked, alarmed. Felix, too, was standing so still it looked as though he had stopped breathing.

"It's calling to me," Finn said in a hushed voice.

Cedar moved so that she was standing right in front of him. His head was turned toward the west; his eyes fixated on a small copse of trees a couple hundred yards away. Cedar strained her eyes to see what he was looking at. One of the trees appeared to be covered in thin strips of colorful cloth tied to its branches. The colors were dancing with the leaves in the wind. It was beautiful, Cedar thought, but that didn't explain why Finn was so fixated.

"What's calling to you?" she asked, placing her hand gently on his arm. At her touch he stared down at her in surprise, as though he had just realized she was there.

"The tree," he answered. "Can't you hear it?"

"Finn," Felix said in a sharp voice. "Snap out of it."

Finn shook his head, like a dog shaking off after a bath. He looked again at Cedar, slightly abashed. "Sorry," he said.

"What was that all about?" she asked.

"It's what they call a fairy tree," he started to explain. "I could hear it. Tara is a very ancient, very magical place—"

"There's someone over there," Jane said, cutting him off. Cedar looked again and saw that her friend was right. Standing near the tree was a middle-aged woman, complete with baseball hat and fanny pack. "Looks like just a tourist," Jane said.

Finn and Felix exchanged glances. "I'll go check it out," Finn said.

"Are you sure?" Cedar said, grabbing his arm. "She's right by that fairy tree. . . ."

"I'll be fine," he said. "We're close to the Mound of Hostages. We don't know what will happen when we find the stone—best not to have any tourists about. I'll tell her we're doing an archeological survey and that the hill is closing to visitors for the rest of the evening."

Cedar watched him trot off toward to the lone tourist, her lips pressed together.

"This place is starting to creep me out," Jane said, and no one disagreed with her.

"Mummy, what's this big rock for?" Eden asked, and Cedar took her eyes off Finn as he approached the tourist. Eden had her arms wrapped around the stone that was in the center of the mound, though she couldn't quite reach all the way around.

"Feel anything strange there, little one?" Felix asked her.

"Nope," Eden answered. "Feels just like a normal rock."

He grinned. "That's because it *is* a normal rock. They call it the Lia Fáil, but we all know it isn't the real thing. It's probably been here for a very long time, but it wasn't always in this position on top of the hill. They moved it here a couple hundred years ago to honor some soldiers who died in one of the rebellions."

Cedar walked around the stone, which came up to her shoulders, and ran her hands across the rough, rounded top. It was cold, just as she'd expected. Felix reached out to touch the stone too, but shook his head. "It doesn't look at all like how Brighid described the Lia Fáil," Cedar said. "Or the stone in Maggie's story for that matter. How could a person even stand on it?"

"Let's find out," Felix said, a playful smile on his face. He lifted her as though she weighed no more than Eden and held her above his head. She set her feet on top of the stone but it was impossible to keep her balance without Felix holding on to her. As expected, the stone stayed silent, and Cedar jumped down after a moment.

"I wish Liam were here," she said. "I'd like to know his thoughts on all of this. I wonder if he's been here before—he didn't say anything about it when we were talking about Tara back at Logheryman's house."

"I'm sure he has," Felix answered. "Tara is a powerful place to do magic."

"Do you think he's a powerful druid?"

Felix looked at her thoughtfully. "I don't know, to be honest. But you really care about him, don't you?"

"I do," Cedar answered truthfully. "I know it sounds strange, since I've only just met him, but I feel like he's . . . kind of a father figure. I've never had a father figure in my life before, and I like it."

"I like him too," Jane said with an affectionate smile. "And you deserve to have someone like that in your life. I see many long conversations between the two of you in your future."

Cedar smiled at that thought, but then realized that Finn had yet to return. "Why is Finn taking so long?" she asked. She walked a few paces forward and squinted at the fairy tree. There was no sign of Finn or the tourist. "Something must be wrong." She started running toward where she had last seen him. Felix scooped Eden up in his arms and followed behind her, Jane trailing behind. The cloth-laden fairy tree was on another ridge surrounded by deep trenches. Cedar crested the ridge and then stopped in her tracks as she stared down into the trench below. The baseball hat-and-fanny-pack-wearing tourist was gone. In her place was a strange woman in a long skintight dress the color of blood. Finn's arms were wrapped around her, and he was kissing her passionately.

Cedar felt the blood drain from her face, and for a heart-stopping moment she believed that Finn was a willing participant in the kiss. But then the blood rushed back through her veins with a pounding force, and she let out a snarl and ran down the hill. "Hey!" she yelled. "Get away from him!" Finn and the woman acted like they couldn't hear her.

Felix dropped Eden and ran after her. "Cedar, no!" he yelled, but she kept right on running. The woman in the red dress had glowing skin and toned arms that were wrapped tightly around Finn's neck. The tops of her breasts were heaving as she pulled him in closer. Cedar was about to reach out and rip the woman away from him when Felix grabbed her by the arm and pulled her back. "She'll kill you," he hissed. "It's a leannán sí—a succubus."

"I don't care what she is; she's doing something to Finn!" Cedar cried, trying to escape his grasp. She didn't know why she felt so certain that Finn wasn't acting of his own free will. She just knew that it was impossible. She had never been so sure of anything. "Finn!" she screamed, though they were only a few feet away. She yanked herself away from Felix and grabbed Finn's arm, but Felix pulled her back again and shoved her behind him.

"Cedar, I'm serious, she could kill you in an instant. You need to stay back. Let me deal with this." He crouched, and then ran at the woman, shouting in an unfamiliar language. The woman pulled herself away from Finn and locked eyes with Felix for a split second before he crashed into her. Finn staggered back, dazed, and Cedar ran to him. "Finn, are you—" she started to say, but stopped short, gaping at the scene in front of her.

The leannán sí had been knocked to the ground by Felix's assault, but when she recovered herself and stood, she was no longer the beautiful woman she'd appeared to be a few moments ago. Her face was a grayish-green that looked like a wax sculpture that had been set too close to the fire. Her eyes were small pricks of red, like stab wounds, and her mouth was a gaping black hole oozing a tar-like substance that ran down the corners of her mouth and dripped off her chin. The chestnut tresses were gone, replaced by a few stray strands of coarse white hair, brittle with decay. Felix ran at her again, but she raised two clawed and withered hands in front of her and met him with a sickening crunch.

Felix staggered back, and Finn ran forward. He grabbed his friend by the shoulders and pointed up to where Jane and Eden were huddled together. "I'll take care of her!" he yelled. "Go protect the others! And watch for druids—she might just be a decoy."

"Finn, no!" Cedar yelled as he sprinted toward the leannán sí. But he didn't slow down. He leapt into the air and hit the ground on all fours as an enormous lion, his great shaggy mane streaming behind him as he lunged toward his prey. Cedar felt herself being lifted off the ground; Felix had scooped her into his arms and was running back up the hill to where Jane and Eden were huddled together. Eden threw herself at Cedar as soon as Felix set her on the ground, and Cedar hugged her close. "Don't watch, baby," she said, turning her daughter's head the other way. Felix circled around them, his eyes wary.

Below, Finn and the leannán sí were engaged in a dance of death. Finn was crouched low, snarling, and the leannán sí was clutching what was left of her arm, black tar dripping off her stump of an elbow. Before Finn could renew his attack, she was on him in an instant, moving so fast that she looked like a red blur in the green grass. He reared up on his hind legs, swiping at the air with his claws, but she was on his back, her legs and remaining arm wrapped around his body and neck. Cedar saw her mouth close in on the fur between Finn's shoulder blades and come up dripping. She screamed. "Felix, please! You have to help him!"

"I can't leave you unprotected!" Felix yelled back, but his face was torn with anguish. As they watched, the Finn-lion reared again, and the leannán sí jumped. He was on top of her in an instant. She struggled to force him off, but then a piercing wail ripped through the air, and Finn raised his shaggy mane, the leannán sí's throat clutched between his teeth. He threw it down on the ground beside her and then staggered back as her body disappeared, melting into the ground. Finn stumbled and then collapsed, himself once more.

Cedar was the first to reach him, but Felix was close behind her. Jane and Eden followed, clutching hands.

Cedar wiped the black tar off Finn's face with the hem of her shirt and pushed the hair off his forehead with her hand. "Finn," she whispered. "Can you hear me?" He didn't answer. His eyes were closed, but she could see his chest rising and falling with shallow breaths. "Is he okay?" she asked Felix, who had knelt beside her.

Felix gently turned Finn and lifted up his shirt. Between his shoulder blades was a deep gash, a sickly green ring around it. Felix cursed.

"What is it?" Cedar asked.

"He's going to be fine," Felix assured her. "But the bite of the leannán sí is even more deadly than her kiss. She's drained him of almost everything. He'll recover in time, but I need to examine the wound more closely, draw out the poison—"

"No," came Finn's voice in a thin whisper. Felix gently turned him over onto his back again, and he opened his eyes. The whites had gone a pale yellow. "Not enough time," he said, so softly that Cedar and Felix had to lean forward to hear him. "Find the Lia Fáil, and then worry . . . about me. Have to . . . get out of here." He closed his eyes and leaned his head back against Cedar's lap. Eden ran up to him and rested her head against his chest.

"Are you going to be okay, Daddy?" she asked in a small voice.

He reached up to put an arm around her, and Cedar could see how much effort it took him. "I'll be just fine, honey," he whispered. "You help your mum find that stone, okay?"

She nodded fervently. "Okay, Daddy. I will." Then she stood up. "Let's go, Mummy!"

Felix lifted Finn and set him on his feet, but Finn swayed alarmingly and looked on the verge of collapse. Felix hoisted him over his shoulder in a fireman's hold and started up the hill. "It's just over here," he said, veering slightly to the north. Cedar could see it. The Mound of Hostages was a small hill about three yards high, covered in grass. A sheep was standing on top of the hill, grazing, but as they got closer it gave a soft bleat and ran off. The sun was going down; soon it would be full dark. Cedar picked up the pace.

"So . . . what was that thing?" Jane asked.

"It's called a leannán sí," Felix answered, "but you would probably know it as a succubus. An evil spirit that seduces young men and drains them of life. I don't know what it was doing here, but I don't like it. It usually only goes after humans—it should have known better than to tangle with the Tuatha Dé Danann."

"Finn said she might be a decoy," Cedar said. "But I don't see any druids here. Maybe they sent her, thinking she could defeat you both?"

"Unlikely," Felix answered grimly. "I say we take Finn's advice and grab the Lia Fáil—if we can find it—and get the hell out of here."

They walked around the mound to until they came to the entrance, which appeared to lead straight into the side of the hill. "Is it . . . a tomb?" Jane asked hesitantly

Felix nodded. "It was, many ages ago. It's been excavated, but if Abhartach says the stone is still here, it's still here." A small gate with four iron bars blocked the passage, fastened into the stone at the top by a padlock. Two large standing stones buttressed either side of the entrance. Cedar walked up to the gate and peered through the bars. She couldn't see where the passage ended, but she knew it could be only a few feet long because of how small the hill was. She reached her arm through the bars and set her hand against the stone wall but felt nothing unusual. Of course it wouldn't be that easy.

Felix set Finn down at the entrance, slumped against the side of the mound. Finn struggled to sit up straight, his eyes trained on Cedar, as Eden ran over and sat in his lap.

"Go in," he told Cedar, his voice thin and weak. "Find the stone. Don't be afraid."

Cedar looked nervously down the dark passage. She *was* afraid. It seemed impossibly simple that she might be able to walk into this passage and claim the Lia Fáil. But it hadn't been simple at all, she reminded herself. They'd survived several brushes with death to reach this point, so maybe this really was it. Maybe it would all be over soon, and they'd finally have the power to stop Nuala for good.

She hadn't really thought about what would happen after that, about what it would be like to be queen. As she stared into the ancient darkness, she thought of Maeve and wondered what kind of advice she would give her. Would she have been proud? Or would she have insisted that she should leave the Tuatha Dé Danann to their own devices and embrace her identity as a human? Cedar would never know, but she resolved to take Liam out for a pint when all of this was over so that she could learn more about her adoptive mother.

"Take Eden," Finn whispered, giving his daughter a gentle nudge to her feet. "The stone is supposed to grow warm if it's touched by a Tuatha Dé Danann, and I'm not sure if your gift of humanity will affect that. But it should work for her no matter what."

"I can't see anything," Eden said, squinting through the bars. "I don't want to go in there."

Cedar dug around in the backpack Brighid had given her and pulled out a small flashlight. "Here we go," she said. "Be brave, my heart. We'll do this together."

"Ready?" Felix asked. Cedar nodded.

"Good luck," Jane said, an anxious look on her face.

Felix snapped the padlock and tossed it away and then set the gate down in the dirt at their feet. "I'll stand guard out here," he said. "Take your time. Feel your way around. If one of the stones grows warm at your touch, tell your mum, okay, Eden?"

"I will," Eden said earnestly, and Cedar nodded, her throat too tight to speak. Clutching Eden's hand in hers, she ducked her head and crept into the passage. Once inside, she found that she could stand, though Finn or Felix would have needed to crouch. She shivered. The air in the tomb was cold, and it was almost pitch-black as they moved away from the entrance. She wondered how many bodies had been interred inside this passage and in the hill surrounding them. She switched on the flashlight and started on her left, running her hands over the large standing stones that created the walls of the passage.

"Eden, look at this," she said. One of the stones was covered in circles, swirls, and a curious X pattern. She traced the largest spiral with the tip of her finger. "I wonder what it means?" she said. "Maybe it's a map of some kind. . . ." She shone her flashlight on the *X* and pressed her hand to it, but the stone stayed cold. Eden did the same, and then shook her head. They continued on, shining the light in front of them, looking for a stone that matched Brighid's description, but touching them all just in case. Eden stayed close to Cedar and ran her fingers over the same stones she did.

Above the standing stones was a layer of smaller rocks that led to the ceiling, which was a few inches over Cedar's head. She lifted Eden up so that she could touch those stones as well, and then she reached her own hands up to touch the ceiling. She felt what seemed to be more carvings on the stones above her head, and she pointed the flashlight up to look at them. Surely the Lia Fáil wouldn't be one of the roof stones, she thought, wondering if there was any heavy equipment hidden in one of Brighid's backpacks just in case. She glanced back through the narrow entryway and could make out Felix's and Jane's figures against the background of the darkening sky.

"Can you see anything that might be it?" she whispered to Eden, not quite sure why she was whispering. It just seemed appropriate in this place, like it would in a funeral home or a museum.

"Just lots of rocks," Eden whispered back. "But none of them feel warm."

"Same," Cedar said. "I wish we knew for sure what it looked like . . . or that it glowed in the dark or something." She had reached the back of the passage, which was only about four yards from the entrance. A large rectangular stone sat right at her feet, in front of the back wall. It seemed like it was about the right size for the Lia Fáil, but it felt cold. "Eden, come here," she whispered, and Eden squatted down beside her. "Touch this one," she said, placing her hands on Eden's and pressing them into the rock. "How does it feel?"

"Like a cold rock," Eden said, standing back up. Cedar stood beside her. She was starting to feel ridiculous, and she wondered if Abhartach had been making a little joke at their expense by sending them here. She swept the flashlight around some more as Eden touched each of the rocks on the other wall. Then something caught Cedar's eye. When she pointed the flashlight at the standing stone carved with the circles and swirls, an odd shadow appeared at the base. She moved in for a closer look. Propped up at a strange angle next to the stone was a flat rock that was about a foot long on each side. Cedar pulled it away, hoping she wasn't about to excavate some undiscovered grave. What she found instead was a large gap behind the carved standing stone. And wedged into this gap was a smooth rectangular stone that roughly matched the dimensions that Brighid had described to them.

"Eden!" Cedar called, forgetting to whisper this time. Eden rushed over. "Did you find it?" she asked, her huge eyes reflecting the beam of Cedar's flashlight.

"Maybe," Cedar said. Trembling, she reached into the gap and set her hand on it. It was cold, and her heart sank. Then Eden squeezed in beside her and laid her hand flat against the stone.

"Ow!" she cried, yanking her hand back and cradling it against her chest. "It's burning hot!"

"It is?" Cedar said, touching it again. To her, it felt slightly cooler than the air temperature around them. "Are you sure?"

"Mum, it's really warm! You can't feel it?"

They stared at each other for a moment, and then Eden threw her arms around Cedar's neck and squealed, "We did it!" Cedar hugged her back, still not quite able to believe it. "You gotta stand on it, Mum, that's how it works!"

"I know," Cedar said, reaching in to try and pull out the stone. It was heavy and firmly wedged. "It's . . . not . . . coming . . . ," she grunted.

"Maybe I can push it from the other side," Eden said, running around the standing stone. "I can see it, I'll just push it with my foot." She stuck her leg into a narrow space and kicked.

"Eden, that's not going to . . ." Cedar's voice trailed off as the stone became dislodged and slid toward her. Cedar peered around the stone at her daughter. "How did you . . . ? Never mind, come around to this side now, and help me lift it." Cedar worked the stone the rest of the way out of the gap.

"Aren't you going to stand on it?" Eden asked.

Was she? Cedar asked herself. Here it was, in front of her—the object they had been pursuing for the past several days. It would only take one step to prove that she was the true queen of Tír na nÓg, the Queen of the Faeries, as Eden liked to put it. But she didn't feel like the queen of anything. She was dirty and tired, her lover and her best friend were sick, and her mother was dead. She felt completely inadequate for such a title, and she knew that when she stepped on that stone, her whole life would change. Again.

"I think . . . I think I'll wait until we're out of the mound," she said, grunting as she tried to lift the stone.

"Here, I'll help," Eden said, grabbing on to one end. The stone became lighter at Eden's touch, and together the two of them carried it to the entrance, where the last rays of sunlight were dying, and where their friends were waiting for them in the darkness.

CHAPTER 14

"**W**e found it!" Eden cried as she and Cedar emerged from the mound. Cedar looked around in surprise. They were alone. Her heart constricted. Had some sudden danger caused the others to flee? She took another step forward, still grasping the stone with Eden. And then she saw them. It was as though a veil had suddenly been lifted from her eyes. She gasped at the same time as Eden screamed, and both of them dropped the stone.

Jane was lying facedown on the ground several feet away, and Felix was sprawled beside her, his arms stretched out toward her. Neither of them were moving. A circle of a dozen cloaked figures surrounded them, silent and unmoving, holding flaming torches that illuminated the scene. Liam stood in the center of them, and at his feet lay Finn, who was staring up at Cedar through pain-filled eyes.

"Cedar . . . go . . . ," Finn croaked. Liam silenced him by putting a foot on his throat.

"Our succubus did her job well," Liam said, as Cedar stared on with horror, trying to make sense of what she was seeing. He looked her directly in the eye without a trace of affection, no crinkling around his eyes, no warm smile. "And so did you, I see." He nodded toward the stone on the ground.

"What are you talking about?" she asked. "What are you doing?" She knew what her eyes were telling her, but her heart was unwilling to believe it. Not this.

"I am reversing centuries—no, millennia—of history," he said, reaching down and hauling Finn to his feet. Huddled behind her,

Eden started to cry. "I am freeing my fellow druids from their lives of servitude or exile. We will return to Tír na nÓg as equals with the Tuatha Dé Danann."

Cedar tried to shake off the shock that was clouding her mind. "*You're* working for Nuala?"

"Not *for* her, no. We have an arrangement. My role is to find the Lia Fáil and prevent you from claiming it. And then, when she's queen, the druids will return to Tír na nÓg as victors, with as much power and status as the Tuatha Dé Danann have always enjoyed."

"Is that what you think? Liam, don't do this," Cedar pleaded. "Nuala is a liar and a psychopath. She's just using you to get what she wants. Can't you see that?"

"I have my guarantees," Liam said calmly. "It *will* happen."

"So all this time, you've just been pretending to help us?" Cedar asked. "None of it was real?"

"I've been keeping tabs on you," he corrected. "How else do you think the druids knew you were going to Scotland? Or coming here? Who do you think opened Eden's mind to Nuala? I was always close, even when you didn't know it."

"And what about my mother? I thought you loved her. She would hate you for what you've done." The depth of his betrayal was beginning to sink in, and she felt sick.

"She wasn't your mother, as you well know. She was nothing but a pawn in one of the many games the Tuatha Dé Danann like to play with mortals. Your father used her like a cheap whore, and then tossed her out like rubbish when he was done with her. She'd be glad that I'm finally putting the Tuatha Dé Danann in their place."

"Liam, Nuala killed Maeve. She's going to *destroy the world*. And you're okay with that?"

"This world can take care of itself," he said, ignoring her first statement. "Or not. Our place is in Tír na nÓg, the land of the gods."

"You're mad," Cedar spat at him. "How did I ever wish you were my father? My father *died* protecting humans, and you don't even care if they're all slaughtered. All you care about is your precious status."

"Let's not be melodramatic, shall we?" His composure infuriated Cedar, but she felt helpless to do anything. If the druids had been able to overcome Felix, what chance did *she* have of fighting them? And she had Eden to protect. There were no nearby doors that they could use for escape, and even if they could, she would never leave Finn and the others behind. She looked down at the stone at her feet. Perhaps . . .

She froze mid-step as Finn gave a scream of pain. "I wouldn't do that if I were you," Liam said. He was pressing a small dagger made of a blue crystal to Finn's throat. Cedar could see no blood, but Finn was in such agony that his whole body convulsed, and Liam had to hold him in place. She took a step back.

"Stop. Please, stop. What are you doing to him?" she demanded.

"I'm torturing him," he said matter-of-factly, lowering the knife. Finn stopped screaming, though shudders continued to run through his body. "The bite of the leannán sí not only drained him of his power, it increased his sensitivity to pain." He pressed the knife to Finn's flesh again.

"Stop!" Cedar cried out, Finn's screams tearing through her as if the knife were pressed to her skin rather than his. "He's done nothing to you!"

Liam lowered the knife again. "This isn't about him, Cedar. It's about you."

"What do you want from me?"

"They call this the Mound of Hostages for a reason, my dear. Give us the Lia Fáil and abandon your claim to the throne, and I will spare his life."

"No," Finn said, struggling to raise his head. "Don't do it, Cedar."

Liam laughed and pushed Finn to the ground, where he landed in a heap on the dirt. "Always so noble, aren't you Fionnbharr?"

Finn ignored him, his eyes pleading with Cedar's. "Why are you waiting?" he asked. "Eden, listen to me. You have to escape. You don't *need* a door, you just need to believe you can do it without one. I know you can. Cedar . . . I'm just one person. Think of all of the millions who will die. *Go*. You *must* do this."

Cedar stared at him in anguish as he lay in the dirt, barely able to lift his own head. She could feel Eden inching away from her, back to the entrance to the mound. They *could* do it, Cedar realized. They could still take the Lia Fáil back to Tír na nÓg. She could stop Nuala by becoming queen.

"Cedar, move away from the stone," Liam said, his voice heavy with hatred. Cedar felt like she was being punched in the stomach every time he spoke. "Eden, I would stop whatever you're doing if I were you. Your grandmother is dead . . . you wouldn't want to be responsible for killing your father too, would you?"

"Eden, don't listen to him," Finn begged. "It's okay! Just go! Cedar, take the stone!"

Cedar looked down at the stone, and then back at Finn, his gold-flecked eyes imploring her to leave him. She remembered the first day they met, when he had saved all of her paintings from the fire at the gallery. She remembered the first joyful years they'd spent together and then the years of pain that had followed. He had only just returned to her life, but she had never stopped loving him. And he had never stopped loving her, even though she'd done her best to push him away after his return. She gazed down at him now, lying helpless at the feet of their enemy, and realized that her noble goal of saving the world paled in comparison to her love for Finn.

She took another step away from the stone.

"You can have it," she told Liam. "Give me Finn, and you can have the stone. He's worth more to me, something I'm sure you could never understand. We *will* stop Nuala, don't doubt that for a minute. But not this way."

Liam shot a look at the two druids who were standing closest to Cedar, and they ran forward and picked up the stone, struggling beneath its weight. Finn groaned, and Cedar started to run to his side, but Liam held out his hand in her direction. She felt herself freeze in her tracks. She tried to move, but was paralyzed. "Not so fast," he said.

"What now?" she snarled. "I gave you what you wanted. Please. Just leave us alone."

A slow smile spread over one side of Liam's face, a smile that sent chills down Cedar's spine. "You could never give me what I want, Cedar," he said. "Can you go back in time and stop yourself from being born? Can you bring back the dead?"

Cedar felt something start to smolder deep inside her. "You want to turn back time? It wouldn't matter. Maeve—my *mother*—would never have loved you, even if I hadn't been born," she said through gritted teeth. "I'm sure she saw you for the snake you are—she wasn't as blind as I was. It's your own fault that she didn't love you. Not mine, not Brogan's. And certainly not Finn's. Now let him go."

Liam had gone pale, and his face was trembling. "You will regret saying that," he said, his hand gripped the blue crystal dagger tightly. He reached down and slashed Finn's chest, making him howl in agony.

"No!" Cedar screamed, trying to break free of the spell that had immobilized her. "You said you'd let him go if I gave you the stone!"

"And I'm having a change of heart," Liam said, slashing at Finn again. "You need to feel what it's like to lose the one person you've ever loved."

Suddenly, Cedar could move again. Liam had stopped slashing Finn with the knife and was staring behind Cedar, at the top of the

Mound of Hostages, his face twisted with rage. All of the other druids were focused on the same thing, their mouths gaping in shock and confusion. Cedar turned and nearly fainted with relief. Abhartach was standing on top of the mound, dressed in clean clothes and washed from head to toe. His black eyes glinted in the sun and the tattoos covering his skin seemed to shimmer. Standing next to him, her chin raised and her eyes flashing in the light of the druids' torches, was Brighid. Eden was huddled inside the entrance of the passage, her eyes wide with terror.

Liam cried out a command, and the druids raised wooden staffs from beneath their cloaks, pointing them at the top of the hill. But Abhartach was faster. He threw up his arms, and the druids all stumbled backward, some of them falling as if they'd been hit by a sudden gust of wind. Their torches snuffed out, and only the moon and stars were left to illuminate the sacred hilltop. Brighid glided down the hill, her long black hair flowing behind her like a cape. Cedar felt someone slam into her, and when she looked down, Eden had wrapped herself around her waist. Together, they ran down to join Brighid, who was kneeling over Finn. Chaos erupted all around them as Abhartach battled the druids.

"I'll be okay," Finn murmured to Brighid, "Felix . . . and Jane . . . they need you." Brighid nodded, her face stoic, and rushed over to where Jane and Felix lay sprawled on the ground. In a show of her incredible strength, she picked them up, one under each arm, and carried them into the mound, delivering a kick to a druid who tried to stop her that sent him soaring several feet in the air.

Cedar felt the wind pick up around them, as though a tornado had suddenly landed on top of the hill. The stars were blocked by dark clouds that rumbled and raged with thunder. Cedar put her hands under Finn's arms and tried to pull him toward the mound.

"I'll help, Mummy!" Eden said, grabbing one of his arms.

"No," Finn said, protesting as loudly as he could manage. He pointed behind Cedar. "Now! Before it's too late!" The Lia Fáil was lying unprotected in the grass. It had been abandoned after Abhartach commenced his attack. Cedar jumped up and ran to it, crouching to avoid the rocks and branches that were flying through the air. She didn't see Liam anywhere, but the darkness made it hard to see anything. She reached the stone, and then looked back at Finn and Eden, who were huddled together on the ground. "Do it!" Finn yelled. Cedar lifted one foot and then the other and stood on top of the stone.

And then the world split apart.

The roar that issued from the stone beneath her feet was far louder than the storm raging all around them. It was a roar of victory that had been contained for millennia. It ripped through the air, above the howling wind, and shook the ground beneath them. And then something happened inside of Cedar that was even more incredible. She had felt it before, on an infinitesimal scale. It was that burning feeling that she felt in the pit of her stomach whenever she felt incensed. She could feel it there now, like a hot coal glowing at the core of her being. But this time, it didn't stay there. It spread throughout her body, down into her legs and up through her lungs and into her throat. She felt as though flames would shoot out if she opened her mouth. The sensation was almost unbearable, but she willed herself to keep standing on the stone, to let whatever was happening to her run its course. Every nerve and fiber in her body felt like it was on fire, but it was strangely painless. She felt stronger, more energized than she had ever felt in her life. She felt like she could do anything.

She felt like a goddess.

She raised her head and took in the scene around her with new eyes. The storm had stopped raging, and the sky was once again an inky black pierced through with bright stars and the glowing moon. Brighid was gaping at her in open-mouthed amazement from the entrance to the passage, Felix and Jane leaning against the entrance stones. Finn and Eden were clutching each other where she had left them. Finn's eyes were filled with tears.

"Kill her!"

Liam stood on top of the Mound of Hostages, a crude wooden sword pressed against Abhartach's throat. Yew, she suspected. He had known that they were planning to free Abhartach and wouldn't have come unprepared.

"Eden," Cedar said calmly as the druids slowly began to surround her, their black cloaks rustling in the now silent air. "Get your father into the mound." She hoped the strength her daughter had shown in lifting the stone would serve her well. Out of the corner of her eye she saw Finn raise himself to his knees and start moving, Eden half-dragging him toward the passage.

She turned in a circle on top of the Lia Fáil and stared down her opponents. She could still feel the fire burning inside her and knew what it meant. She took a deep breath, and then she slowly lifted her arms out from her sides, her fists still clenched. She felt the fire course through her veins and opened her hands.

White-hot flames erupted from her palms, shooting six feet into the air. She felt no heat, only the release of energy that had been restrained for far too long. The flames roared like blowtorches, and the druids who had been closing in on her took a step back. She pointed her palms toward the ground and created a ring of flames around her. The flames continued to burn in their protective circle even when she lowered her arms. Then she turned back to face Liam, who was still pressing the yew sword to Abhartach's neck. She narrowed her eyes slightly and focused on the wooden handle of his weapon. It burst into flame, and Liam dropped it with a shout. Abhartach immediately swiveled around and advanced on his opponent.

Cedar turned away. Let Abhartach deal with Liam; she had a dozen other druids to fight. She felt the ground shake violently beneath her; they were trying to knock her off the stone, and she jumped down before she could fall. Still, her circle of flames held, and none of the druids could breach it. She remembered how quickly they had scattered when Finn unleashed his dragon fire at the castle. She tried to see the faces shadowed by their dark hoods. Who were these nameless enemies who had hunted her and tormented her child? Were they just pawns in Nuala's game, embittered by centuries of servitude? They were shifting around nervously, staying clear of the flames, seemingly unsure how to proceed without the direction of their leader, who was still engaged in vicious combat with the dwarf. She opened her arms again, spreading them wide, and sent fire sweeping around the druids in a circle, drawing them into a tight huddle.

She started to shout for Eden, but then she stopped. *I should be able to do this*, she thought, wondering if she would need a door . . . or anything at all. She stared at the empty air behind the druids' prison of white flames. They were screaming from the heat, though the flames had yet to touch them. Cedar concentrated with all of her might. Then suddenly she saw it happen, feeling a sudden rush of power. The air glimmered behind them like a spiderweb thick with dew. She opened the ring of fire so that the sidh she had created was their only exit, and then, moving her hands slowly together, she started to shrink the circle. One by one, the druids were forced through the sidh. When the last one disappeared through the shimmering air, she concentrated hard again, and the sidh closed. Cedar lowered her arms and let out a deep breath, and the fire extinguished in a puff of white smoke. Another wave of her arms, and the ring of fire around her also vanished.

In the sudden silence she heard a victorious growl. Abhartach was standing over Liam's limp body on top of the mound. Then she lowered her eyes to the mound's entrance, where Finn, Eden, Jane, Felix, and Brighid were standing motionless, their faces perfect masks of relief and sheer incredulity.

"What?" she asked them, a small smile playing at the corner of her lips. "You didn't think I could do it?"

She heard a loud guffaw from the top of the mound. Abhartach jogged down the side of the hill on his short legs and pounded Cedar on the back, a broad grin stretching across his face. He turned his head and yelled something to Felix and Brighid, who were the only ones who could understand him.

Felix closed his mouth, which had been hanging open. "He says that you were spectacular," he translated in a hushed voice. "He's right."

And then Eden rushed toward her, and Cedar caught her up in a spin. "You've grown lighter!" Cedar cried.

"You've grown stronger," came Finn's voice from beside her. She set Eden down and took his face in her hands.

"Are you all right?" she asked.

"I am. Brighid is a damn good healer. Way better than you," he said with a wink to Felix.

"I have never claimed to be better than Brighid at anything," Felix said, hugging Cedar.

Cedar looked at Brighid and Abhartach, who were standing slightly off to the side. "Thank you," she said. "Your timing was perfect." Brighid smiled graciously, but she didn't quite look Cedar in the eye. "What convinced you to come?" Cedar asked. "I thought you didn't want to get involved?"

Brighid tossed her sheet of her dark hair behind her shoulder and straightened her chin. "Well, it's not like I hadn't already done several things to help you, now, was it? The house seemed very empty after you all left. I wanted to make sure you could come back and visit. Which means I needed to make sure you stayed alive. And obviously, you needed me."

Cedar laughed. Brighid's self-centeredness never ceased to amaze her, but she was grateful that she had come, no matter what her reasons were. Abhartach looked up at Brighid and said something, waving his hands and gesturing in the air. "What's he saying?" Cedar asked.

Brighid rolled her eyes. "He is insisting I tell you that he persuaded me to help you. He had a change of heart after he left you by the Giant's Grave. He thought being a hero might help repair his damaged reputation, and he figured that I might like to join him. We knew each other many years ago, you see. And since I *am* the most magical being in the world, it was fairly easy for him to find me. Of course, once I realized how easy it was for him to breach my home's regular defenses, I had to increase security, which is why you were unable to return."

"Well, please tell him that I am very grateful for his assistance. And for yours," Cedar said.

"So . . . can someone please explain to me what just happened?" Jane asked. "I knew the stone was supposed to roar, but what was with the crazy white fire? You're like the freaking Human Torch. How did you do that?"

Cedar stared at the stone, which rested innocently in the grass. It seemed completely unremarkable, and yet she had experienced its overwhelming power for herself. "Remember how some of the legends we read claimed that the stone had the power to 'rejuvenate the king'? And how the stone revealed Utain's true self? I think that's what happened. I think it restored me to how I was meant to be. Maybe it was the only thing that could break the spell that Kier and Maeve used to give me the gift of humanity."

"I can hear you now," Finn said. "Your Lýra. It's beautiful." Cedar paused, and realized that she could hear his too. A faint musical signature emanated from Eden, Finn, Felix, and Brighid. It sounded so natural that she wondered how she'd never heard it before.

"Well, I think it's dreadful," Jane said with a smile that belied her words. "Now I'm *really* the only human here." She nudged Felix in the ribs with her elbow. "Can't you bite me or something and turn me into a Tuatha Dé Danann?"

Cedar laughed. "I don't think it works that way. But tell me, what happened to *you* guys? When we went into the passage everything was fine, and then we came out, and . . . it wasn't."

"That's a mild understatement," Finn muttered.

"It happened quickly," Felix said, staring at the ground. "They were already here, waiting for us—we just couldn't see them. Finn had already been weakened by the leannán sí, so he couldn't fight back or transform. And they were targeting Jane, so I had to stay close to her."

"They were targeting me for that very reason," Jane said. "You'd have been able to defend yourself otherwise."

"It wasn't enough," Felix said, his eyes haunted. "You could have died." The way he looked at Jane made Cedar blush. She felt as though she were intruding on a very private exchange.

"Oh, stop with the dramatics," Brighid said. "You saved her life. She couldn't possibly have survived the force of the spells you absorbed. They nearly killed *you*. Apparently the druids have lost none of their power during their exile on Ériu."

"Where did the druids go, Mummy?" Eden asked. "And how did you make a sidh without a door?"

"I . . . I don't know how I did it, baby," Cedar said. "I just knew that I could. Maybe it's because I'm older. But I think your father is right, and that you don't need the doors either. As for where the druids went . . . well, all I can say is that I hope it worked."

"What worked?" Finn asked.

"I remembered something Liam told me the first day I met him, when I was trying to get into Maeve's workshop. He said that even if I somehow got in, I'd never be able to get out. So . . . that's where I sent them."

Jane looked slightly sickened. "So they're stuck in there . . . forever?"

"I don't think so," Cedar said. "I was able to make a sidh to get them in there, so I'm sure we'll be able to get them out once we've decided what to do with them."

Under the light of the moon Cedar could make out the body lying on top of the Mound of Hostages. She climbed up the hill and crouched down beside it. She knew she should be glad he was dead, but she felt her eyes prick with tears and an uncomfortable tightness in her throat. She felt Finn's hand on her shoulder.

"It's okay to be upset," he said.

She shook her head. "It was all a lie," she said. "I was so foolish. *You* didn't trust him. I should have listened to you. He almost killed you."

"He fooled all of us," Finn said. "Don't blame yourself. You've always wanted a father, and he pretended to be one."

Cedar looked at Liam's face, which was softer and kinder in death. Maybe he would have been different if Maeve had returned his love. Maybe he really would have been the gentle, wise man she'd thought him to be. She touched the bracelet on her wrist and wondered if it had really belonged to her adoptive mother, or if that, too, had been a lie. She took it off and was about to toss it onto the ground, but instead she tucked it into her pocket. Perhaps someday she would find the truth.

"What are we going to do with the body?" Jane asked. She had come up the hill and was standing beside them, while Felix had stayed below with Eden and was talking with Brighid and Abhartach.

"Well, we are standing on top of a tomb," Finn pointed out. He lifted Liam's body and carried it down the hill. "Cedar, do you think you could give us a little light? Without burning us to a crisp, that is?"

Cedar opened one of her hands, and a tower of white fire shot up from her palm. Her companions jumped back, and Cedar snapped her hand shut. "So cool," Eden whispered, opening her own hand and scowling at it in disappointment.

"Sorry," Cedar said. "Let me try again." Slowly, she opened her fist again, and a small ball of white fire rose up from her palm. She walked into the passage ahead of Finn and led him all the way to the back. There he laid Liam's body down. He called out to Felix, who translated his request to Abhartach, and then several melon-sized rocks floated through the entrance of the passage. Finn plucked them from the air and placed them over Liam's body. "There," he said when the body was completely covered. "A cairn inside one of the world's oldest tombs. A better burial than he deserves."

They walked out and Cedar propped the gate back up against the entrance. "I suppose this is where we say good-bye for now," she said to Brighid and Abhartach. "We need to take the Lia Fáil back to Tír na nÓg."

"You don't seem to be in any hurry," Brighid said with a sly smile. "You're the queen now, Cedar. Time to start acting like it."

Cedar laughed nervously. "I think you'd be better suited to be queen than I am, dear Brighid. But . . . we still have Nuala to deal with, so yes, I suppose I need to go and claim my throne."

"That sounds so weird," Jane said. "So listen . . . I know I'm not one of you guys, but . . . can I come? To Tír na nÓg? I have the rest of the week off from work anyway, since, you know, you made me miss my geek convention."

"Of course!" Cedar said at once, before swiveling around to look at Finn and Felix. "I mean . . . she can, can't she?"

"You make the decisions now," Felix said with a grin. "But yes, it should be fine. We've had humans in Tír na nÓg before. Of course, it's been a few centuries, but they all seemed to have a good time."

"I'll be able to come back to Earth, though, right?" Jane asked, eyeing him with suspicion. "I'm not going to age a hundred years while I'm there or anything? 'Cause I do have a life to come back to and all."

Felix laughed. "You'll only age a hundred years if you stay for a hundred years," he said. "Brid, Abe, you coming too?"

"Tempting," Brighid said. "But I think I'll wait until you get things sorted out. Abhartach and I have a lot of catching up to do."

"Don't take too long to visit," Cedar said. "Okay, let's go. But first, I think the three of us should have a drink of this." She rummaged in the backpack and pulled out the bottle Brighid had given her, filled with the potion that would protect them against Nuala's power.

Brighid nodded in agreement. "A small sip should do it," she said. "There may be others who will need it before this is finished." Cedar tilted the bottle to her lips and felt the sweet, honey-like substance trickle down her throat, then passed the bottle to Felix, who took a sip and then passed it to Jane.

"Okay," she said, slipping the vial into her pocket. "*Now* we're ready."

She picked up the Lia Fáil, which now seemed light in her arms. "Eden, do you want to try opening the sidh without a door? Let's go right to the Council room in the Great Hall."

Eden scrunched up her nose in concentration. She focused her eyes on the air in front of her, as though staring down some invisible person. And then it happened. The air in front of her started to shimmer and dance, and through the veil Cedar could see the Council members seated in their circle of white chairs.

"I did it!" Eden said, jumping up and down.

"I knew you could," Cedar said, and kissed the top of her head. She took a deep, steadying breath and thanked Brighid and Abhartach one more time before turning to give Finn a wry smile. "Why do I have the feeling that the hardest part is yet to come?" Then, clutching the Lia Fáil in her arms, she stepped through the sidh.

CHAPTER 15

Cedar would always remember the scene they walked into when they stepped through the sidh and into the Council chambers. The Council was sitting in their customary circle, goblets of wine in their hands or on small glass tables between their chairs. Trays of fruit rested beside them. They were engaged in a heated discussion.

"We said we'd give her a week! We must honor that!" Gorman was saying.

Sorcha, the tall, reedy blonde, tossed her hair behind her shoulder. "We're wasting time," she snapped. "It is impos—"

She stopped mid-sentence, her mouth gaping open as she stared at the group that was emerging from thin air in front of her. Some of the Council members jumped up, others sat frozen in shock. Someone knocked over a tray of fruit. A large grin formed on Gorman's face, but the rest looked as though they had been sucker-punched.

It was a very satisfying reception.

Cedar strode forward, holding the Lia Fáil in her arms. Eden and Finn flanked her, and Felix and Jane followed behind. "I have done as you asked," Cedar said, holding out the Lia Fáil as though it weighed no more than a baby. "I have brought back the Lia Fáil."

"Impossible," Sorcha seethed, trying to glare at them all at once. "Where did you find it?"

"Hidden in the Mound of Hostages at Tara," Cedar answered calmly.

"Is this a trick? This cannot be the true Lia Fáil," Deaglán said dismissively. He strode forward. "It has been lost for centuries. If it was truly at Tara all this time, someone would have found it. You have brought us a fake. The Council does not look kindly on those who try to deceive us, Miss McLeod."

"Airgetlam," Cedar said.

"I beg your pardon?"

"My name is Cedar mac Airgetlam," she answered loudly. "I am the daughter of Brogan and Kier mac Airgetlam, and a descendent of Nuadu of the Silver Hand, one of the first kings of the Tuatha Dé Danann. Do not mock me or call me a liar, councilman."

He looked at her through narrowed eyes. "You might feign confidence, but you are still human, no matter who your parents were. And no human will ever rule the Tuatha Dé Danann. Fionnghuala is our rightful queen!"

"Listen closely, and you will hear that I have the Lýra, just as you do. And if that's too subtle for your stubborn ears, then maybe you'll be able to hear this." She threw the stone down at Deaglán's feet, where it slammed into the ground with enough force to rattle several of the goblets of wine. Then, casting her gaze around at all the Council members, she stepped up onto it.

The roar of the stone was as thunderous as it had been on Earth. Cedar could feel the power of it coursing through her body. Any of the Council members who had remained seated were now on their feet. Then Gorman fell to his knees, his head bowed, and the elf-like councilwoman called Maran did the same. The stone continued to roar, and Cedar made no move to step down.

"What the hell is going on?"

Cedar didn't have to look to know who had just arrived. The roar of the stone was unmistakable; she was sure it could be heard all over Tír na nÓg. Slowly, Cedar turned and met Nuala's enraged eyes. She was standing outside the circle of Council members, her face like a stone but her eyes blazing.

Cedar stepped off the stone, and it fell silent. "You lost," she said simply.

For a moment, Nuala seemed bereft of speech. Then she recovered herself. "You have tricked the Council," she said loudly, her voice rich with power. The ivy-haired woman who had fallen to her knees stood up, looking at Nuala in confusion. The others looked bewildered too.

Cedar reached into her pocket and wrapped her hand around Brighid's potion. She heard a commotion over her shoulder and turned to see Rohan, Riona, and Gorman's wife, Seisyll, rush into the courtyard.

"We heard the roar, and we knew it must be the stone," Riona said, her face glowing with pride. "You did it!" Cedar seized her opportunity. She pulled Riona in for a tight hug as Finn and the others accepted their friends' congratulations.

"Everyone on the Council needs to drink this," she whispered into Riona's ear, slipping the vial into her hands. "The wine is our best chance, I think." Riona paused for only a heartbeat, and then nodded.

"You heard the stone roar," Cedar said, facing Nuala once more. Out of the corner of her eye she saw Riona whispering to Seisyll. "You know what it means. If you doubt me, why don't *you* come and stand on it. Then we will know for sure."

Nuala tossed her hair behind her shoulder and marched forward, stopping just shy of the Lia Fáil. "I don't need to prove that I should be queen of the Tuatha Dé Danann. Who else will restore Ériu to us? Who else will bring back the druids? Not you. It doesn't matter that you can make this old rock roar—probably using a spell your druid mother taught you—what matters is what's best for our people. *I* am best for our people"

Some of the Council members were nodding and murmuring their agreement. Seisyll had pulled Gorman aside and was speaking to him in a hushed voice. He returned to the circle, and cleared his throat. "This matter can be settled later!" he cried jovially. "For now, let us celebrate the return of one of our most sacred treasures—the Lia Fáil, which our forefathers brought from Falias. Now all the four treasures have been reunited, and it is an occasion of great joy! I propose a toast. Seisyll, if you would be so kind . . ."

Seisyll nodded graciously and raised her hand, causing the decanter of wine to soar through the air and freshen the glasses of everyone in the courtyard. "To the Lia Fáil!" Gorman cried, lifting his glass in a toast, and then draining its contents. Still looking shell-shocked, the other Council members hesitated for a moment but then followed his example. Cedar let out a breath she hadn't realized she'd been holding. Even Nuala accepted a glass and muttered, "To the Lia Fáil," before taking a small sip.

After setting her glass down on one of the tables, Nuala smiled dangerously. "Thank you, Cedar, for returning the Lia Fáil. You have done us a great service once more. But this one act does not entitle you to the throne. The Council has already made their decision."

"Uh . . . that's not quite true," Gorman said, clearing his throat once more.

"Silence, you idiot!" Nuala lashed out. "Deaglán, I command you to remove this fool from the Council. We no longer need his advice." Nuala turned to face Cedar, clearly confident that Deaglán would carry out her orders without question. Cedar watched Deaglán flush, but he made no attempt to approach Gorman, who looked outraged.

"You . . . command me?" Deaglán said, as though he wasn't sure he had heard her correctly. Nuala sighed and rolled her eyes before glaring at him over her shoulder.

"You heard me. Get rid of him."

"I don't take orders from you," he said softly.

"Since wh—" Nuala stopped short, then slowly turned to face him. Cedar could feel her uncertainty. She watched as Nuala's face hardened. "Sorcha, was it not decided that I should be queen?" Nuala said. She spoke clearly and loudly, venom tracing every syllable.

Sorcha looked affronted. "We . . . we determined that if Cedar could complete the quest and return with the Lia Fáil, she would be the rightful queen."

"This isn't happening," Nuala muttered to herself. She pointed a shaking finger at Cedar. "She is a *human*! She is trying to trick you! She is completely unfit to rule our people." She took a deep breath. "Make me your queen. Now."

No one moved. Cedar held out her hand and allowed a burst of flame to rise up from her palm, shooting several feet in the air. Then she closed her fingers and it was gone. All eyes in the room were fixed on her. Concentrating hard, she opened a sidh in the air in front of her and walked through it—reappearing on the other side of the courtyard. Finn was grinning as he closed the sidh behind her. "Show-off," he muttered. Cedar resisted the urge to smirk at the look on Nuala's face.

"Does anyone still think of me as human?" she asked. There was silence. "I'm afraid that Nuala is right," she continued. "You have been deceived. But not by me." Her meaning hung thickly in the air.

Amras, the tall, elf-like councilman, stared at Nuala and asked, "You would dare use your ability on the Council?"

"Of course not," Nuala snapped. Her voice was confident, but her eyes darted around nervously. "She's lying."

"She's not," Sorcha said, a look of disgust on her face. "You deceived us all, didn't you? I can see it clearly now." Beside her, Deaglán was trembling.

"Deaglán," Nuala pleaded, moving toward him. "Deaglán, my love, you must believe me, I would never . . ."

"Believe you?" he said. "*Believe you?* How could you? I thought . . ." Cedar watched as the reality of Nuala's betrayal started to sink in; his expression transformed from shock to disbelief to hurt to—very quickly—rage. He started advancing on Nuala. "You made a fool out of me," he snarled. "You used me!"

"I didn't, I swear," Nuala said, taking a step back. Cedar watched as Gorman pulled Seisyll close to him, within the protection of his shield. Finn walked up behind her, and whispered in her ear. "Stay back."

"Why?" she asked, unable to take her eyes off Nuala and Deaglán, who was still raging at her. Finn didn't answer—he just led her back a few paces, beside Rohan and Felix.

"I loved you, I truly did!" Nuala was saying. "It wasn't a trick!"

"*Liar!*" Deaglán bellowed. He picked Nuala up by the front of her dress and held her a foot in the air.

"Put me down!" she demanded, kicking at him, but it was like kicking the side of a mountain and expecting it to move.

Finn and Felix stepped forward at the same time. "Deaglán, let her go," Finn said. "There are other ways to deal with her."

Deaglán ignored them. "Tell them the truth," he snarled at Nuala.

"I only did it to help you!" she said. "You wanted it—Ériu, the return of the druids—I know you did. You just needed a little . . . help to make it happen."

"Who else did you deceive? What else have you made us do against our own will?" he demanded.

"Nothing!" she said, still struggling fruitlessly to free herself from his grasp.

"Deaglán . . . ," Gorman said in a warning voice. "You need to put her down. The Council will address her crimes."

Deaglán opened his fist, and Nuala crumpled to the floor.

"Did you force Liam to help you?" Cedar asked, stepping forward. Nuala looked up at her with absolute hatred. Slowly, she stood and brushed off her dress.

"Liam didn't need any persuading," she said. "The promise of revenge on Brogan's people was enough for him."

"What are you talking about?" Deaglán snarled.

Cedar answered him. "She promised the druids on Ériu full equality with the Tuatha Dé Danann if they helped her become queen. They attacked us several times as we looked for the Lia Fáil. They tormented Eden and nearly drove her out of her mind. They tortured Finn and nearly killed my friend Jane. They would have killed all of us in the end, I think."

"She's a lying bitch!" Nuala cried. "Deaglán, you have to protect me! You *must* love me!"

That was the wrong thing to say.

Deaglán let out a roar of fury, and before anyone could react, Nuala lay facedown on the ground. Deaglán was standing over her, blood dripping off his elbows, his fist clenched around her heart.

There were several moments of shocked silence. Deaglán stared at the heart in his hands, his expression tortured. Finally, after several long seconds during which no one moved, Amras and Gorman slowly approached him. Silver shackles bound themselves around Deaglán's wrists, but he didn't resist, not even when Amras and Gorman led him from the courtyard. Seisyll covered Nuala's body with a robe and then levitated it in front of her, following Amras and Gorman out of the room.

"Eden," Cedar whispered, whipping around to look for her daughter. She wasn't there.

"Riona took her away a few minutes ago," Finn said, and Cedar breathed a sigh of relief. Her daughter had witnessed enough gruesome things in her short life.

"Cedar." She turned toward the voice and saw Sorcha looking back at her. Then Sorcha sank to her knees. The remaining Council members joined her. "Forgive us," Sorcha said. "You were right. I didn't think it was possible, but we were deceived, all of us except for Gorman, whose shield of protection made him impervious to Fionnghuala's power."

Cedar was still absorbing the fact that Nuala was dead. It was over. They had won. And now, these great beings who had mocked her were kneeling before her, asking for her forgiveness. She felt acutely uncomfortable. "Please, stand up," she said hurriedly. "It's okay—I know how you must feel."

"But how is that we could see through her so clearly now?" asked the ivy-haired woman as she got to her feet. "I could see exactly how I had been deceived, and yet I felt none of her power, even though she was obviously trying to use it."

"It was the wine," Cedar admitted. "Brighid gave me a potion that negates Nuala's powers. It was the only way to show you the truth."

"You have proven yourself a thousand times over," Sorcha said. "There is no doubt. You are our true queen."

❧

"I feel ridiculous," Cedar said, staring at her reflection. She was wearing a long emerald dress the color of her eyes. It was the most elaborate piece of clothing she'd ever owned, all silk and lace and fine embroidery, with glittering jewels on the sleeves and bodice. Despite its ornate appearance, it was as light and comfortable as a cotton nightgown. Her hair was woven through with tiny glowing pearls, and her feet bare. Her skin was glowing, and she didn't know if it was because she was now truly one of the Tuatha Dé Danann, or because she was just so happy that their ordeal was over.

"You look like a goddess," Finn said, coming up behind her and wrapping his arms around her waist. He rested his head on her shoulder.

"Are you feeling okay?" she asked. The torture the leannán sí and Liam had inflicted upon him had had lingering effects, and he still sometimes experienced moments of pain and weakness.

"I'm fine," he answered. "I know I've said this before, but . . . thank you. For saving my life even when you weren't sure what the cost might be."

"You would have done the same for me," she said, reaching up and wrapping her fingers through his hair. "And I would do it again in an instant."

"But the risk . . . ," he started to say. She spun around to face him and silenced him with the look in her eyes.

"You still don't get it, do you? *You* are worth the risk. What we have together is worth the risk. Do you know how rare this is? People who love each other like we do? I would give *anything* to protect that. It's like I told Liam—we would have found some other way of stopping Nuala. But I never would have found another you."

He regarded her carefully for a long moment and then nodded, a smile playing at the corner of his lips. "When I first met you, I knew I was getting myself into trouble. I just didn't know how much. And in case I haven't made it clear enough, I feel exactly the same way about you. Although . . . it *would* be nice if our lives were less exciting for a little while."

"A week, at least," Cedar agreed.

Finn laughed and spun her around. "Shall we go get a crown for your beautiful head?"

"If we must," Cedar said. They had been given a few days to rest while preparations were being made for the coronation. But the time had not been spent idly. Cedar had freed the druids from Maeve's workshop and brought them to Tír na nÓg for questioning. She had placed Rohan in charge of determining how much they had been acting of their own free will and how much they had been controlled by Nuala's power.

The change in the land over the past few days was remarkable. It was as though spring had finally arrived after a long, dark winter. The gray sky was showing patches of blue, and tender green blades were making their way through the dry, brown grass. Eden had reported seeing a trickle of water making its way through the cracked riverbed, a discovery supported by the fact that she was covered in mud.

Cedar couldn't resist spinning around once in the emerald dress, and she laughed as it floated around her like a swirl of mist. "Shall we?" she said, holding her hand out to Finn. He pushed open the door of their room and they stepped into the willow-lined courtyard, where they both stopped short.

"Oh, for goodness sake, you guys—don't you have your *own* room?" Cedar said, her voice full of amusement.

Jane blushed and peeked out from around Felix's arms, which had her pinned against the trunk of one of the willow trees. "Well, we do," she said with a wicked grin, "But I wanted to see how many places in Fairyland we could, ah, experience before I go back to Earth."

Felix, who didn't seem to notice that Cedar and Finn were there, ended the conversation by covering Jane's mouth with his own.

"Best leave them alone, I think," Finn said, guiding Cedar toward the door. "Don't be late!" Cedar called over her shoulder as they stepped into the common room. Riona and Rohan were waiting for them with Eden, who—to Cedar's astonishment—floated into the air at the sight of them.

"Look! I have wings!" she cried, fluttering around their heads in a pale yellow dress that had two large golden wings attached.

"They're not real," Riona whispered. "But I have a friend who can do these sorts of enchantments, and I thought Eden might like it for today."

"I think we can safely say that she does," Cedar said with a broad smile as Eden squealed with delight from above them.

A few minutes later they were entering the Hall, a much grander entrance than any Cedar had made before. The colored banners that usually hung limp from the Hall's twisted spires were fluttering in the gentle breeze. Music could be heard from within, and people everywhere were straining to see Cedar, to touch her, and to see if the stories were really true. Cries of "The prophecy has been fulfilled!" and "The lost princess has returned!" rang out from the crowd.

Cedar and Finn walked hand in hand. Eden was trying to walk regally behind them, but every once in a while she couldn't help but unfurl her wings and flutter into the air. At last, they reached the inner courtyard, where the crowd parted around them as they moved toward the dais. When they reached it, Finn released her hand and whispered, "Enjoy this—you deserve every bit of it. Just don't trip on your way up." Cedar tried to hide a grin as she climbed the steps onto the raised platform. The Lia Fáil sat just in front of the throne, which was made of intricately woven branches. Standing beside it was Brighid, a delicate crystal crown in her hands.

"I didn't think you'd be back so soon," Cedar said quietly as Brighid nodded at her.

"I go where the excitement is," Brighid replied, a glint in her eyes. "Besides, *someone* has to crown you, and I *am* the most important person here."

Cedar laughed. She reached out and laid a hand on the arm of throne, and felt a strange sensation course through her. Suddenly the dry branches beneath her fingers started turning green, as though life was being poured back into them. The change rippled through the woven branches. The courtyard was silent as all eyes watched the transformation take place. Then brightly colored blossoms erupted along the newly green vines until the entire throne was covered in large, fragrant flowers.

"Ahh," Brighid said softly. "Now *that's* how it should be. Have a seat, Cedar."

Cheers erupted from the crowd as Cedar lowered herself onto the throne of flowers. She looked out at the sea of faces that surrounded her, most of whom she had never seen before, and thought, truly believing it for the first time, *These are my people.* Her eyes sought the only ones who really mattered. She wasn't even listening to what Brighid was saying as she locked gazes with Finn, whose eyes were brimming with tears, and then Eden, who was beaming with pride and waving at her enthusiastically. Then Brighid gently placed the crown on Cedar's head, and she stood from the throne. She gave Brighid a questioning look, and the other woman nodded. "One more time," she said.

Once again, Cedar stepped up onto the Stone of Destiny, and its roar blended with the roar of her people as they accepted her as their queen.

ACKNOWLEDGMENTS

The creation of this book couldn't have happened (at least not by deadline!) without the assistance of several key people. First and foremost was my husband, Mike, whose support was invaluable not only to the writing of this book but also to my own sanity. I'm also grateful to Janice Hillmer for helping me with my day job so I could have time to write; to Dwight and Denise Friesen, Lesley Winfield, and Liam Steele for their insider info on Edinburgh Castle; to Suzie Evans, Charis Rowan, and Kevin Hearne for their help with pronunciations; to Sarah Cook for traipsing all over the Hill of Tara with me in the bitter cold; and to the wonderful team at 47North, including David Pomerico, Patrick Magee, Katy Ball, Justin Golenbock, and all the others working behind the scenes. My editor, Angela Polidoro, is a genius at finding (and fixing) my blind spots and will probably edit this sentence and make it a better one. And as always, thank you to Chris Hansen for teaching me how to tell a story and sending me on this journey in the first place.

ABOUT THE AUTHOR

JUSTIN SHERWIN, 2012

Jodi McIsaac grew up in New Brunswick, Canada. After stints as a short-track speed skater, a speechwriter, and a fundraising and marketing executive in the nonprofit sector, she started a boutique copywriting agency and began writing novels in the wee hours of the morning. She currently lives with her husband and children in Calgary.

MCISA
McIsaac, Jodi.
Into the fire

0006117685575

Dayton Metro Library